THE UNDERDOG PARADE

MICHAEL MIHALEY

ODDITIES KJB

This is a work of fiction. All names, characters, places, and incidents are a product of the author's imagination. Any resemblance to real events or persons, living or dead, is entirely coincidental.

Published by Akashic Books

Paperback ISBN: 978-1-61775-711-2
Hardcover ISBN: 978-1-61775-712-9
eISBN: 978-1-61775-713-6
Library of Congress Control Number: 2018960658

First printing

Kaylie Jones Books Oddities
www.kayliejonesbooks.com

Akashic Books
Brooklyn, New York, USA
Ballydehob, Co. Cork, Ireland
Twitter: @AkashicBooks
Facebook: AkashicBooks
E-mail: info@akashicbooks.com
Website: www.akashicbooks.com

Also available from Oddities/Kaylie Jones Books

The Kaleidoscope Sisters by Ronnie K. Stephens

Angel of the Underground by David Andreas

We Are All Crew by Bill Landauer

Strays by Justin Kassab

Foamers by Justin Kassab

This book is for my mom.
Something small, compared to all the love she gives.

WILLOW CREEK LANDING

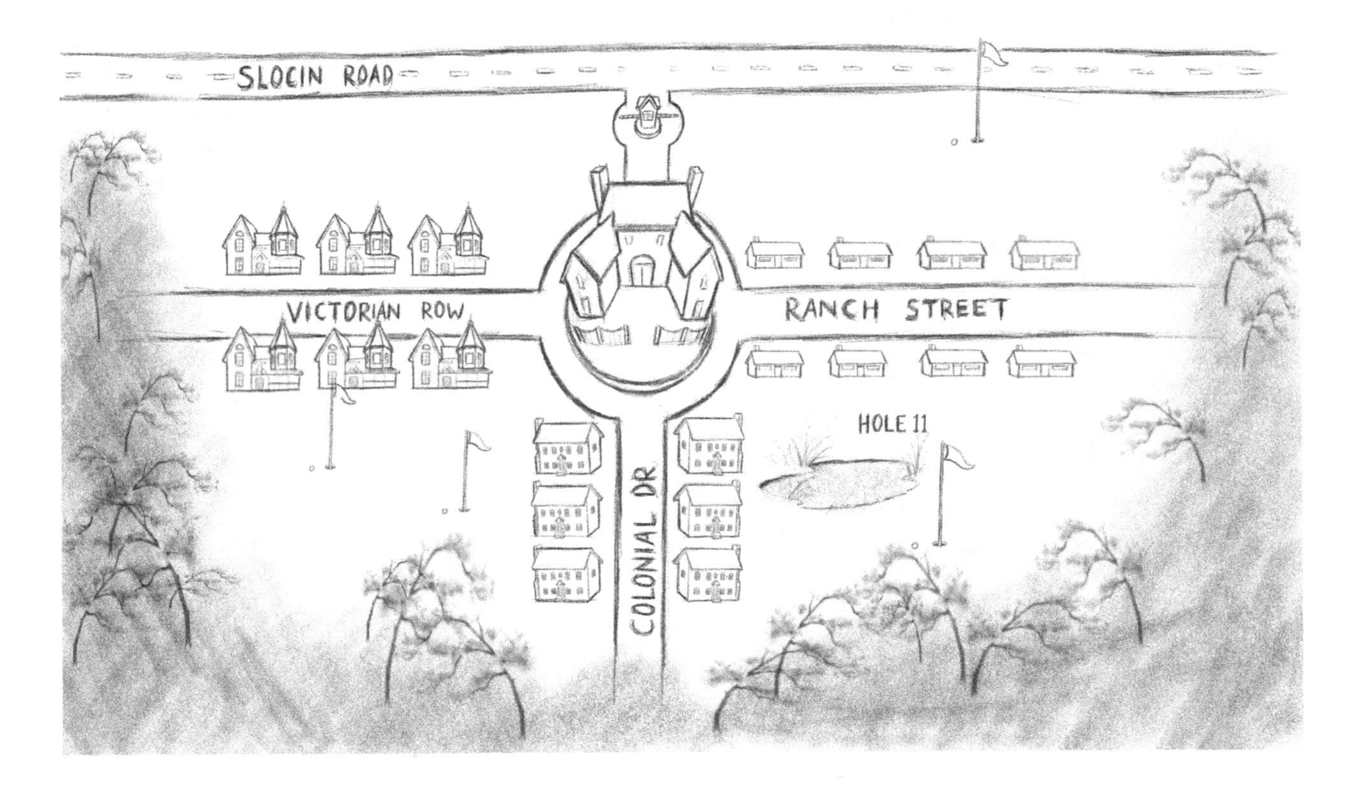
SLOCIN ROAD
VICTORIAN ROW
RANCH STREET
HOLE 11
COLONIAL DR

All the world is made of faith, and trust, and pixie dust.
—J.M. Barrie, *Peter Pan*

PART I

Day 57

It was the summer of the drought.

This drought ranked sixth on Peter Grady's list of reasons to stay in his room and add another sweat stain to his pillow. Peter created lists regularly—it was his way of putting his feelings on paper. He treated his lists like pop music charts with entries changing positions often. The major difference between the pop charts and his lists was the number of people polled. Peter's lists had only one.

Through his locked bedroom door, Peter heard the muffled, fake laugh of his mother. Her bogus chuckle was easy to detect; it sounded like the added laugh track of an old television show. When his mother laughed really hard, things found a way of shooting out her nose—water at the dinner table, snot during the winter, stuff like that.

Peter would bet his Mike Piazza–signed catcher's glove that his mother's nose would lie dormant for another full hour at least. Mrs. Keeme, the next-door neighbor, was visiting. She was funny like the chicken pox.

Earlier, Peter made it out of the living room just in time. Before the doorbell had even rung, a whiff of Mrs. Keeme's powdery scent—like something you'd use to cover the stench of an old, damp sneaker—entered Peter's nose. He took flight to his room and started formulating this new list of his at his desk. He gave Mrs. Keeme today's top honors, subject to change depending on how the rest of the morning turned out.

It was not like Mrs. Keeme was mean. She just complained on and on, usually about her husband, soon to be ex-husband, Bernie. From her visits, Peter learned too much about Bernie. He was fat, lazy, and stupid—pretty much a slug with black socks. Peter never had a problem with Mr. Keeme. He was one of the few neighbors who would wave to him.

No matter how much Peter tried, it was nearly impossible to escape Mrs. Keeme's every word. Their new house had no hiding spaces. Her voice tumbled down hallways, crashed down doors, and smothered Peter's ears and weighed down his shoulders until he felt his knees turn to jelly, as though he and Mrs. Keeme were partners in a chicken fight and Peter had the unfortunate bottom position.

There was a bang on the door and the knob rattled—CJ.

"Peter, the door is locked," she said.

"I know."

"I want to come in."

"I know."

After a pause, CJ said, "Are you going to let me in?"

"I moved," Peter said, glancing at the globe on his desk for a reference, adding, "to Bangladesh."

The knob rattled again then stopped, followed by a jarring thud pushing out the bottom third of the door. Peter pictured the pink-and-white sneaker slamming into the door. It had happened a thousand times before.

Peter waited, watching the door. CJ never gave up easily. She was relentless in her pursuit to drive her brother nuts. It was her calling. The ensuing silence had a slightly unsettling feel, similar to a horror movie when you're waiting for something to jump out, but the door remained still.

The window shades were closed as they had been all summer, blocking the sun and heat during the day and anything (or anyone) from looking into his room during the night. Mrs. Keeme continued to drone on, but she said something that now had Peter's undivided attention. Mrs. Keeme told Peter's mother she was moving out of "the Creek"—the pet name that residents gave their gated community, Willow Creek Landing.

Peter stared impatiently at his bedroom wall. He wanted dates, a time frame on Mrs. Keeme's departure, but as she so often did, she went off on another complaining rant, this time about her son, Joshua. Apparently he would be staying in their home until it was sold. Mrs. Keeme said she already rented an apartment for herself outside the Creek. Bernie was already gone. It was like a jailbreak.

Peter didn't care about this Joshua. He had never even seen him before, though due to Mrs. Keeme's visits, he felt like he'd known him for years. When Peter's family had moved into the Creek a year ago, Joshua was away at college. Through a succession of home visits, Peter learned Joshua had run into some sort of trouble while away, and then Mrs. Keeme stopped mentioning him altogether. Until today.

Thumps and scratching noises came from outside Peter's window. He stood and sighed. He pushed aside the shade and shielded his eyes from the ever-present sun, then saw the familiar, gold tiara with a red star in the center covering a mop of yellow curls. A leg kicked over the window sill outside, and Peter saw the full getup: a sparkling, red-and-gold top, white stars on blue shorts, and golden, plastic-coated lasso wrapped around the shorts like a belt.

"You know the screen opens only from the inside, right?"

"Right," CJ grunted, trying to hoist her body up to the window with her elbows.

Shortly after coming to the Creek, Peter came to the overriding conclusion that the move was a horrible mistake, but one easily rectified if he could convince his family of their erroneous ways. So he made a list—"Reasons Why Willow Creek Landing Sucks Rocks"—and supplied this four-page document, complete with bullets, to his parents.

Nothing happened.

"Living on a ranch" was reason twenty-seven. Peter felt a lot more secure living in his old home where you needed at least a ladder to get to his room on the second floor. Here he was as accessible as a McDonald's drive-through.

He opened the screen to help CJ inside. Though the fall was no more than four feet, the height would still be a hard fall for CJ.

"I can do it," CJ said, slapping away at his hand.

Peter helped her anyway. "I know, I know. You're Wonder Woman."

The Great Willow Creek Race

It's only fair to note that Peter had never been in favor of the move to Willow Creek Landing. He liked his old neighborhood where he had friends on his block and friends in school. Though Willow Creek Landing was only a twenty-minute car ride away, it might as well have been Iceland. There was a whole group of unfamiliar neighbors and a new school district. It was no big deal for CJ; she was entering kindergarten at the time they moved. Peter came in at sixth grade, a year before middle school, when groups of friends were already established.

Peter's skepticism of his new neighborhood was born when his father, Nick, had brought home a glossy, full-color brochure advertising Willow Creek Landing, "a community for the twenty-first century." His old neighborhood didn't need that sort of promotion. Peter wasn't impressed with the private golf course (he hated golf), luxurious new homes, on-site restaurant and catering facilities, or the general store where you can shop without leaving the wrought-iron gates. Big deal.

The community also hosted several events throughout the year for the residents, which was the reason Mrs. Keeme cut short her visit earlier. Today was the Great Willow Creek 5K, a 3.1 mile run through the development—which the residents made into this huge deal. Mrs. Keeme wanted to get outside the gates before the community's security team closed the streets to traffic.

When the front screen door slammed shut, announcing Mrs. Keeme's exit, Peter unlocked his bedroom door and walked down the hallway to the living room with CJ at his heels.

Their mother, Abby, was in the kitchen loading the dishwasher and going over the conversation she had with Mrs. Keeme in her head. Abby would miss the cranky, old lady; in a strange way, she enjoyed her company. There was a part of Abby that understood and felt for Mrs. Keeme. The urge to drop everything and start anew was not groundbreaking—Abby had felt it several times standing at this very spot, loading or unloading the dishwasher. The damn machine required the attention of an infant.

"You can come out now, the coast is clear," Abby said, hearing the kids' footsteps.

"Is Dad coming to the race?" Peter asked.

"He's hiding in his room too. You can tell him she's gone. He'll be happy to hear all the news."

The neighbors were one of the few things Peter's father didn't absolutely love about their new surroundings. On several occasions, he said they lived in the "fruits and nuts" section of the Creek. At first Peter thought his father was talking about the trees lining the block, though his father was never the nature-loving type. He later realized his father was referring to the neighbors.

CJ drifted into the living room and turned on the television.

"Did you take your meds, Peter?" Abby asked.

Meds, Peter thought. It used to be *did you take your pill*; now it was a concoction of different orange vials soon to be changed again since this recent recipe hadn't worked either.

Peter had taken his meds with his Cheerios in the morning, scarfing them down as quickly as he could, hoping the bitter aftertaste or smell of the pills wouldn't revive the horrible memory of his last seizure. But they always did: gym class, end of the school year.

He had done a good job up to that point of melting into the background. Fitting in was Peter's ultimate, but highly improbable, goal at school. He'd planned on settling for remaining invisible. But after the seizure, even that goal was no longer possible. He shuddered when he pictured himself flopping around the gymnasium's Lysol-stinking oak floors in front of all the other students, lying on his back with his arms and legs flapping about as the gym coach removed any objects near Peter that could harm his out of control body. They had nicknamed him "Nemo" after that. Indeed, Peter was a fish out of water.

Peter, CJ, and their parents walked down Ranch Street—named, rather unoriginally, after the style of homes on the block—toward the pavilion in the center of the Creek. The pavilion was like a town hall where all the big events were held. People were already gathered near a huge, white banner that read *FINISH LINE* in big, blue letters. Two men held a thin tape taut, ready for the winner to break through. The runners started at the cart path of hole one on the golf course and continued along the perimeter of the development. Willow Creek Landing bordered on the Pine Barrens, a huge nature preserve that Peter was excited to explore once the drought broke. From an aerial view, the preserve shaped Willow Creek Landing like a bushy beard.

Peter lagged behind his parents, and CJ lagged behind him, dragging a small, stuffed dog in her lasso. Over the last few months Peter developed an acute sense of when his parents were fighting. Recently, they had provided him with ample resources to polish this talent. He couldn't understand when they'd found the time to forge this new fight since his father had just returned home late last night from another one of his business trips. They faced one another only to speak in hushed, forceful bursts, and then turned away after tossing whatever verbal grenade they threw, unconcerned by the damage it would generate. It was like a dance of the angry.

Thankfully, the dancing stopped as they approached the growing crowd. Peter found himself in the awkward position of standing between his silent parents as CJ lingered behind them, whispering indecipherable words of either encouragement or threats to her imprisoned fluffy animal. Every once in a while, a resident would stop and greet either Peter's father or mother or both, and wide smiles would crease their faces only to disappear once the neighbor left. Peter couldn't wait to go home. He'd add *parents seemed a lot happier in old home even if they didn't realize it themselves* to the list of reasons why he hated Willow Creek Landing.

"This is fun," Peter lied to his father, just to break the silence.

"Oh, yeah. Holding a race in August in ninety-five-degree dry heat, during a drought. Brilliant idea," his father said, returning the icy stare of a lady in front of him who overheard his answer. Nick looked around with disdain at the faces of the crowd, detaching himself from the people surrounding him.

Peter could feel only relief as a smattering of applause turned into a steady stream of cheering as the lead runners came into view from down Victorian Row one hundred yards away, for the final stretch. The sweltering sun had apparently taken a greater-than-obvious toll on the runners, and the two men in the lead, with their arms and legs flailing, looked more like they were falling off a cliff than sprinting to a finish. The spectators started to cheer.

Peter cheered because everyone else was doing it, not counting his father. He held little interest in the outcome of the race until, just ahead of the runners, a figure broke suddenly from the throngs of people on the sidelines and started sprinting toward the finish line. From a distance, Peter thought this unofficial runner was a tall, skinny girl because of the long, flowing hair, but then he saw a flimsy beard bouncing up and down in the air. His beard didn't have that rough look of iron wool, but seemed soft and fragile. He wore blue jeans hastily cut into shorts and a T-shirt with many different, bright colors melting into each other like a kaleidoscope. His eyes were wide and alert. He wasn't running that fast—the open sandals on his feet were designed for a more leisurely pace. The lead runners, with barely enough energy to register a look of surprise or anger, tried to catch the bearded fellow but eventually withered and faded farther behind.

The crowd, fuming at this stranger who was ruining their great event, shouted things as he passed, but the stranger continued to run with a determined grin to the end. He skidded at the finish line, almost tripping into the tape, then contorted his body into a limbo-type maneuver and passed cleanly underneath. He pointed to the crowd and held a finger to his lips, similar to a reprimanding librarian, and shouted, "Your wealth is rotted! Restore, people! Restore!"

Willow Creek Landing's security team, color-coordinated in dark-blue pants and collared polo shirts, surrounded him immediately and escorted him off the course by his elbows. His sandals skimmed the ground.

"Live righteous, people! You have been forewarned!" the bearded guy shouted before being swallowed up by the crowd.

No one noticed who really won the race.

CJ giggled, thinking the act was part of the day's planned festivities.

Nick looked sickened. "Don't tell me that's the Keeme kid."

Abby nodded slowly, having watched the scene play out in disbelief. She glared at her husband. "Joshua. Product of a broken home, exhibit A."

Day 58

Most of the trees in the Creek were no older than ten years and were neatly arranged—not by nature's plan, but by some developer with an Italian last name. But on the edge of Peter's front lawn, bordering the Keemes' property, stood a giant pine tree, one of the remaining remnants from the original landscape. No one knew why this tree survived the developer's master plan. Cost maybe—there was speculation that the developer had cut corners in the end after hemorrhaging money.

Peter now sat high in the tree, skimming the pages of *The Outsiders*. It was one of his favorite books, though lately he wondered how "outside" this group of boys really was. Maybe they were poor and social outcasts, but at least they had a strong-knit group of brothers and childhood friends who banded together. Right now, all Peter had was CJ circling the tree below dragging a branch with her lasso.

Peter couldn't stop thinking about Joshua, the sandal-wearing runner from yesterday. The fact that this guy lived thirty feet away now made him even more interesting. Peter wondered if Mrs. Keeme had already left the Creek.

CJ stopped and stared high in Peter's direction. "Are you coming down soon? I'm bored to death."

Sunlight poked through the limbs and leaves, dotting the pages of Peter's book. He loved this tree. It kept both the sun and CJ at bay.

A burst of sharp laughter came from down the block and Peter felt the hairs on his neck tingle. His list, "Reasons Why Willow Creek Landing Sucks Rocks," instantly popped into his mind. That sharp laughter came from reason number two: Chipper Kassel.

Chipper was a constant presence on most of Peter's lists these days, but he had rocketed to the top since Peter's seizure at school.

Chipper would have made his rock sucking list, though further down, even if he *didn't* live in Willow Creek Landing just for the sheer terror and humiliation he brought Peter during his first year at the new school. Knowing that Chipper roamed freely within the Creek's gates made Peter feel like he'd slipped and fallen into the lion exhibit at the local zoo.

Chipper was with his two constant companions, Jason Franco and Eddie Doane, but Peter preferred to call them Goon A and Goon B. They came down Ranch Street from the direction of the pavilion, tossing a football. There was no real reason that Peter could think of for Chipper to make this walk since Ranch Street was a dead end that emptied into the Pine Barrens. Chipper's family lived in a big home on Victorian Row, the other side of Willow Creek.

Peter prayed for the power of invisibility, or an earthquake.

CJ stopped pacing and watched the boys approach. With CJ near, her brightly colored outfit and tiara sparkling in the sun, the chance of going undetected was nil.

One of the goons, either Jason or Eddie—they were interchangeable—noticed Peter first, nudging Chipper and pointing into the tree as if they were bird-watchers and had just spotted a rare, exquisite bird. Chipper handed off the football and led the goons in the direction of this bird, who was now highly nauseated.

Out of fairness, even Peter would begrudgingly admit that his old neighborhood hadn't been perfect. There were bullies there too, but they were clearly marked and usually on the fringe of the school's hierarchy. They were easy to ignore, or their actions could be simply chalked up to a Neanderthal upbringing or low intellectual horsepower. Chipper was different—the new-and-improved version of the modern-day bully. He was the class president, popular with students and teachers, and he cleaned up all those "most" awards at the sixth grade graduation. Peter wanted to submit a write-in award for Chipper, *most likely to tie an M-80 to a cat when no one is looking*, but he couldn't trust the student council, which would probably do everything in their power to unveil the disreputable student who dared to tarnish the name of their beloved class president. Chipper wielded that kind of power and influence. His back pocket was filled with people. Worst of all, the playground behind the pavilion, where CJ loved to play, had a gold plaque attached to the climbing gym that read: *This playground is the Boy Scout Service Project of Kenneth "Chipper" Kassel, Jr.* It was enough to make vomit rise to the back of your tongue.

Peter never understood why Chipper enjoyed lashing out and terrorizing the "lesser" kid. The world was his oyster. The only conclusion Peter came to was terrorism gave Chipper enjoyment and satisfaction. It was a hobby like collecting stamps.

"Are you coming down?" CJ asked.

A small noise came from Peter's mouth.

"Howdy," Chipper said, hopping the curb and crossing the lawn. "If it isn't our friend Peter Grady."

Peter kept his eyes locked on his book.

"Hey, Nemo," one of the goons said from behind Chipper. He dropped on the ground and started shaking.

"That's not nice," CJ said quietly.

Chipper's arms shot in the air. "Whoa, watch out guys. Wonder Woman is here to protect Nemo."

The shaking goon stood up. All three acted like they were laughing so hard they had to hold one another up.

No matter how hard he tried, Peter couldn't bring himself to look up from the book. He felt a hot wetness forming in his eyes.

Then the tree spoke.

"Get lost, midgets. You're decreasing my property value."

Now, Chipper was in no way vertically challenged. There was a rumor he was going to be the captain of the middle school football team as a seventh grader, but he suddenly seemed small as Joshua appeared from the other side of the tree.

Joshua was dressed in the same cut-off shorts from yesterday but was now shirtless and barefoot. A rubber band shaped the bottom of his beard into a triangle. He stared down at Chipper and the goons, an unlit cigarette dangling from his lips as he scratched a small tuft of chest hair. His face was expressionless.

Chipper and the goons coagulated. The goons looked to Chipper for representation, but Chipper looked prepared to defer to anyone else. He shifted his weight and bit his lip. Peter had never seen this side of Chipper.

It was the tone in which Joshua spoke that struck Peter—a combination of menace and boredom, as if he'd swat them dead like mosquitoes without thinking twice about it, maybe while eating a ham sandwich.

Chipper and the goons continued to hold their position until Joshua barked, "Get lost!"

They didn't stay to see if his bite was worse.

Joshua yawned as he watched them run down the street. He scoffed, "Like I give a rat's ass about property value."

Peter didn't know if he should thank Joshua or offer him the three dollars and change in his pocket. Joshua made the decision for him. He walked away, tiptoeing down the sun-scorched driveway to his mailbox. Peter watched from the tree as Joshua riffled through the stack of mail, saying, "Bills, magazines, advertisements. You know what these are?"

Not sure if the question was directed at him, Peter didn't answer.

"Spiritual handcuffs," Joshua said, and shook his head in disappointment. "What a waste."

On the way back to his house, Joshua stopped short as if he'd just remembered there was someone sitting high in the tree next to him. He shielded his eyes from the sun.

"C.S. Lewis depicts hell as this bureaucratic hole where everyone is forever concerned about his own dignity and advancement, and everyone constantly lives with deadly serious cases of envy, self-importance and resentment. What do you think?"

Peter was lost after the word *depicts*. He found it difficult to maintain eye contact but saw that Joshua had no such problem. His eyes were wide and white and danced like pitched Wiffle balls.

"I don't know," Peter responded.

Joshua nodded slowly, as if he was digesting Peter's nonanswer. "I like someone who is man enough to say 'I don't know.'" His hand scrambled in his pocket and he pulled out a lighter.

"You smoke?"

"I'm twelve-and-a-half."

Joshua nodded again, satisfied with the answer. He pointed up at him. "Good man. Promise me you never will."

Peter was too confused to answer. He was always being told by adults not to do things, just not at the precise moment the person was doing the exact thing they were telling you not to do.

"What is your name, young man?"

"Peter."

"I'm Josh."

Peter nodded, making the mental note of calling him Josh instead of Joshua.

"Okay, Peter. Another question. Why is Wonder Woman hiding behind the tree?"

In his panic, Peter had forgotten all about CJ.

"She's my sister. I think she might be afraid of you, but I've never seen her scared of anyone," Peter said, which was the truth.

"I'm not scared," a small voice said from the tree's trunk.

Joshua's smile was thin and showed no teeth. "Last question. Don't your grapes hurt from sitting on that tree limb for so long?"

Peter didn't have time to process and reply to the question. His mother called to him and CJ from the front door.

"I have to go," Peter said, apologetically.

"I know," Joshua answered.

Peter hopped down from the tree and ran after CJ. They scooted in past their mother, who stood stiffly in the door, pointing inside the house. She didn't watch as her children approached but stared curiously beyond them at the shirtless, long-haired neighbor, even after the screen door closed.

Day 59

The sun started its climb, backlighting Willow Creek Landing in soft tones of peach and pink. The low moans of tired air conditioners drifted from up and down the block. Since the drought started, the predawn hours had grown as a popular time for leisure and social activities, and many walkers and joggers now dotted the streets.

Peter sat on the living room couch, still in his pajamas, somewhere between the state of sleep and wakefulness. His father was leaving on another one of his business trips, and Peter always liked to see him off.

In addition to his growing number of lists, Peter kept a running tab of three additional things, all on his desk calendar in his room. For each day of rainless sunshine, he drew an orange circle under the date, which was now fifty-nine in a row and counting. He drew a black circle on the days he had seizures. And recently he'd started keeping track of the days his father was away on business with blue circles, which wasn't as consistent as the orange circles, but not too far behind either.

"The fruitcakes are up early," Nick noted, peering over the couch and out the window facing the street.

Peter didn't need to look; he knew his father was talking about Mr. James and Mr. Terry, the neighbors across the street. His father was always calling them a variation of the word fruit: fruit sticks, fruit platters, fruit loops, etc.

Nick rolled his eyes. Dressed in pressed khaki slacks and a plain black T-shirt, arguably a size too small, he felt confident in what he called his "business travel" attire. In one of the many men's magazines he devoured religiously—especially now that he could actually afford a $300 pair of brown leather loafers—he'd read that "confidence radiation" was mandatory in a CEO, and a CEO was what he was since he'd opened his business, though he only had four employees. He checked his confidence radiation level as he caressed his freshly shaven head and patted his abs. The constant maintenance to look good was a necessary evil, especially now that he was pushing forty, but he read he couldn't radiate confidence with a horseshoe hairline and a doughy body. He packed his salmon dress shirt with a matching tie in his carry-on for his trip to Colorado.

"I guess the Fruit Roll-Ups think they're above everyone else," Nick said, nodding to the window as he zipped his carry-on and threw it over his shoulder.

This made Peter rise from the couch and nose close to the window.

Mr. Terry's short and portly frame scooted back and forth across his lawn like a plastic duck in a shooting gallery. Sweat pasted his fire-engine red silk pajamas to his body.

"He said he had very expensive flowers in his garden that he had to water or they'd die," Peter said, trying not to sound too much like he was defending him.

"He's not watering his very expensive flowers, Peter."

Sure enough, at closer look, Mr. Terry held a garden hose discreetly lodged into his ribcage, dragging behind him like a tail. His head swiveled up and down the block, further indicting himself and his actions. It sure seemed Mr. Terry was fully aware of breaking the county's moratorium on water usage that had been enforced since the drought had caused the water reserve to sink dangerously low.

Peter refused to hold this against him. He liked Mr. Terry.

"And how do you know about his very expensive flowers? What, are you buddies now with the fruits?"

"No," Peter said, with such force that he felt an instant and solitary guilt, betraying two of the small number of people in Willow Creek who were friendly to him. He couldn't help it. Anytime his father spoke with such disdain, Peter's response was knee-jerk.

Abby appeared behind them, her hair messy from sleep and still in her robe. She yawned and shuffled to the kitchen for coffee.

"What day you coming back, Nick?"

"Friday, if nothing pops up."

"Are you *expecting* things to pop up, Nick?" she asked, her voice quickly losing the early morning lubrication.

Nick looked away from the window to stare coldly at his wife's back. "Don't start with me now, Abby. The taxi will be here any minute."

It wasn't even six a.m., and Peter could tell the day was sure to be another scorcher. He felt the urge to go outside and play before the sun took over and just blinking made you sweat. He glanced over at his father and rallied for the nerve to ask.

"Dad," he finally mustered, "do you want to play catch before you leave?"

Nick was texting on his phone and his brow furrowed as it always did when he was being distracted. "Not today, slugger. I don't want to get all sweaty before I get on the plane."

Peter tried to shake his head like he understood, but he couldn't hide his disappointment. *Slugger, my butt*, Peter thought. He could have been the next Mickey Mantle (though he was 99.9999 percent sure he wasn't), but his father would have no idea. They hadn't played catch since his father started the Business. His father probably thought if he had a glove on one hand and a ball in the other, how could he hold his phone? Peter was tired of hearing about the Business. It was the Business that brought him to this new home. It was the Business that changed his Dad. The Business was another staple on several of Peter's lists.

Once, desperate to play catch, Peter asked Mr. Terry. Mr. Terry immediately said no but agreed after Mr. James persuaded him. Mr. James looked a little younger than Mr. Terry and definitely was in better shape, but Peter was more comfortable with Mr. Terry. He was always smiling and talking loudly, waving his arms and making animated faces. Mr. James once told Peter that Mr. Terry used to be a character actor. When Peter asked what that was, Mr. Terry said it meant he was too fat and ugly to be a star. Then he laughed.

For catch, Peter had to loan Mr. Terry CJ's mitt. Mr. Terry's first throw missed horribly, sailing high over Peter's head and down the street. Mr. James, who Peter had seldom seen smile to that point, laughed and slapped at the arm of the lawn chair he had set up for the occasion. The added dimension of having a spectator excited Peter even though Mr. Terry seemed less than thrilled.

"You come over here and try this," he shouted at Mr. James. "This is opening old wounds. I'm going to have to see my therapist later." Peter threw a bullet that hit Mr. Terry square in the chest, freeing the air from his body with an exploding *OOOMPH*! Mr. James doubled over in his lawn chair, choking with laughter. "There's a big leather glove on your hand for a reason, Terry. It's not an accessory," Mr. James said, wiping tears from his eyes. Mr. Terry ignored the heckling, gently rubbing the center of his chest.

For an hour, they both constantly underthrew and overthrew each other, but not once did Mr. Terry show any sign of aggravation. He actually grew quite serious, concentrating on each throw, the tip of his tongue visible, and rejoicing in lottery-winning style when he threw a catchable ball. They played until the sun sank under the homes and Mr. Terry collapsed on the curb, begging the violet-streaked sky for a mimosa IV.

A cab slowed in front of the house and pulled into the driveway. Nick gathered his belongings and told Abby he'd call once he landed.

"Herb might be here when you get back, Nick, depending on when you get back," Abby said. She'd purposely held off on this information until this time.

"Uncle Herb is coming over?" Peter asked. That was news to him.

Nick threw his bag over his shoulder. "Well, that's why we bought this ranch, for Herbie. Right, dear?" The word *dear* dripped from Nick's mouth.

"Hurry home," Abby said, flatly. She went back to kitchen and Peter followed her, waving one last goodbye to his father.

Nick jogged to the cab and threw his bag, then himself, into the backseat. He leaned toward the driver and tapped the top of the driver's seat. The cab sped off. It was like the classic chase scene in a movie and Nick was hot on the tail, the pursuer. But anyone watching would have no idea what he was chasing.

Uncle Herb

After the cab pulled away, Abby sprinted through her morning cleanup routine, taking minutes to accomplish what normally would take her through lunch. She chose to avoid the everyday distractions that dragged her routine out: television, phone, magazines, children.

She dashed between rooms, dropping dirty coffee mugs into the kitchen sink, picking puzzle pieces off the living room floor, and lugging the laundry basket to the basement. She had energy. She moved purposefully. This was not a common weekday.

Peter took notice but pretended not to, stealing glances at her from the couch as she darted past.

"Peter, after we get Uncle Herb, I have to go out for a bit. I need to take a shower now."

"Who is staying home with us?" Peter wanted to know. If she said nobody or gave a line saying how he was old enough now to be trusted, that meant he was babysitting CJ. Kids got good money to babysit, and that's where he wanted to lead the conversation. Plus, these handsomely paid babysitters weren't watching CJ; there should be some extra combat pay for that.

"Uncle Herb will be here," she said, as if this was the most ordinary thing in the world.

"Really?" Peter loved his Uncle dearly, but he was not what you'd describe as the typical babysitter.

Abby stopped what she was doing and placed her hands on her hips. "Really. Problem?"

"No," Peter said. Unlike CJ, he knew when not to push his mother. The hand-on-the-hip thing was a dead giveaway. The topic of monetary compensation would have to wait.

"Please wake up your sister now. I'm in a hurry," Abby said.

Peter's shoulders sagged. He had just given in to his mother, and this was how he was rewarded?

The Worst Things To Do In The Morning—A List by Peter Grady.
1. Wake Up.
2. Wake Up CJ.

A tornado outbreak from the minute she woke, CJ slept on her back, totally still with her hands folded over her chest. Her resting pose always freaked Peter out, as if his little sister was part vampire or something. And she slept hard. You could shake her, and she'd roll a little like a large log, only to return to the original resting spot. She had resisted a set bedtime since she was two, and now that their father was out of town a lot, Abby didn't have the energy at night to battle and enforce. So she let CJ run and run until she was totally out of gas, then she'd find her curled in some random spot—the middle of the hallway, under the kitchen table—and Abby would carry her to bed.

Peter hovered over her bed. He sighed.

"Wake up, CJ."

Baby Vampire didn't respond. Her interwoven fingers sat motionless on her chest.

He stood on the bottom of her mattress and jumped up and down, chanting "Wake up!" but CJ's body just moved with the waves.

Frustrated, Peter jumped off the bed and headed to the door. "All right, CJ, we're picking up Uncle Herb. See you later."

CJ bounced into the air. "Where's my lasso?"

Peter had CJ buckled into her car seat, eating a granola bar and drinking a juice box, when their mother crashed out of the front door running to the car, buttoning her blouse and pushing her wet hair over her ears. A look of bewilderment crossed her face as she reached the car.

"You got her dressed too?" she said, pointing to the Wonder Woman outfit on CJ, accumulating bits of granola crumbs by the mouthful.

"She slept in it."

Abby dropped her purse at Peter's feet in the passenger's seat. She shook her head, impressed. "I don't know, Peter. Sometimes I think you're more cut out for this gig than me."

Uncle Herb lived in a group home, a twenty-minute ride from the Creek. Peter didn't know the exact definition of a group home; it's what his mother had always called the place, but from what he could gather a group home was where several people lived, related only by the fact they all were disabled, and the house had staff acting as caretakers.

Back when they were house hunting, Abby's conditions were a ranch home for its wheelchair accessibility and no farther than a half hour from her brother. She wanted her brother to feel welcome, though Herb hadn't spent any significant time there as of yet. They had moved in right after Peter's summer vacation last year, and during Christmas, Nick was adamant about going skiing over the holidays. He was so stressed out over the new business that Abby didn't fight him on it, but she wished she had. She spent much of Christmas morning feeling guilty, thinking how her brother had to spend it with only the staff who worked in his home. It was the first Christmas they'd ever spent apart.

In turn, Abby's conditions annoyed Nick, who didn't like the location limitations or the nixing of his dream to buy and restore an old Victorian, though Abby's rebuttal that it was too much of a project for them was valid. Nick would never admit it, but DIY was a letter combination that didn't agree with him. He was hapless with a hammer, and his only experience and knowledge of construction had been gleaned from watching home improvement shows on television.

"How long is Uncle Herb staying with us?" Peter asked as he fiddled with the air conditioner vents, then the radio station presets—anything to distract him from his mother's aggressive driving. Cars in the process of being towed had more distance from the bumper in front of them than the poor car Abby was tailgating now.

It didn't help Peter's nerves that his mother was applying eyeliner as she drove.

The car in front braked and Peter winced.

"Mom, can you pay attention to the road?"

She pointed to Peter with her eyeliner pencil. "Hey, the driver controls the radio," she said and pressed the button setting for the "all news, all the time" station. "Uncle Herb has two weeks of vacation. Hopefully, he'll stay the whole time, but I'll leave that up to him. Sometimes it's easier for him to be in his own environment."

"Uncle Herb, yay!" CJ cheered from the backseat.

Listening to the all news station was a form of torture on Peter's ears. What a broken record, repeating the same things every twenty minutes, especially now with the drought and all. *Today will be super hot and super dry outside. Tomorrow the same. The next day, ditto. And the next day, well, you know where I'm going with this, right?* the radio host blabbed.

A citrus scent floated under Peter's nose. He turned to his mother and noticed the pressed slacks and expensive blouse. It wasn't unusual for his mother to wear sweatpants the entire day.

"Why are you so dressed up?"

She smiled. "Do I look pretty?"

Peter hated when she asked him that. She was his mother.

"Well, if you need to know, nosy pants, I might be going back to work. Just part-time though. Mrs. Stewart is doing quite well in real estate, and she wants me to come in today and talk to her boss. I can work a flexible schedule, and to tell you the truth, I think I might be good at that type of work. We met a lot of those agents when we were looking for our house. They weren't anything special. I'll just need to get my real estate license, but I can cobroker some deals for now."

Peter turned around to see if CJ was listening. She was off in her own world, rigging her lasso into some sort of pulley system, stringing it through the seat and around the seat belt latches. Peter turned back to his mother.

"Why?" he wanted to know.

"Because you need a license to sell homes, silly."

"No, why do you need to go back to work? Dad makes a boatload of money now. He says it all the time. Why do you have to work too?"

She seemed taken aback by the question, but Peter didn't see anything wrong with it. He was confused, so he asked. Whatever happened to "there's no such thing as a stupid question?"

Abby's eyes darted back and forth from the road to Peter. "Maybe because I want to, Peter. Is something wrong with that?"

Peter sensed his mother getting angry, so he abandoned his question to hang and slowly die in the air-conditioned car. He stared out the window, and they drove the rest of the way in silence, though at times he could feel his mother's eyes glancing over at him.

They pulled into the half-circle driveway of Uncle Herb's group home, parking next to a large van. The home was in a wooded area—the only house on the block. Abby had once told Peter that a lot of people don't want to live near group homes even though the homes and properties were immaculately kept. Some residents fought fiercely to keep group homes out of their own neighborhoods. Abby said that people feared *different,* even in this day and age, and there was still a stigma on people with disabilities. Peter couldn't understand it, but considering Herb was one of the first names he could speak, his experience was unlike other people's.

"Uncle Herb will be so excited to see you guys," Abby said, putting the car in park.

CJ kicked the back of Peter's chair. "Uncle Herb! Uncle Herb!"

Peter said nothing, and his mother looked over at him as she stepped out of the car.

"Is everything all right, Peter?" she asked.

Peter didn't look at her as he unbuckled his seat belt. "Yeah. I'm just tired of the sun, I guess."

Uncle Herb was waiting in the shade of a tree with a suitcase on one side of his wheelchair and an aide from the home on the other. His button up shirt drooped down from his atrophied muscles as if it was wet.

Abby said, "Sorry we're late, Maria. Traffic."

The aide acknowledged the apology with pursed lips. Maria was a stump of a woman, barely an inch over five feet, but built solid from three decades of working two, sometimes three jobs at a time—always physical work, because it made the day go faster. She looked imposing compared to the man in the wheelchair next to her, his body swallowed by chrome and padding. In Maria's four years working for the group home, Hoobie—as she liked to call Herb—had become her favorite resident. He had handsome, gentle features, and she playfully flirted with him as she helped him eat, go to the bathroom, or bathe. Unlike some of the lazy and stupid college kids she had to work with, Maria had found it easy to understand him. Her English was average, but Hoobie had such trouble speaking that he broke down his thoughts into the simplest terms, which was helpful in overcoming the language barrier. Maria's anger would surge when her coworkers acted surprised and delighted when Hoobie said something smart or funny, those patronizing fools. Maria knew that Herb was a thousand times smarter than they or their children would ever be. *Young people are so visual*, Maria thought. *They see drool and wheelchair, they think stupid.* Hoobie might not be able to walk by himself, but Maria recognized early on he could run circles around people with his mind.

And now Maria felt like she should be slapped for not protecting her loyal friend. She was letting him go with this woman who was constantly chasing her own tail—always in a rush, always late! Always talking, never listening. Who cared if she was his sister? How could she take care of Hoobie for two weeks around the clock? This wasn't Christmas dinner. She couldn't even take care of her own children. The boy walked around with his head down like a kicked puppy. And the girl in her crown and holding a rope, *loco rematado*, raving lunatic. She was cute, though, you have to give her that, with her blond curly hair and big blue eyes. The mother was a hound dog, always chasing an invisible scent just out of reach.

Maria frowned as she watched Hoobie's family spill out of their car. "Are you sure you want to go, Hoobie?"

But Herb was too occupied to answer, smiling and waving at his approaching niece and nephew, his fingers and arms crooked and rigid like those of a conductor cueing up his orchestra. He smiled at Maria, and she shook her head disapprovingly as she had done thousands of times to her adult children, knowing that they too had to make their own decisions. She pulled a napkin from her pocket and dabbed at bubbles of saliva forming at the corner of Herb's mouth.

When Abby and Herb's mother died seven years ago—not even a year after their father—the first thing Abby bought with her portion of the inheritance was an oversized SUV with large trunk space to hold Herb's electric wheelchair. They had standardized vans made for this type of transportation, but Abby couldn't bring herself to buy such an unattractive vehicle.

Abby leaned down to kiss her brother, which was followed by a gentle hug from Peter. CJ came at him with a flying hug, almost leaping into his lap.

Maria yelled, "He no piece of furniture!"

CJ paid her no mind until her hug was finished, and then she scowled at Maria as she let go. Maria, after getting over the initial shock of the little girl's brashness, scowled in return.

They all followed Abby to the SUV. Maria helped them load and buckle Herb into the center seat of the back row. CJ and Peter would sit closely on each side of him for support. Maria leaned in and patted Herb on the chest. She whispered, "See you soon, Hoobie."

Herb smiled. "*Ew-ill.*"

"I know I will." Maria turned to Abby, "Two weeks is long time. Any problem you call me, right?"

Abby was struggling to lift the electric wheelchair into the back of the SUV, and this time, Maria didn't offer any assistance; she was done helping. After much effort, Abby had the chair over the lip of the trunk and slammed the door shut. She pushed the hair out of her eyes and glared at Maria, who despite her cool appearance was laughing hysterically on the inside. Abby marched past her and slid behind the wheel. "I appreciate your concern, Maria, but I think I can take care of my own brother."

Maria turned and walked away without saying goodbye. Abby noticed her roll her eyes.

They were on the expressway heading home when Abby finally finished cursing Maria in her mind. In the rearview mirror, she could see the three of them sandwiched in the back, the kids leaning toward the center to keep Herb upright. CJ was making silly faces at him, crossing her eyes and distorting her mouth. Abby said, "After this vacation, Herb, you might need a vacation."

Herb smiled at the joke even though he didn't share the sentiment. He had been looking forward to this for weeks, months maybe. The kids were growing up so fast. Usually he saw them once or twice a month for lunch or dinner, because it was easier on Abby not to have to take care of another body. But this time Abby was adamant about him staying for an extended period, and she didn't have to twist his arm too hard. His group home was okay; he had fun with some of the staff, like Maria, and he got along with all the other residents, though most of them had more developmental disabilities than physical ones, but nothing could replicate time with Peter and CJ. They were his blood. The group home wasn't bad at all if you looked big picture. If he'd been born twenty years earlier, he could have ended up in an institution.

"What's that, Uncle Herb?" CJ asked. She was pointing to the indentation on the side of his forehead.

Peter groaned. "You ask that every time, CJ."

"It's his birthmark, honey," Abby answered.

Herb didn't mind CJ's asking at all. It wasn't a visit until she did. He loved how CJ's fingers softly traced the horseshoe impression that started near his eye and curved above his ear and into his hairline, left by the forceps during his delivery. He was an "instrument baby" of the late 1960s. At birth, he was wearing his mother's umbilical cord like a scarf. The loss of oxygen during that critical time left Herb with spastic tetraplegia, unable to walk and with limited arm control, so despite his age—he was turning forty-two in a couple of months—his muscles had withered to the point that his frame was pretty much equal in size to Peter's.

"So," Abby said, trying to get everyone's attention. "Like I was telling Peter before, I need to go out for a little while, and Uncle Herb is going to watch you, if that's okay with you, Herb."

Herb nodded. Watching was no problem, it was one of the few the things he *could* do well. His only concern was if something happened that required action.

"So, despite Uncle Herb's presence, Peter, you should still look after CJ and go to Uncle Herb for guidance. Uncle Herb is there only to supervise, and under no condition do you leave the yard. Understand?"

Peter had no problem with the directions, but he turned and glared at someone who would. CJ wasn't listening of course, busy tracing her pointer finger down the window as she gnawed at the plastic top of her travel cup.

Herb took it all in, smiling.

"Did you hear that, CJ?" Peter said, looking for some sort of affirmation.

CJ couldn't be bothered.

"CJ?" Abby said, stressing each letter as she usually did.

CJ's stared at the back of her mother's head. She seemed perfectly content to let her wait.

"Mommy's talking to you," Abby added.

"I-I-I-I know-w-w-w," CJ said, parroting the inflection of her mother's voice.

Peter's head dropped, exhausted by his sister's defiance.

"CJ!" Abby said sternly.

Herb didn't care if this car ride never ended. He was enjoying every second of it. CJ turned to him as if she was appraising his value, her squinty eyes fixed on his face. Then she turned back to her mother and said, "You talking to me?"

Uncle Herb let his chin fall to his chest, in hopes of hiding the smile that cracked his face.

Abby shot back, "Young lady, I don't know where you learn these expressions, but I strongly suggest you unlearn them quickly."

CJ ignored the threat, choosing to stare at Uncle Herb, who looked like he was choking but was really trying to prevent his niece from seeing him bottle his laughter.

"She's always like this, Uncle Herb," Peter said.

A string of saliva dropped from Herb's bottom lip to his lap. CJ bowed her head to get a better look at Herb's face, so he turned his head toward Peter's window. When he thought he could keep a straight face, he glanced over at CJ, but she was waiting for him, smiling. His body then bobbed in uncontrollable laughter, falling forward like a puppet dropped from the top of a building. Only the constraints of the seat belts and Peter's grip kept Herb from falling face first onto the floor of the car.

At home, the family had barely dropped Uncle Herb's suitcase, and him into his chair, before Abby jumped back into the car and left. She was late for her first day of work. Peter found himself in the front yard, a willing captive of CJ and her lasso. Uncle Herb sat parked on the driveway, thinking how lucky he was to get a front-row seat for this show.

As Peter let himself be tied, he heard shouting. He looked up and saw an attractive young woman storm out of Josh's house. Josh followed, not looking in a particular rush, and taking his time to look at the sky and his yard.

"Waste away your life if you want to, but I'm not going to be around to see it," she shouted at the air, but Peter guessed her words were aimed at Josh.

"I'm sorry you feel that way," Josh said. He looked over at Peter and CJ, but didn't acknowledge them.

"Don't give me your self-righteous crap. You piss away everything, that's what you do, you and your crazy ideas and beliefs. There is just too much collateral damage with you. You leave it in your wake."

"I don't think that is a fair assessment," Josh calmly replied.

The woman threw her arms up the air. Her pocketbook, which was wrapped around her shoulder, hit her square in the head on the rebound, fanning her anger. "You know what, Josh? Me wasting my life waiting for you to grow up, that's not fair."

She opened her car door, sat, and slammed the door shut. She stared at Josh as if she was taking a mental snapshot, and for a second, her anger seemed to turn into something sadder. "I'm sorry," she said. The engine roared and the tires screeched. The back end of the car fishtailed as she sped away. Counting Dad's taxi and Mom's car, Peter noted it was the third car today to speed off down Ranch Street.

Across the street, Mr. Terry had watched the entire scene from his knees in his flowerbed. When the car was out of sight, he shouted, "Girlfriend needs some medication, I believe."

Josh waved and headed back toward his house. From the ground, Peter craned his neck to watch Josh's every step. Josh stopped at the stoop in front of his door and looked over their way. "That didn't go too well," he said, and flashed the peace sign before disappearing inside.

Day 60

Uncle Herb paid casual attention to the cartoon on television: this big, blue octopus was living in an apartment complex in the city, hanging out and getting into exciting adventures with his buddies—a wiener dog, a penguin, and a talking flower. It was a dated cartoon, considered a "classic" by the cable network, but much newer than the cartoons he had grown up on—and a lot less creative, in his opinion. It was like *Friends* for the kindergarten set.

It didn't matter what was on; Herb's enjoyment stemmed from his proximity to CJ. She sat at his feet, her back leaning against his knees as she ate raisins out of the container.

"Look, Uncle Herb, Oswald always wears a life preserver near the water," CJ pointed out.

It was in moments like this when Herb wished that speaking wasn't such a frustrating effort. He wanted to joke with her, tease her, and make her think: *why does Oswald need a life preserver? He's an octopus!* But Herb knew by the time he pushed the words into the air, the payout wouldn't be there, and both CJ and Oswald would be far from the water, flying a kite or eating ice cream. The last thing he wanted was to slow them down.

His first night of vacation at his sister's home had gone as well as expected. He soaked in CJ and Peter, shared in Abby's enthusiasm about getting a job, and spent a night of horrible sleep, which was nothing new.

The room Abby had set up for him was comfortable enough. The mattress was firm and didn't swallow him, and Abby had installed bed rails—probably CJ's old set—to prevent Herb from rolling off and falling to the floor. The troubling aspect was the small desk and unopened boxes piled high in the corner. The room was evidently intended as a home office for Nick.

Herb had to admit he wasn't overly upset when he found out

Nick was away on business. The comfort quotient rose exponentially. When Nick was around, Herb felt like a visitor. He didn't know if Nick made him feel this way on purpose, if it just came naturally, or it all was in Herb's head, but they were brothers by law only.

Herb knew this was partly his fault. He had felt this unsettling ping in his gut since Nick and Abby started dating. Early on, Herb tried to chalk the pings up to Nick being awkward around a person with a disability. Herb experienced it every day. But then there would be a look in Nick's eye, a discreet facial expression or a conversation where the things left unsaid weighed heavier than the spoken words, and the pings rattled around like pennies in a cookie tin. He wanted to embrace Nick for the person he was, flawed like everyone else, but there was something more, something slippery that prevented Herb from getting to that point.

Herb felt awful about the situation, the strain it put on his sister during his visits, but the pings never disappeared. He hoped the plans for this visit hadn't caused too much trouble. He also hoped that at some point he could salvage some sort of relationship with his brother-in-law, but right now he hoped Nick's business trip was a long one. He was getting very selfish in his old age.

Peter entered the living room and plopped down on the couch. "Mom said she called in my medication prescription this morning. Can I bike into town and go get it, Uncle Herb?"

"I want to go too!" CJ said.

Peter melted into the couch. "No."

"Why?"

"Because Uncle Herb can watch you now. You don't have to bug me all the time."

Herb knew CJ's insistence on shadowing Peter had to be a drain on the boy, but for a split second, Herb himself felt insecure, trying to gauge if Peter had reached the age when he'd be embarrassed to be seen publicly with his disabled Uncle. It was bound to happen, but Herb's sudden and sharp anxiety unsettled him. *Maybe this vacation wasn't such a great idea*, he thought. His home and work (delivering interoffice mail at a nonprofit agency) kept him sheltered and safe. Complacency and routine had its advantages.

Now the emotions being stirred were things he hadn't felt in over two decades.

Herb tried to be diplomatic; this was all so new to him. He asked Peter if it was okay if they all went.

Peter gave in reluctantly.

"I-gush-e-shoe-oh," Herb said. *I guess we should go.*

As Peter and CJ removed their bikes from the garage and strapped on their helmets, Herb wondered if his anxiety was something more. If he unconsciously knew he was in over his head. CJ ran to the garage and returned with two tall, bright orange fluorescent flags. She stuck one on the back of her bike and wiggled the other between the seat padding and metal frame of Herb's wheelchair.

"There, Uncle Herb. So cars can see you. Peter won't use his anymore."

This did little to ease Herb's uncertainty, but he appreciated the gesture.

Peter checked his tire pressure with a hand squeeze and CJ followed suit, even with her training wheels which were plastic to the core. They headed out: Peter and CJ circled the slow surge of Herb's motorized wheelchair like sheepdogs. Herb's nerves were getting the best of him, with the worst-possible scenarios playing out in his head. They were good kids, great kids even, but still kids. If CJ had one of her excited lapses in judgment and ran into the street or something—his limitations as a chaperone made him shudder.

These feelings only escalated as the group made the right turn off Ranch, passed the pavilion, and headed to the exit. Beyond the hedges and gates separating Willow Creek Landing from the rest of the world, cars flashed by, zipping down the two-lane road at high speeds.

Peter pedaled ahead, then stopped his bike at the guard booth and waited. He didn't like biking so slow, giving the sun ample opportunity to roast exposed areas of skin. He saw the queasy look on his uncle's face as he approached.

"Maybe I should go by myself," he said.

Selection seventeen on Peter's "Sucks Rocks" list: Slocin Road.

Peter had two recurring dreams since moving into the Creek, both involving balls. In one, he sat in his backyard minding his own business, when a sharp whistle would crack the air. He'd look up to see a small marshmallow, the ones found in instant hot chocolate packets, hurtling toward him through the sky. He'd hear a distant shout of "Fore!" but it was always a split-second after realizing the marshmallow was a golf ball that had just penetrated his eye socket with a sickening slurp. The rest of the dream usually consisted of Peter knocking into trees and lawn furniture, trying to acclimate himself to the life of a cyclops. In the other dream, he chased a rolling tennis ball. He was either on a tennis court or the elementary school in his old neighborhood where he and his friends played stickball. The second he lifted his eyes with the ball in hand, he was standing on the divider line in the middle of Slocin Road with a giant tractor trailer barreling down on him—the truck's thick, steel grille the exact height off the road as Peter's face.

Peter understood why the color drained from his uncle's face; he felt the same way the first time he biked on Slocin.

"It's not too bad," Peter said as they reached the gates and silently contemplated the width of the road's shoulder. He pointed to a side street fifty yards away. "We just have to make it to there, and then we can take the back roads to town."

Herb studied the traffic pattern: two lanes in each direction with a steady flow of cars, and the nearest traffic light a half mile down the road. Cars would have no reason to drive under sixty miles per hour.

"Great," Herb muttered to himself. All the consequences of his next decision circled like a carousel in his head. Turning around and going home would certainly disappoint the kids and maybe even set the tone for the rest of Herb's stay. But going? He refused to let himself imagine the unimaginable. He was paralyzed enough.

So, Herb did what he always did when he felt himself at a crossroads. He lowered his head in prayer.

Cars slowed as they entered and exited Willow Creek Landing, lowering their sunglasses or phones to peer at the man in the wheelchair, his head bowed, and the two children on bikes huddled around him. One or two drivers came close to stopping and offering assistance, but then the boy would smile bashfully or wave, and the drivers would wave back and continue on their hurried way, relieved on several levels while still feeling a personal rush for reaching out enough to achieve Good Samaritan status in their own minds.

"Uncle Herb?" CJ asked, after several minutes of silence.

Peter stuck a finger to his lips to quiet her.

CJ leaned in closer to the wheelchair, shooing her brother.

"Uncle Herb," she whispered, "don't worry if you're scared. I'll protect you. I have my lasso. I'll walk right next to you."

Peter rolled his eyes and threw his hands in the air. "Like a lasso will do anything against a speeding car."

"It will!"

The lasso discussion had little time to spiral into an argument. Herb's head rose.

"Eddie," he said. *Ready.*

They waited until there was a break in traffic and no vehicles could be seen as far as the nearest bend. This would give them at least five seconds of car-free travel. Herb motioned for Peter to go, warning him to stay completely to the outside of the shoulder. When Herb was praying, asking for help, a sign to lead him, it was CJ's interruption that dictated his decision. By "protecting him," she would remain on foot and on the inside of Herb, a barrier preventing her from getting any closer to the road. There would be no losing control of her bike or judgment. Caution was in Peter's nature, and Herb felt confident as Peter hugged the grass outside the shoulder, pedaling straight and steady.

But then Herb heard the sound of approaching cars in the distance. He prayed with his eyes open for traveling mercies as he braced himself for the deafening roar and manufactured wind gusts.

"It's okay, Uncle Herb," CJ said in a soothing voice. She led her bicycle on foot in perfect stride with Herb's wheelchair.

The deafening roar never did come. An elderly couple driving a hatchback economy car passed first, their eyes nowhere near the road but staring stupefied over at Herb and CJ and the parallel orange flags sagging lifelessly from their poles above them. The couple muttered declarations like, "in all the years" and "I never," and unwittingly turned into the grand marshals of a parade of rubberneckers, filled with slow-moving floats of curiosity, amusement, or mild annoyance. Herb praised the good fortune.

The group reached Main Street, and Herb decided he had lived through enough adventure for one day. He parked next to a shaded bench and told Peter he could run to the drugstore on his own since he would be in sight the entire way. CJ had packed some picture books in the mesh storage unit underneath Herb's chair, and she grabbed one and headed to the bench.

The sun's glare washed out the colors of the bouquet shops and restaurants dotting both sides of Main Street, constructing an image resembling a collage of overexposed photographs.

"When is it going to rain, Uncle Herb?" CJ asked, peering to the sky.

"Ah-de-no."

The picture book played music, and CJ hummed along with the song. Main Street buzzed with cars, and a periodic honk would produce a face and waving hand behind a window of a passing car.

"Wow, how does everyone see us over here? We're not even on the sidewalks," CJ wondered aloud.

Herb looked up at the obtrusively bright orange flags, but only smiled.

As Peter reached the plate glass window of Handley's Drug Store, he braced himself before opening the door. He knew the magazine rack of Handley's was a local hangout for some of his schoolmates until Mr. Handley would whisk them off for loitering. The store was air-conditioned—a reason to go anywhere these days. Peter was thankful for Uncle Herb's suggestion to go solo. This way he could move stealthily. Just like his list of goals for the school year, the summer was more of the same: if Peter couldn't fit in, he wanted to be invisible—entirely impossible if he, CJ, and Uncle Herb had all went to the drugstore. In Wonder Woman attire or not, attention followed CJ like dirt to Pigpen. Ladies would approach her in the supermarket to comment on her big, golden curls or her large, blue eyes. Only her family commented on her largest feature, which drew the most attention: her mouth.

Peter stared at his shoes as he entered the store and beelined down the cosmetics aisle to avoid the magazine rack in the front of the store. He took the milliseconds of silence as a good sign, glancing behind his shoulder once he was halfway down the aisle.

He reached the pharmacy department at the back of the store and saw Mr. Handley behind the counter. Mr. Handley was called the Wizard, though never to his face. From the elevated platform behind the counter, Mr. Handley looked like he was seven feet tall, but when he stepped down from the counter, usually to help a customer find a product, one could see that he was no larger than the tallest shelf in the store, providing an Oz-like moment.

"Hello, Peter. I was expecting you. Your mother called this morning," Mr. Handley said, as he smiled behind the glasses that dangled from the edge of his nose.

Peter looked up at the Wizard. "Yes, sir."

Mr. Handley handed Peter a stapled, small, white bag. "Your mother asked me to run a tab. I usually don't do that, but for you . . ." He smiled at his joke and winked.

"Thanks, Mr. Handley."

Peter stuffed the bag in his front pocket and raced back down the aisle with his head down. When he reached the exit doors, he let out a sigh of relief as he pushed, until he collided with Chipper entering the store.

"Howdy," Chipper said, his usual greeting in its low, ominous tenor.

"Sorry," Peter said, sliding fluidly around Chipper and out the door only to bump into one of the goons. The quick change of temperature, and Chipper, dizzied Peter. He quickly considered retreating into the store, saying he forgot something, but Chipper grabbed his shirt and ushered him down the sidewalk. The safety of the store aisles closed with the door.

"Maybe Nemo could help us out, guys. What do you think?"

The goon shook their heads eagerly. Peter didn't like where this was heading. He concentrated on a crack in the sidewalk as Chipper and the goons formed a triangle around him.

"Hey Nemo, yoo-hoo! I'm up here," Chipper said, trying to get Peter to look up.

No way, Peter thought. *Just do what you're going to do.*

"Nemo, Jason here is working on his first aid merit badge. We need someone to practice splinting and slinging. Can you be our dummy?" Chipper said, which evoked an eruption of goon laughter.

"I have to go," Peter said. The words fell limply to the ground with no force behind them.

"C'mon, Nemo. I promise no tourniquets."

Peter shook his head and tried to walk away, but Chipper grabbed him firmly by the shirt with both hands. He wasn't going anywhere.

"First step, immobilization," Chipper said in a scholarly voice as one of the goons grabbed Peter from behind.

"Let me go!" Peter said, trying to sound forceful but failing miserably.

Chipper slapped him on the side of his head, the demeaning act more painful than the actual slap.

Chipper glanced down the block. "Oh, I see what the rush is all about, people are waiting for you. Why didn't you say something?"

Like that would have mattered, Peter thought.

"Who's that with your Looney Tunes sister, anyway?"

There was no way Peter was answering that question, but then Chipper grabbed Peter's nipple and turned it like a volume dial.

"My uncle," Peter said through clenched teeth.

Chipper let out a whooping laugh. "It just keeps getting better and better. What were you doing in Handley's, buying him a drool bucket?"

The goons' laughter was delayed, as if they first had to ignore or push down and bury something before rejoining the ridicule.

"You know, Nemo, you should save up and buy a little yellow bus for the entire family."

Underneath the heavy layers of fear, Peter felt anger boil. He could take the personal attacks, but his uncle should be off limits. His face reddened and his vision blurred. A sudden bang startled them all. Peter felt the grips release him. Mr. Handley was pointing from behind his store's window.

Chipper waved and smiled. He said under his breath as he waved, "Hi, Mr. Wizard. We're just taking a stroll down the yellow brick road." He looked at Peter with disdain. "First your druggie neighbor, now the wizard. You have some luck."

Peter didn't agree, but he had no plans to debate the issue. He made a break for it, dashing down the street.

"Run, Nemo, Run!" he heard Chipper mocking him.

Peter didn't stop until he reached CJ and Uncle Herb. He hid his wet face as he loaded himself on his bike. Uncle Herb and CJ followed naturally.

Herb had seen the end of the altercation. At first, he'd hoped they were friends of Peter, but he was beginning to realize friendship might be a rare commodity for his nephew. Between Slocin Road and watching those boys torment Peter, Herb felt like day two of his vacation had already stripped him raw. He would have loved to rescue Peter, to make him feel protected while instilling a deep fear into those kids, enough to make them think twice the next time they decided to pick on Peter. The painful feelings of inadequacy rushed into Herb, emotions he hadn't experienced since his own awful adolescence. He was a penguin cursing his flightless wings. He thought being around the kids was a good thing; now he wasn't so sure.

Peter, CJ, and Uncle Herb traveled home in silence; only the sound of the wheelchair's motor could be heard above their thoughts.

Night

The carcass of Peter's air conditioner sat defeated on the carpet below his window, having burnt out over three weeks ago. Peter's father had promised to fix or replace the AC right after returning from his Arizona business trip, but then it was the New Orleans trip, followed by the most recent trip to Texas. It was depressing for Peter to think of the endless number of cities and states in the country.

Things you can do with a dead air conditioner—a list by Peter Grady. One: stub your toe in the dark. Two: makes a suitable small table or chair. Three: use as an extra hamper.

The heat was relentless, nudging and crowding him. Peter lashed out in bed as if trapped in an invisible net. He peeled back the white elastic band of his underwear and kicked the lone sheet to the bottom of his bed as he sweated and stared into the darkness while imagining himself in an igloo, or making a snow angel in his bathing suit.

Then Peter heard the sound of a footstep, a hardwood plank wheezing in the hallway. Then another. Peter sat up and peered underneath his bedroom door for light. CJ and his mother had the habit of turning the hallway light on when they woke in the middle of the night. No light, but another footstep. Uncle Herb's room was next to his, and he debated calling out just for show, to let whoever it was in the hall know he wasn't sneaking up on anyone. It occurred to Peter that he was doing the second dumbest action of victims in horror movies—sitting there. The dumbest, of course, being to look for the cause of the sound. He heard the footstep again, closer this time, and slipped out of bed, tiptoeing to the closet. He stepped over a row of shoes and hid in the back corner. He grabbed the aluminum baseball bat leaning in the corner and lifted it to his chest, feeling the cool metal against his skin. The steps stopped in front of Peter's bedroom door.

"Peter, are you awake?" CJ whispered from outside the door.

Peter exhaled. He crawled back into bed with his heart still racing, leaving the bat in the closet. The door creaked open and CJ appeared at the foot of his bed above the crumpled mountain of sheets.

"Go back to bed, CJ." Peter turned on his side. The smoldering large numbers of his digital clock read 11:53 p.m.

"Wake up, please, Peter. There is someone in front of the house, a man. I heard him. He's right outside."

CJ's eyes were egg shaped, and she bit at her bottom lip. She moved around to the head of bed. "I'm serious," she said, and Peter could smell her breath, an extraordinarily strong, sweet scent.

"Were you eating marshmallows?" Peter relaxed.

She looked away sheepishly.

Then it made complete sense to Peter: why the hallway light wasn't on, how she could hear someone in front of the house when her room faced the golf course in back. She was making a late-night visit to the kitchen's snack stash. Marshmallows were CJ's weakness. Peter was wondering how long she had been doing this when he too heard a low mumbling from outside.

CJ whipped her pointer finger to the window, and leaned her face into Peter's. "He's coming this way."

Peter rolled to the floor and crawled over to the air conditioner. He carefully lifted the shade enough to dip his head under, and CJ did the same, their noses inches from the mesh screen. The one streetlight lit the block in a rusty tint. No signs of movement except for Mr. Terry's miniature windmill on his side lawn, the sails turning over lazily in the still night.

"I don't see anything," Peter said.

"There was someone there, I swear." CJ's eyes darted from side to side in disbelief.

Peter sighed, "I'm going back to bed," but as he started to back away he heard the low, incoherent mumbling again, like a witch reciting a spell in front of a cauldron.

CJ pointed to the window and mouthed, "I told you."

Their pajamas hugged the contours of the air conditioner. They allowed only the features above their noses to rise up the windowsill.

"Where is it coming from?" CJ said, softly.

A garbage can rattled down the street—obviously the voice did nothing to stop the raccoons' pillage.

"I'm getting Mom," CJ said, and she turned, but Peter grabbed her and nodded with his head. A shadowy figure appeared from beyond the hemlock tree. The man walked with the muscled tautness of a stalking tiger, the hair bouncing gently off his shoulders.

"It's Josh."

"Josh?" CJ asked.

Peter brought his finger up to his mouth. In this light, Josh reminded him of an animal in the wild. Peter felt like a photographer for *National Geographic*. Ever since the race, Peter held a fascination with his neighbor—the way Josh decided to do something and did it without caring what anyone else would think or how much he stood out. Peter would never have done that in a million years. This presented a perfect opportunity to study him. Even the way he walked was unusual, and Peter wished he could walk the same way. Josh's gait possessed a menacing grace; one that would make you feel protected if you walked by his side through a crowd of strangers, but more than uncomfortable if you crossed his path on an empty street.

CJ said, "Who's he talking to? He's by himself."

Josh was pacing slowly in the middle of the street, his head bent to the sky. He was dressed only in jeans.

"He needs shoes for his birthday," CJ whispered.

Getting a little bolder, they pressed their faces against the screen to hear his words. He spoke in streams.

"He makes me to lie down in green pastures; he leads me beside the still waters. He restores my soul; he leads me in the path of righteousness for His name's sake."

"*Who* does that to Josh?" CJ asked, her words muffled and constricted by the screen.

"Shhhh."

"Yea, though I walk through the valley of the shadow of death, I will fear no evil; for you are with me; Your rod and your staff, they comfort me."

Peter was pretty sure Josh was quoting the Bible, but he made a mental note to ask Uncle Herb in the morning. Uncle Herb would definitely know.

Just as Peter started to relax, Josh stopped chanting and turned his head quickly in the direction of their window. Noticing this, Peter and CJ collapsed to the ground, their heads colliding on the way down. They rolled around the carpeted floor, both cupping their impacted skulls, their mouths drawn in hushed cries.

There they remained in silence until the pain subsided. After minutes of silence and hearing nothing but the crickets, Peter desperately wanted to know if Josh was still standing in the middle of the street or if he was closer now, maybe at the window screen looking in. Peter couldn't get himself to look up from the rug. He nodded to CJ and pointed to the window. She stared at him as if he was crazy and shook her head no. She then pointed at Peter and thumbed the window. Peter shook his head diagonally, neither a confirming yes or no. It occurred to him that remaining on the carpet until morning sounded like the best alternative.

Day 61

Peter woke to CJ's big toe greeting him and the heel of her left foot resting on his cheek. They had slept the entire night on Peter's carpet. The early light of day peeked through the shades. Peter pushed CJ's foot away, and CJ groaned in protest before turning on her side.

Peter sat at his desk as he did at the start of every morning and removed the colored pencils from the top drawer. On his desk calendar, he drew an orange circle and blue circle on yesterday's date: another day without a drop of rain or his father being home. He counted back twenty days with his finger; his father had been away on business for thirteen of them.

The mean-spirited buzz of his mother's alarm clock intruded on the quiet morning. Peter heard his mother's slaps at the clock followed by the shuffling of her slippers against the floor. Seconds later, Abby appeared in front of Peter's door.

"Morning. What happened here? Was she having nightmares?" Abby said, nodding in the direction of CJ on the floor.

Peter shrugged. He didn't know how to label last night. He had fought the urge to look behind his shades even after he woke; if Josh was still there, that would *really* spook him.

Abby yawned and rubbed her eyes. "I need some coffee, and then I need you to help me toilet Uncle Herb."

"Is Dad coming home today?"

"Tomorrow, I think," she said, and disappeared down the hallway.

Peter followed and joined his mother at the kitchen table, armed with a box of Cheerios and a half-gallon of milk. He ate in silence as she sipped from a mug of coffee and stared into space.

"I never thought I'd say this, but I'm getting pretty sick of sunshine," she said.

"Are you staying home with us today?"

"Peter, I just started working. I don't think it would be wise to take a day off so soon."

Peter didn't answer. This sounded like more than a part-time job.

She added, "You guys are doing okay with Uncle Herb, right?"

Peter smiled and nodded. He stood and walked to the counter, dumping his half-eaten bowl of cereal in the sink. He was reaching for his medication on the shelf when CJ appeared, dressed in full Wonder Woman attire with the lasso uncurled and dragging behind her. Even the indestructible bracelets were on her wrist this morning.

Abby watched her, smiling. "Are we going to save the world today, Wonder Woman?"

Peter knew the reason for full armor. Wonder Woman was in self-preservation mode against neighbors who go boom in the night.

Abby didn't sense the anxiety in her children, the quiet looks shared between the two, the glances out the windows. She was thinking about her day ahead, hoping for a call from a contact she'd made during the first day of her job, a young family looking for a home. Despite being a novice in real estate, Abby was confident she could sell to a young family. She knew the talking points: good school district, low crime, a neighborhood with a lot of parks and fun things to do in the surrounding area. She was experienced with young families herself—a pro, actually—and she felt certain she could thaw that realtor-client relationship into something personal. She'd make them feel like she was one of them and they could trust her. *That's what a good salesperson does, right?* She looked at the clock.

"Let's go wake Uncle Herb, Peter. I need to leave in twenty minutes."

Walking down the hallway, Peter felt an unexpected and sharp longing for a house with stairs. In his old house, a flight of stairs ran up the center of the house. He remembered when his mother was pregnant with CJ. She'd have horrible back pains and often sat on the lower steps, because the stiff, upright position softened the throbbing. Peter recalled sitting next to his mother often, and she'd caress his head for what seemed like hours as they talked about the new baby or sat in a content silence. This was before Willow Creek Landing, before his father started his own business, before it stopped raining. Peter missed those stairs. The new house had a hospital wing feel, each bedroom branching off from a main corridor.

Uncle Herb's room was the first branch down the hallway, closest to the living room. He'd been awake for a while now, and he thanked God when he heard voices growing stronger and heading toward him. Help couldn't arrive soon enough. His bladder was about to burst, and that meant a bath his sister probably didn't have the time or energy to give, plus an extra load of laundry. He was doing his part now by thinking about anything that didn't involve water. "P-e-e-e," he said, as loud as he could while maintaining bodily control, when he felt like he couldn't go a second longer.

Abby and Peter broke into a jog. "Oh, shoot, sorry, Herb. Hurry up, Peter. Help me get him in his chair."

Herb was thankful that Peter was experienced with lifting and moving him. Within seconds, they were in the bathroom propping Herb on the toilet.

"Boy, you really had to go bad, Uncle Herb. It sounds like a waterfall," CJ said. She was tying her lasso to the bathroom's doorknob. Herb smiled at her from above Peter's forearm. CJ waved, and the door slammed shut with a tug of the lasso.

Happy that he hadn't created more work for his sister before she left for work, Herb smiled as Peter dressed him.

"What's so funny, Uncle Herb?"

"Ew." *You.*

Peter led Uncle Herb's crooked arm through the shirt hole.

"Uncle Herb, something really strange happened last night."

Herb was all ears.

"CJ woke me up in the middle of the night. She heard someone outside. It was Josh. I think he was praying."

"Ut wong it hat?" Uncle Herb said, smiling. He tried to poke Peter in the ribs with his free hand but missed. Peter laughed and pulled Herb's other arm through his shirt and over his back.

"There's nothing wrong with praying. You know what I mean. It's just that he was doing it outside in the middle of the night, and it was also the way he was praying, like he was scared or in trouble and needed help."

"Hats hi e-ray." *That's why we pray.*

Peter stepped back and appraised the ensemble he'd picked out for his uncle. Satisfied, he nodded and glimpsed himself in the mirror before heading toward the kitchen with his uncle in tow.

"I know. It was just, just strange, I guess."

After breakfast, Peter, CJ, and Uncle Herb sat on the brick patio in the backyard. Uncle Herb read from the Bible in his lap as CJ colored in the chair next to him, stopping every so often to turn the page when Uncle Herb asked. Peter was in a lawn chair a short distance away, working his way through *The Three Musketeers*. Last year Peter's teacher told him that he was reading above grade level and gave him a recommended reading list for summer. He thought an adventure book with sword duels sounded interesting even though it was a really old story. He was near the beginning of the book: d'Artagnan had just left home with hopes of becoming a Musketeer of the Guard and stopped at an inn, where a well-dressed man ridiculed him for the odd color of his horse.

Peter dropped the book to his side. He looked beyond the white, vinyl fence that separated the backyard from the golf course. The three grass hills of hole four had turned a shade of yellow from the lack of water, giving the golf course a desert-like quality. The heat didn't stop the constant parade of golfers from playing through.

Peter looked further down the golf course and could see the furthest home on Colonial Drive. There were two types of homes, which the residents labeled the ranches and the manches (short for mansions, the Colonials and Victorian styles), but they all shared similar landscaping down to the brick patios in back. Only three shades of paint were available for the exterior of the home, and they were all muted colors, ones you could find if you picked up a handful of sand at the beach. This had something to do with providing no distraction for the golfers. It was all about the golf. These fine details made the neighborhood look fake, like a town surrounding a toy train set. Everything was too symmetrical for a real town. There were four roads in the community, but actually only two long perpendicular lines. At the center where the lines met stood the pavilion.

Chipper's presence in the Creek further isolated Peter from the real world. Chipper's dad was on the board of directors at Willow Creek Landing, and his name and picture were plastered throughout the neighborhood and the community newsletter, *The Creek*. He was some super-successful businessman who overtook small and weak companies, then tore them apart, somewhat similar to what his son did in school.

A whistling hiss sliced through the air, then stopped with a solid thud as a golf ball bounced off the vinyl siding of the house and rolled to a stop not three feet from Peter.

"I got it," CJ said, jumping out of her chair.

Number nine on the "Sucks Rocks" list: incoming golf balls. You were never completely safe in a golf course community, especially outside, but that was also true inside near windows that faced the golf course. CJ, on the other hand, loved when some hack sent a ball into the yard. Her father gave her a quarter for every ball she collected.

Two men in a golf cart pulled up to their back fence. CJ dropped the ball discreetly in the cupholder of Uncle Herb's wheelchair.

A pot-bellied man wearing a collared sports shirt and sunglasses on top of his salt-and-pepper hair stepped out of the driver's side of the cart. A much older and shriveled man in plaid pants remained seated, a thick cigar sticking out from the center of his mouth like a lever. The driver leaned on the fence, and his eyes searched the ground of their backyard. He didn't acknowledge the man in the wheelchair or the two children sitting in the yard until he grew impatient with his search.

"You guys see a golf ball come through here?"

CJ looked at Uncle Herb and then turned toward the golfer. "No," she said.

"Let's go, Dean. The other foursome is up at the tee already," said the shriveled man with the plaid pants from the golf cart. The sweet-smelling cigar smoke drifted into the yard.

The man named Dean dismissed his partner with an abrupt wave. "They can wait. That was my St. Andrew's commemorative ball. I could swear it was this house here. You guys didn't see anything?"

Peter sensed an accusatory tone. He stared at the grass in front of him.

"Nope," CJ said.

"They're hitting up on us, Dean," plaid pants said.

The man named Dean stared at CJ the same way childless people looked upon a kid having a meltdown in a store, though CJ was completely calm.

"Dean! C'mon, you can drop a ball where I am."

"All right, all right." Dean jogged back to the cart. He shot a quick hard look at CJ one more time before speeding off.

When the sound of the golf cart hushed, CJ pulled the ball from the cup holder and inspected the St. Andrew's insignia. "Maybe Dad will give me a dollar for this one," she said, tossing the ball in the air and cupping her two hands to catch it. She bolted inside to add the new treasure to her collection.

"Her mouth is going to get her in real trouble someday," Peter said.

Uncle Herb looked at Peter but said nothing.

"They knew she was lying, Uncle Herb. She shouldn't have done it. What would happen if he jumped over the fence and started looking for the ball? He could have seen it in the cup holder."

Peter crossed his arms and waited for a reply, but Uncle Herb just smiled at him.

A thunderous rumbling came from the front of the house as a flatbed truck plodded down the street carrying stacks of lumber. The truck's hydraulic brakes screeched to a stop in front of Josh's house.

"Can I take a look, Uncle Herb?"

Uncle Herb nodded, yes.

Peter watched as the truck driver, a stubby guy in a baseball hat and T-shirt with wet stains under the arms, stepped down from the truck and pulled leather gloves from the back pocket of his dirty jeans. He squinted in the direction of the sun, then at Josh's front door. A shirtless Josh appeared in jeans with similar grime as the driver's. Josh pushed his hair back and tied a bandanna to his head.

"Where do you want it?" Peter heard the trucker ask.

"I'll be working here on the driveway, makes sense to keep the wood close. Let's drop it all on the front here, the neighbors will go ballistic. Have you ever seen such manicured lawns?"

The trucker nodded and wiped his brow with his forearm. Peter found himself making his way to the front yard, hugging the perimeter of his house. Josh and the truck driver unloaded long planks of wood from the back of the truck, two or three at a time. They worked in silence, and Peter studied them as he moved closer, not stopping until he reached the giant pine tree. He squatted and peered from behind it, nibbling at a fingernail as he watched.

The trucker broke the silence by asking Josh what in high heaven he was building with all this wood. Josh found this to be the most hysterical question for reasons beyond Peter and, by the confused look on his face, beyond the trucker. The trucker stepped back and stared as Josh's body quivered, then erupted again in laughter. This went on for a couple of minutes. The trucker distanced himself from Josh. When they continued unloading, the trucker worked with newfound energy.

Peter waited, but Josh never did answer the question.

After the truck was empty and the front lawn layered with stacks of wood, Josh had to chase after the trucker to tip him, and the trucker accepted the crumpled bills at a trot, heading quickly back to the truck's cab.

Peter slid further behind the tree and sat down, his back against the bark. With the trucker gone, there was no longer safety in numbers. It was the middle of the day, but the nighttime-roaming, prayer-chanting Josh was not far from the front of Peter's mind. However, Peter couldn't get himself to leave; he was drawn to Josh, an invisible pulling, but maybe that wasn't such a good thing. The trucker sure sensed something and couldn't leave fast enough.

Peter heard the sound of a twig snap and looked up to see Josh standing above him. The sun behind him shaded his face.

Peter scurried to his feet, his height barely reaching Josh's chest. "Oh, hi."

Josh looked around Peter's yard. Peter maneuvered his body to see the expression on Josh's face. There was none.

"Where's your mother?" he asked.

Peter fought the initial and strong urge to lie. He figured Josh already knew the answer; the empty driveway gave it away. "She's at work, but my uncle's in the backyard with my sister." He rushed the end part of the sentence.

Josh nodded, and Peter squinted up at him. Peter didn't know why he always thought of wild animals when he saw Josh, but standing in front of him now was like crossing paths with a bear in the woods—should he make a lot of noise to show a lack of fear, or play dead?

"I forgot your name," Josh said, not apologizing but merely stating a fact.

"Peter."

Josh nodded again. "How old are you again, Peter?"

"Twelve and a half."

Josh scratched the side of his face. "Wow. I wouldn't have pegged you for a day over twelve, but a whole half."

Peter felt his face redden. "How old are you?"

Josh leaned down toward him and whispered, "Twenty-three and three quarters."

Peter had known older people, his parents for one, but out of uncertainty toward the person he was speaking to, he acted impressed.

A man in designer sunglasses and a black, sleeveless vest sped down the street in a golf cart. Many residents traveled this way, even if they weren't off to a round of golf.

"Listen, Peter. I have four really long pieces of wood that I need to move from my lawn to my driveway. I should have had the trucker help, but I wasn't thinking. He seemed in a rush anyway. I don't think it's a job for anyone under twelve, but maybe a really strong twelve and half—"

"I can do it." The words rushed out from somewhere inside Peter, not his brain.

"Maybe we should wait until your mother comes home so we can ask her if it's okay. I don't want—"

"It's okay, really."

Josh puffed out his right cheek, then his left as if he was debating against himself. A slow shrug of his shoulders signaled he'd come to some sort of verdict. "Heck, I've always found it easier to ask for forgiveness than for permission anyway. Let's go."

Peter followed closely behind Josh, his two steps equaling one of Josh's. The wood planks in question were indeed a two-person job, the length of two diving boards and as thick as Peter's fist. They spanned most of Josh's front lawn. Josh instructed Peter to bend down and lift with his legs for more strength and less strain on the back. Peter felt his arms quivering as they carried the first board. He studied Josh's arms, searching for a sign of struggle, but saw only the blue veins streaking through his locked arms.

Peter's father used the gym in the pavilion when he was home. Peter had started to notice changes in his Dad's body. It was impossible not to, really. Peter and CJ had caught him several times admiring his shirtless body in the mirror. Sometimes he'd flex and make them grab his arm or punch his stomach. There was something different in Josh's lean yet perfectly curved muscles, something genuine—not store-bought.

After they placed the first plank on the driveway, Peter held his one arm to stop it from shaking and asked, "Josh, how will cars get in and out of the driveway?"

"What cars? I don't own one."

"What about when your parents visit?"

Josh looked at Peter as though he was an old clock and his face could be easily opened to display the inner workings. A slight smile appeared on Josh's face. "Visit? So, you know about my parents? I figured everyone must. This place is like a small town. A small, fenced-in town." Josh laughed. "Sounds like I could be describing a prison."

Peter had no intention of explaining to Josh the visits from his mother. They walked across the lawn to the next plank. Peter made sure to lift with his legs.

"Good," Josh said. They walked several paces, Josh moving backward and facing Peter. "So, I guess you know about the race then too."

Peter nodded. "I was there. I saw it."

Josh didn't seem the least bit embarrassed. He smiled, "Don't hold it against me. Sometimes I act before I think. I guess you could say I was inspired."

Peter would never hold that against Josh. If Peter acted on just a small portion of his thoughts, especially when he tried to rally himself to oppose Chipper, his life would be a lot better.

"I'm only here for a short time. Until my parents sell the house, or something else," Josh said, pausing.

"What do you mean, 'something else?'" Peter asked.

Josh wiped the sweat from his face and looked toward the sky. "That's a conversation for another day," he said, and from his tone, Peter knew Josh was done talking.

They dropped the second plank and slid it across the driveway until it touched the other plank. From the dead-end direction of Ranch Street, the golf cart from a couple minutes earlier puttered toward them, now carrying two men. Josh lifted his arm over his head to stretch his shoulder. The cart slowed as it passed, the passenger leaning his head across the lap of the driver to get a better view. He looked like a carbon copy of the driver with his sunglasses, khaki shorts, and sleeveless vest. The driver rested his arm on the steering wheel as he drove. The Plexiglas windshield was folded over, and his hand dangled in the open air.

The expression on Josh's face changed. He dropped his hands to his side and returned the golfers' stares with a hard, vacant look. Suddenly, the simple conversation and Josh's small grins seemed miles away, and again Peter saw the wild animal in his neighbor.

"Do you know them?" Peter asked.

Josh's eyes followed the slow-moving golf cart. When the golfers were gone, Josh just smiled at Peter without answering.

Most of the interactions Peter had with the golfers and residents of Willow Creek Landing were similar to the exchange with the guy who'd lost his ball. They either ignored Peter or treated him like he worked for them.

CJ appeared in the side yard between their houses, swinging the lasso over her head. She let the loop fly, barely missing the shrub she aimed to rope in.

Josh watched, the dark cloud that had enveloped him now evaporated. "She's pretty good with that thing."

"She thinks she's a superhero."

CJ tried to rope the shrub again, casting glances at her audience as she wheeled the lasso over her head. She let go and the loop landed over the top of the shrub.

"Gotcha," she shouted. CJ pulled from her end and the shrub bowed.

"You better be careful before the shrub gets mad and catapults you across the street," Josh shouted.

CJ stopped applying pressure on the rope. She had no idea what catapult meant, but it didn't sound good.

"What's Uncle Herb doing?" Peter said, hoping his sister would get the hint and leave. Peter knew she wanted them to welcome her over. Usually, CJ wouldn't wait for such formalities, forcing her presence wherever Peter might be, but Peter knew she wasn't completely sold on Josh yet. Neither was Peter.

"He's napping," CJ replied.

Peter sighed. Where was it written that big brothers had to include little sisters in everything they did? Peter made a mental note to himself that once school starts he would poll his classmates and take the results back to his mother.

As if on cue, his mother's car pulled into the driveway at the usual high speed.

"Mom's home, Peter!" CJ said.

Peter didn't want to leave. He was enjoying helping Josh, one of the few people he had spoken to this summer who wasn't related.

Peter noticed his mother looking at him as she put the car in park and removed the keys from the ignition. She stepped out and waved. Dressed in a gray business suit and with her hair pulled back into a knob, Peter thought she looked very pretty. Recently, Peter had rarely seen her with makeup or jewelry. He remembered how his father made her very angry once when he'd told her the pink sweatpants she wore every day "would walk on their own soon." Her response was something like *If you had my life, you'd do the same.* His father, as usual, made a joke, further infuriating his mother. He'd love to wear pink sweatpants, he said.

Abby stopped next to CJ in the middle of the strip of grass that separated the two houses. She rubbed the back of her head.

"Hi, Joshua. I'm Abby. We met briefly when we first moved in last summer. You left for college shortly after," she said.

"Josh," he said, and bent down to pick a twig that stuck out of his sandal like a flag.

Peter sensed uneasiness in his mother. She waved Peter over and he obeyed, wondering if she had a problem at work. When he reached her, he whispered, "How did it go today?"

"Good. I think I have my first client." She looked at Josh. "I recently started working again. As a realtor."

Josh nodded. "Congratulations." He twisted the cap off a water bottle. "I asked Peter if he could help me for a minute. I hope you don't mind."

Peter noticed the pause before his mother answered.

"Of course not. What are you building? A third floor or a ladder to poke the clouds for rain?" she said and laughed. The laugh didn't sound right to Peter. It was the same fake laugh she used with Josh's mother.

"Just a project," Josh said with a shrug.

Abby nodded, though visibly not satisfied with the answer. "I'm really sorry to hear about your parents. Is there anything we could do to help?"

Josh shrugged again.

Abby shifted her weight from one leg to the other. "Yeah, well . . . if you can think of anything. What do you say we go check on Uncle Herb, guys?"

CJ took off. Peter half-waved to Josh as he left, avoiding eye contact mainly because he felt Josh's eyes on him. Inside, Peter ran to the kitchen window facing Josh's house and watched as Josh pointed at the bundles of wood, counting.

From behind, Peter heard Uncle Herb's wheelchair buzz into the house from the backyard and his mother saying, "I'm so sorry, Herb."

"Me too, Uncle Herb," CJ added.

Peter turned to the French doors in the kitchen that led to the back patio. Uncle Herb was there smiling, half of his face and hairless head completely sunburned, while the other half, his normal shade. He fell asleep on the back porch only partly protected from the sun. He looked like a fishing bob.

Abby left the kitchen and returned with a jar of moisturizer and dropped the container in CJ's lap. She held a small mirror in front of Uncle Herb's face. He laughed at his reflection.

She patted Herb's arm, then asked, "Did anyone call?"

The answer came in chorus: *No, nope,* and *no-o-o.*

By the way she paused before grabbing the cordless phone and marching out of the kitchen, Peter knew *anyone* meant his father.

CJ dragged a stool over to Uncle Herb and climbed to the top. Standing on the circular seat, she opened the moisturizer jar and starting rubbing cream on her uncle's head.

"The burn might not have been so bad if you had more hair, Uncle Herb," Peter said. Uncle Herb had only a few strands, each combed over to the side.

"Anks, Pita."

For every glob of moisturizer that managed to reach Uncle Herb's head, twice as much fell on the floor or on some part of CJ. With the back of one hand, she wiped at a smudge on her cheek, only to smear it down to her earlobe. She asked, "What is Josh building?"

"I don't know," Peter said.

"Did you ask him?"

"No," Peter said, defensively. "You should have seen what happened when the truck driver asked."

CJ wiped her hands on her shirt. "Josh is weird," she said. She jumped down from the top of the stool, landing on her feet, then fell on her knees. She placed her hand on Uncle Herb's leg. "All done, Uncle Herb."

Uncle Herb pushed the joystick of his wheelchair and it jerked forward, almost hitting CJ.

They all found this to be the funniest thing in the world.

Bath Time

After dinner Peter helped his mother bathe Uncle Herb. The setting sun immersed the bathroom in golden hues as they lowered Herb slowly, propping his back against the back of the acrylic tub. Peter held him steady. They worked fast and in unison like a pit crew.

Uncle Herb watched the bathwater engulf him. *"Tie-umin-in,"* he said. *Tide coming in.*

Peter remembered the first time he'd helped bathe Uncle Herb, so nervous he could've puked on the spot. It felt so unnatural seeing a naked adult so close. His mother, annoyed at his transparent awkwardness, yelled at him. "There's nothing that he has that you don't," she said, which embarrassed Peter because she'd said it right in front of Uncle Herb. It wasn't even a true statement. Peter's chest was as hairless as a baby chicken, and before the water and bubble hid half his body, Peter noticed another patch of hair on Uncle Herb where he had none.

Peter held his uncle by his thin arms as his mother ran a soapy sponge along Herb's chest and shoulders. Peter watched in silence as she cleaned Herb's stomach, and then sank her arm into the bubbles to clean his legs and privates. He wondered how many times she'd bathed him. Did she start after their parents died, or was she always helping out like Peter was now? Peter barely remembered his grandparents now; they both died before he turned five. The strongest memory was the color of the orange juice in their house: a murky brown. That was right before they moved into a nursing home.

His mother handed Peter a dry washcloth. "Can you get Uncle Herb's back, honey?"

Peter sank the cloth into the bubbles. "What time is Dad coming home tomorrow?"

His mother sat back on her heels and stretched her back. "No idea."

CJ appeared in the doorway. Right before dinner she'd jumped off the couch, tripped and hit her head against the wall, causing no harm to her but leaving a hotdog-shaped dent in the side of her Wonder Woman tiara. "He's never home," she said, as she tried to push out the dent with her palm.

"CJ, please. I'm tired," Abby said.

CJ turned and headed back to the living room. She casually said, "You're always tired."

Abby sank to her elbows, and her hands enveloped her face. She stared at the empty doorway, rubbing her forehead. "I swear, you guys are putting me over the edge."

Peter squeezed the lukewarm water from the washcloth. A hot bath these days would be considered a form of torture.

"I got your back, Uncle Herb," Peter said.

Uncle Herb nodded. He stared straight ahead at the tiles above the shower handles. *I got yours too, buddy,* he thought to himself.

They lifted Herb into a crouching position, and the water dripped off Herb's body. Abby held Herb upright as Peter gave his uncle a final rinse with the shower nozzle. Together they lifted him above the tub's rim and sat him on the covered toilet seat. Then Peter towel dried Herb as Abby slid Herb into his underwear, white undershirt, and pajama bottoms.

For Christmas last year, CJ and Peter gave Uncle Herb a combination clock and CD player, a gift he wanted because he liked to take audiobooks out of the library. Peter thought it the perfect gift since his uncle had trouble sleeping.

Herb liked to listen to audiobooks while in bed—spiritual topics, sometimes history or biography, subjects that made Peter's eyelids heavy with boredom. But Uncle Herb loved the disks, sometimes asking Peter to change them in the middle of the night if he heard Peter paying a visit to the bathroom.

One of Peter's daily chores during his uncle's stay was to set up the player. As his mother folded clothes and put clean socks and underwear in Herb's dresser, Peter flipped through the CDs that Herb had brought with him. "Uncle Herb, tonight's choices are

The Purpose Driven Life by Rick Warren, or *Into the Wild* by Jon Krakauer."

Abby closed the top drawer and opened the middle one. "How about the Purpose Driven Life Drove Me into the Wild," she said.

Uncle Herb shot his sister a playful look. He said to her, *Sounds good.*

A *rat-a-tat-tat-tat-tat* came from the bathroom. Now it was CJ's bath time. Though Peter couldn't see her, a vivid picture filled his mind. CJ, with bubbles in her hair and on her chin, surrounded by her loyal army of plastic, yellow ducks, which she'd nominate for kamikaze missions to destroy the floating tug boat. CJ's baths were often flood advisories.

Peter said goodnight to Uncle Herb and retreated to the living room, away from the orders of General CJ. He sank in the couch and turned on a baseball game. He half-listened to the announcers as they wondered aloud if baseball would go an entire season without one rain delay. History in the making.

Abby walked past the couch zombie-like on the way to the kitchen. Peter heard a sigh, then the click of the dishwasher's latch.

Peter rolled over and looked above the cushions and out the window at the lavender sky. As if Peter caught the sky by surprise, an ear-rattling scream echoed in the distance, followed by a long high-pitched cackle. Peter pushed himself off the couch and looked at his mother, who was standing in the middle of the kitchen holding a plate.

"What the hell was that?" Abby said, placing the dish on the counter. She moved quickly across the kitchen tiles and past Peter to the open front door. She looked out the screen and down the street. Another scream followed by a high-pitched laugh. Peter had once heard a rabbit scream in the middle of the night. His dad said a cat must have got to it. Peter thought that was the worst sound he ever heard. This new noise topped it. Then a different voice punctured the air, deeper than the first, shouting muffled commands.

Abby closed and locked the front door. She moved faster than usual back into the kitchen.

"I'm sure it's nothing, but get CJ out of the tub, Peter," she said, grabbing her phone midmovement and hurrying to the window at the end of the kitchen—the window facing Josh's house.

When Peter entered the bathroom, CJ was sitting still in the tub, holding a duck in each hand and staring at the empty doorway.

"What's a matter?" CJ asked.

"Get out. Where are your pajamas?"

Peter held CJ's wrist as she stepped out of the tub. He handed her a towel and ushered her down the hallway in the direction of her bedroom. She stopped and pulled out of Peter's grip. "Wait, I need my lasso."

Her towel fell as she ran back into the bathroom and grabbed the lasso hanging from the robe rack behind the bathroom door. She sprinted past Peter to her room, completely naked besides the lasso wrapped around her shoulder like a fireman carrying his hose. Peter sighed then ran after her.

CJ stood in the middle of her room, looking trapped. "Are people trying to break into the house?" she said.

Peter opened CJ's pajamas drawer and picked out something that would be easy to put on, to save time. He tried to remain calm, but the yelling on a usually quiet summer night had unnerved him—this was more than the normal *fore*! "No. Just get dressed."

"I hope Josh is home. He'll help us."

Peter had to admit Josh did cross his mind. Then he heard a door slam and more yelling from somewhere outside.

"I'll be right back. I'm going to check on Uncle Herb."

"Oh, no. I'm coming with you," CJ said. She trailed Peter, bumping into him as she tried to run while squirming her legs into her pajamas bottoms.

Uncle Herb's room was dark, only a soft and rugged voice describing a cloud formation around a mountaintop coming from the CD player. Peter whispered his uncle's name from the hallway. No response. His sleep patterns were so strange. If this were three in the morning, Uncle Herb would be wide-awake. Peter looked at CJ, nodded, and pointed down the hallway. They sprinted toward the kitchen.

The kitchen table and counters had come alive. They danced in dark yellow, the color of cough medicine. Abby had turned all the lights out and now stood at the kitchen window, peeking out. Peter and CJ stayed in the hallway until Abby waved them over.

The security car for Willow Creek Landing was parked at an angle in front of Josh's house, the flashing yellow light glowing from the top of the hood. A tall, thick, shadowy figure stood at Josh's front door, knocking.

"It's Brutus," Peter whispered.

"Uh oh," CJ said from somewhere behind Peter.

Brutus was a legendary figure at the Creek. Peter placed him to be somewhere older than Josh, but younger than his father. One of the residents had dubbed the shadowy figure Brutus, and the name stuck mainly because no one knew his real name or felt particularly comfortable asking him. Brutus wasn't the chatty type. He shaved his head like Peter's father, but it looked a lot meaner on Brutus. His head had a sharp shape as though a bullet was shooting down into his neck. The goatee and the hint of a black-ink tattoo peeking out from under his sleeve didn't hurt his image either. Peter loved making lists about Brutus—his real name (favorite choice: Rattlesnake), his tattoo (a raven, the small black part that always showed from under his sleeve reminded Peter of a beak), where he lived (a tie between a cave and a dark mansion on top of a foggy mountain where only one treacherous road led to the top).

Brutus knocked again, harder this time. The sound of static came from a walkie-talkie in his other hand.

Josh's house was completely dark. Mr. Terry approached from down the street, holding a bag of groceries. He slowed as he passed the security car.

Abby pressed her face to the window screen and quietly called him over. When he stopped in front of their window Peter could smell the musky, strong scent of sweat mixed with cologne. "Brutus is on the case," Mr. Terry said.

"What's going on?" Abby asked.

He shifted the bag of groceries from one arm to the other, then placed them at his feet. His face came so close to the screen that his nose almost touched. "The scuttlebutt at the general store is someone who closely resembled our new friend over there was skinny dipping at hole eleven, causing quite the stir out of the Canadian geese and the people eating dinner on the concourse—how do they get those window seats anyway, you must need some pull—"

"We heard yelling."

Mr. Terry laughed. "There was a chase from security, which apparently one said skinny-dipper made a mockery out of."

"Was it definitely Josh?"

Brutus knocked on the door again, louder this time.

Mr. Terry gave her a look. "I guess it could have been a hairy-legged, flat-chested girl, but there were things swinging where that shouldn't have been, if you catch my drift."

Abby smiled and shook her head in understanding. "I guess the golfers frown upon skinny-dipping on their course."

Mr. Terry smirked. "Prudes."

Brutus stepped away from the door and spoke into the walkie-talkie. He slowly walked the perimeter of Josh's house, making no attempt to hide that he was looking in the windows.

As Peter watched, he felt this pulsing from the corner of his eye, the flashing yellow of the security car. He made the mistake of looking directly into the rotating lights, and the rhythm hypnotized him. His head started to bob slowly in sync, and he felt his vision start to blur into an ocean of golden waves. His jaw and nostrils tightened. There was a smell of something burning. In a dreamlike sequence, his skin started to itch, his fingers twitched, and his tongue felt like it was growing. He heard CJ say his name, but she sounded like she was yelling from the bottom of a canyon. Then the black clouds started to come, and he knew what was about to happen, but it was all so dreamlike, and he was powerless to stop it. The clouds first came from the bottom of his left eye, then the top of his right. He sensed their plan was to meet to in the middle. That was the last thing he remembered.

Day 62

Nick opened his eyes when he felt the cab slow down in front of the gates and guardhouse of Willow Creek Landing. He never got bored with his community's presentation.

"Let me out here," he told the taxi driver.

Nick pulled up the handle to his luggage and started to roll the bag home. If the gates and guardhouse were not discouraging enough for uninvited visitors, the sight of Brutus and his beefy arms sitting in his metal fold up chair would do the trick. Nick knew this was why the community board loved the guy. He'd tried several times himself to engage with Brutus, thinking he'd be a good guy to get on his side but always to no avail.

Nick nodded as he rolled up. "How ya doin'?"

Brutus didn't answer from behind his dark sunglasses. He never responded to the greetings of the residents.

Nick pointed back to the taxi sitting at the red light, waiting to turn back onto Slocin Road. "Nothing like sitting in a car for a half hour that reeks of cumin and body odor, you know what I mean?"

Again, nothing from Brutus, and Nick thought that was a pretty good line—in a jocular, guy-to-guy type of way. As far as Nick knew, Brutus could have been sleeping behind those dark sunglasses, the rest of his face was so devoid of emotion, but as Nick passed, Brutus' head tilted ever slightly. It freaked Nick out a bit, like those portraits in a haunted house where the eyes follow you.

Nick thought about getting a drink in the clubhouse before heading home but decided to shower first and wash the trip off of him. The faint murmur of golf carts hummed in the distance as Nick turned onto Ranch Street. He could smell the cooking of some mass-produced dinner coming from the pavilion's catering hall—one fish entrée, one chicken, and one beef, though it was impossible to distinguish the smells. He beamed with community pride until he came upon the stacks of wood planks covering the Keeme front lawn. He glared at each pile as he passed, hoping someone, anyone, would notice his level of disgust. The front door to his own home opened, and Abby marched down the lawn.

Nick pointed to the stacks. "What is this?"

"Why didn't you call me back?" Abby stopped inches from his face.

Nick remembered the six voicemails, and the fact that he hadn't listened to a single one. "Oh, I forgot to turn my phone back on after the flight."

"How long was your flight, Nick? I've been calling you since last night."

"I had it turned off for meetings, maybe I forgot to check. What's your problem?"

"Oh please, that stupid phone is like an oxygen mask to you. You wish you could forget about your phone. Or do you wish you could forget about your family?"

"Whoa. Uh, hi, Abby. How are you? Oh, my trip? Just fine. What's the matter with you?"

"What's the matter?" She spoke through clenched teeth and tilted her head in the way that Nick knew meant she was primed for a fight. He wasn't up for one—he would have drunk more.

Abby looked to the sky as if making a mental list. "Well, let's *see*. I feel like a single mother, because my husband is off to God-knows-where and God-knows-when, because he never calls. Our son had another seizure, and they seem to be getting worse. Our daughter almost poked my brother's eye out with that frigging lasso of hers, and, oh yeah, we had the cops in front of the house last night. Apparently our neighbor was too hot to wear any clothes and decided to go for a dip somewhere on the golf course. How's that for starters?"

Nick hardly tried to stymie his laugh. "Which water hole?"

"Listen, Nick—" Abby moved closed and poked her finger into his chest, "—I don't know what's going on in that little head of yours and, honestly, I don't have the energy or patience to guess. But it's been going on for a while now. I want to know." She poked him harder, "No, I deserve to know if you're checking out. You understand me?"

Nick held his hands up in surrender. "Easy."

Abby was heading back to the house. "I'm tired, Nick. I'm really tired."

Abby headed toward the bathroom and, without turning around, she said, "Peter is resting. CJ and Uncle Herb are napping. I'm taking a shower."

Nick tossed his jacket on the living room couch and left his suitcase in the foyer. It was hot outside, but the inside of his house seemed stifling. He rubbed his open hand over his mouth, nose, and eyes, and he squeezed his forehead. He walked slowly down the hallway toward Peter's room. The lights were out and the shades were drawn. A portable fan was spinning at full blast. Nick looked at the action figures on the floor, a map of the United States, a poster of some baseball star on the wall, and the desk calendar with all the dots that Peter drew on (Nick had no idea what they symbolized). *Here was a perfectly normal boy,* Nick thought, *besides the fact that his brain was wired just a little off, a stalling car not firing on all cylinders.*

Nick sat at the edge of the bed and stared at his son. He wiped Peter's sweaty hair away from his face. It suddenly dawned on him that it had been a very long time since he just sat and looked at his son. He was getting very handsome, looked like his mother.

"Peter. Are you awake?"

Peter remained motionless, his chest rising in a slow rhythm. Seizures usually wiped him out for days. Nick stood and headed for the door, thinking that maybe if he could smooth things over with Abby, he could possibly get nine in before dinner, when he heard a soft, weak voice say, "Hey Dad."

"Hey, buddy," Nick said. He stood at the doorway. "How ya doing?"

"Tired. Mom said it was a bad one."

Nick leaned against the doorway. "I heard, buddy. Mom told me. But it's not the first time, and you always bounce back stronger, right? Just get some rest and get your strength back."

"Okay, Dad."

"I was thinking on the flight home, before I heard and everything, I was thinking, 'Hey, it's time that Peter and I get out on the golf course together, just me and him.' I was planning it in my mind, and then Mom told me the news. We'll have to reschedule once you get your strength back."

"That sounds great, Dad."

At that second, Nick wished he could see Peter's eyes—to see if his son had turned. He hoped Peter's lack of enthusiasm was because the seizure zapped his strength, not that his son realized his father was lying to him (even though part of Nick believed what he said). He could always get away with saying stuff like that to Peter, who tended to see his father in the best light. He could see that his word carried less weight with Abby, and CJ had developed the "I can take you or leave you" attitude the second she could move around independently. But his son was his son.

Nick sat at the kitchen table and thumbed through the newspaper. "The East End farmers' dismal crops due to the drought" on page one. "The president's upbeat message regarding the drought having no correlation with global warming" was on page three. "The subdued but gleeful responses from the owner of the island's only water park—Business has never been better! Thank God we recycle all our water!"—in the entertainment section. He slid the paper across the table when he heard Abby's footsteps coming from the hallway.

"We need to change Peter's medication. Mr. James mentioned a good doctor he knows. Maybe we should make an appointment," she said.

This irked Nick. "Oh, and that fruitcake knows a lot about my son's problems."

"He's a doctor, Nick."

"For Chrissakes, Abby. He's a freaking podiatrist."

Abby sighed and shook her head. "He was just giving neighborly advice. He likes Peter. He did go to medical school. He knows a lot."

"Sure."

Abby opened the refrigerator and poured a cup of orange juice. "I need to wake Herb. Can you help me bring him into the bathroom?"

Nick rubbed his face. First class flying, luxury hotels, and cute little secretaries seemed like worlds away from this place: an institution with doctor visits and direct care workers doing bed checks and bathroom breaks. "Jesus," he muttered.

"What did you say?"

"Nothing."

"No, what did you just say, Nick?" Her words shot out like BBs.

"Nothing."

She left the room only to storm back in. "You know what, Nick? We were doing just fine without you," and then she left again.

Nick sat alone in the kitchen. When he finally stood, he grabbed his suitcase, took his golf bag from the closet, and walked out the front door.

Day 63

The sun jutted out of the colorless, hazy sky like a blister. Peter sat next to Uncle Herb in a plastic lawn chair underneath the garage door overhang, not nearly as comfortable as the back patio with the heat radiating off the driveway tar, but it was Peter's idea. He wanted to keep a close eye on next door.

He had stayed inside the house all day yesterday, leaving his darkened room only at night to eat a small bowl of cereal and drink a glass of water. His severe headache had softened since yesterday, but his body still ached, and he felt as if he could fall asleep at a moment's notice. These were typical post-seizure symptoms.

Peter sighed. Today, number one on the "Sucks Rocks" list—no, correction, number one across the board on most every list ever created by Peter Grady—was . . . drum roll please . . . the seizure. Dealing with the physical effects after a seizure was difficult enough, obviously harder than the actual seizure since he never remembered that part (only the witnesses did and, unfortunately, they never forgot the sight), but there was a mental tax too.

It was dealing with the disappointment. As each day passed seizure free, there was this glimmer of hope building inside of Peter that the last seizure he experienced would indeed be his last. A few years ago, the doctors had told his family of a possibility that Peter would outgrow his seizures as his brain matured, and Peter started reading extensively and playing concentration games in the hopes of speeding up the maturing process, but to no avail. His mother said only time would tell. Two years seizure-free was the goal. Once Peter hit that mark the doctors would try to wean him off the medication, and he'd be normal. Eight months was his record. After each seizure Peter would find himself again at ground zero, a hit streak that came to another crushing and immediate end.

According to his mother, Peter's seizure the other night was a long one. This made Peter feel even worse. Two seizures in two months meant another round of doctors' visits filled with blood tests, pee tests, brain scans, and a change of medication. Then more doctor visits to monitor the new recipe. During the last visit, there was talk about changing his diet, and Peter was sure that would be brought up again. The diet didn't sound that bad—his mother said he could eat a lot of bacon and cheese, something about the fat being good—but there were things he'd have to cut out that Peter would miss desperately, like soda.

Peter had called his bouts *Grandma Seizures*. Of course, that was not the clinical term, but early on Peter had misheard the term *grand mal*. Another medical term for his seizures was tonic-clonic, which sounded more appropriate to Peter in a funny sort of way. Peter pictured shaking a liter of soda and then watching it explode. That's what his seizures felt like.

Uncle Herb had his Bible in his lap, but he was listening to the news on a small, portable radio he always had near him. *Old school,* Abby always teased him, *no iPhones in Herb's life*. There was a report on the weeklong forest fires in California followed by a taped interview with a Malibu resident who had lost his house to the sprawling wildfire shortly after undertaking a major renovation to rebuild his home after the last wildfire a few years ago.

"Hat inks," Uncle Herb said. *That stinks.*

The man took it in good spirits; at least that's what came through during the radio interview. He joked about being happy that he didn't waste time putting up the molding.

There's nothing you can do against an act of God, Herb thought. *It's not like he was smoking in bed.* California was going through a drought worse than the one they were living through on the East Coast.

Uncle Herb remembered the last wildfire that hit Long Island, over a decade ago by now. The Sunrise Fire, named after the blaze that engulfed both sides of Sunrise Highway, was a series of major brush fires that devastated the Pine Barrens regions of central Long Island, threatening many area homes and businesses. It closed down the highway and stopped train service, effectively cutting off a portion of the South Shore from the rest of Long Island. It took firefighters from all over the island and the city to extinguish the flames.

Uncle Herb wondered how far that fire was from here. Willow Creek Landing abutted the Pine Barrens regions, but the Pine Barrens was bigger than most people think, covering almost a hundred thousand acres. As far as he knew, the developers had not even cut out their vision for Willow Creek Landing at that time, but they were probably thrilled that the preservationists did not beat them to the punch for the property. Uncle Herb thought the woods behind the golf course would be a fun place to explore with Peter and CJ, but it was probably not handicap-accessible—he pictured his chair getting stuck on a giant tree root, lifted off the ground like a small fishing boat on the top of a giant whale.

CJ kicked open the screen door and rumbled out, wiping a white, sticky substance off her lips and cheeks.

"Marshmallows," Peter answered as if he read Herb's mind. "She can't help herself."

CJ trudged across the front yard, kicking up a cloud of dust in her wake. The remaining grass looked like hay, and it crunched under her step. Peter had told Herb that the neighbors across the street watered their lawn on the sly, sometimes with spray bottles, but even their grass now had the color of faded leather and was swallowed in the sea of brown.

"Have you read the entire Bible?" Peter asked unprompted, bored with watching CJ lasso anything that could be hooked.

Uncle Herb held up two crooked fingers.

"Wow," Peter said. He'd read *The Outsiders* four times, his personal record, but that wasn't nearly as thick the Bible.

CJ wiped her forehead with her arm, her tiara tipped to one side. "I'm sweaty."

A golf cart zipped by with two men and their golf clubs, triggering a recent experience in Peter's mind.

"Is Dad home?" he asked, suddenly remembering the foggy conversation shortly after his seizure.

CJ collapsed to a sitting position against the garage door. "Who knows?" she said as if an answer required too much energy on her part.

Uncle Herb sat in silence, looking into the distance. He knew the answer but decided to plead ignorance. He'd heard Nick come in and leave like a summer shower—*a quick thunderstorm was more like it,* Herb thought. The neighbors' garage door opened, and the kids' attention turned away from their father.

Josh appeared from the garage, dressed in a maroon T-shirt with a white inscription reading *Who's Your Daddy?* Without missing a beat, he corralled his unruly hair into a ponytail, dropped two wooden horses on one of the few open spaces of lawn, and ran an extension cord from the garage back to the horses, all with a stream of cigarette smoke trailing him. Then he noticed he had spectators.

A thin smile pushed his cigarette to the corner of his mouth. "He has risen."

Peter half-waved.

Josh flicked his cigarette to the ground and stepped over the bundles of wood, slowly walking their way. His jeans, stained with dark blotches, were ripped in places where you could see the underlying threads. He grabbed what looked like an oversized, plastic, yellow ruler off one of the bundles.

Josh squatted down in front of CJ and handed her the ruler. "Do me a favor, hold this on top of my head."

CJ hesitated, looking over at Uncle Herb before holding the giant ruler over Josh's head. She gave it back, and Josh studied a small, clear cylinder in the middle of the ruler. A black liquid washed back and forth inside the tube.

"Let me see here. Yup, just what I thought," Josh said.

"What?" Peter wanted to know.

"It's called a level. Its purpose is to make sure things are even and square." He looked gravely at Peter. "I'm a little off."

Peter thought he was joking, but there was no hint of a punch line in Josh's straight face.

"Those dudes over there," Josh said, pointing across the street to the home of Mr. James and Mr. Terry. "They said you had a seizure the other night."

Peter felt his face flush. He avoided Josh's eyes.

Josh continued without waiting for a response. "Yeah, well,

I'm here to say I'm sorry. The guys said the lights from the rent-a-cops might have tripped it off."

"It's okay," Peter said, just wanting to move on. Josh made him sound like a circuit breaker.

"Peter has epilepsy," CJ said.

"Hee-hay," Uncle Herb said.

Josh smiled and stepped past Peter to Uncle Herb's wheelchair. "I'm Josh," he said and gently held the gnarled knots of Herb's fingers in both hands.

Uncle Herb nodded. Peter wished he had said something, anything. He wanted to see if Josh could understand his words. It was one of those weird barometers Peter used to judge people, though he didn't know what the test measured.

Josh stared at the Bible in Uncle Herb's lap, long enough for Peter to notice. Then Josh looked away.

"What are you doing over there?" CJ asked.

Josh looked over at the piles of wood on his driveway and laughed, as if from this view he finally understood how crazy it all must look.

"Long story," Josh said, looking at Peter. "I'm working on a project, an extremely time sensitive one. I could use some help if you're up for it. An assistant."

Nobody ever asked Peter for this sort of help, and he looked away, feeling both embarrassed and pleased. Even his father never asked, which was fine with Peter. His dad's frustration with his inability to fix things was usually taken out on the nearest person.

Uncle Herb didn't seem too thrilled about the idea. Peter could tell he was mulling over his decision. Peter wondered what Josh's reaction would be if Uncle Herb dropped his head in prayer.

"Please, Uncle Herb," he said.

Uncle Herb slowly nodded okay.

"I want to help too!" CJ said as soon as Peter received permission.

Peter looked over at Josh. "She always wants to do what I do."

"No problem," Josh answered, in a way that made it seem he was answering everyone's questions.

"Are the police going to come?" CJ asked, hopeful.

Peter covered his face with his hand.
Josh smiled and opened his palms to the sky.

The Project

The tool belt Josh handed Peter wilted down below his waist even on the smallest setting, so Josh created a new hole with a leather puncher. CJ wanted a tool belt too, but Josh gently placed his hand on her shoulder and guided her to the garage. "I have a very important job for you," he told her.

Peter's eyes widened as he took inventory of the garage. The place looked like a Home Depot. Josh cleared his throat and said since Peter and CJ were his assistants, it was of the utmost importance for them to know the names and uses of each tool.

"Where did you get all this stuff?" Peter asked.

"It's my father's, an accumulation over a lifetime."

Josh showed them the garage. When Peter or CJ would ask Josh the name or purpose of a specific tool, Josh would mostly shrug and say he had no idea. He did point out the different types of saws and warned them to stay away from them if they "liked all their digits."

"And here, CJ, is your first project," Josh said, pointing to a large, square piece of wood leaning against the wall. It was at least three CJs high and wide. "This is the door for my project. I need you to paint something, a mural, dress it up."

CJ's head shot back. "What should I paint?"

"Whatever you want."

CJ twisted her face in thought. Josh pulled several paint cans from a shelf. He opened all of them and handed her several paintbrushes. "It's not every color in the spectrum, CJ, but it should suffice."

CJ didn't hear a word he said—colorful images fired through her mind like shooting stars.

Peter followed Josh out of the garage, and they started rearranging the wood to Josh's instruction. Peter held a long piece of wood vertical in the air as Josh opened and locked a stepladder. He climbed it with another piece of wood lying on his shoulder. At the second to top step, he asked Peter to hand him the nail gun.

"The what?"

Josh smiled and pointed with his chin. "The scary looking thing over there. I guess I'm not that good of a teacher. Keep your finger off the trigger."

Peter lifted a heavy gun-shaped instrument and carefully handed it to Josh, who considered the tool before leaning into the ladder for support and pressing the tip of the nail gun against the point where the two boards met. He looked down at Peter.

"I guess I should tell you I never used one of these before," Josh disclosed.

The look on Josh's face was one Peter never saw before in the short time he knew his neighbor: uncertainty. Peter stepped as far away as could without letting go of the beam and closed his eyes.

BAM! Peter flinched, and the sudden angry outburst of the nail gun startled Herb, sending the Bible on his lap into the seat's crevice. A group of birds scattered from the cable wire running high in front of the homes. Josh stepped down off the ladder. The board that had rested on his shoulder now hung suspended in the air connected to the vertical beam.

"Wow!" Josh shouted, and his amazement made Peter cringe a little, as if even Josh himself wasn't sure how everything would turn out. "Sure beats a hammer, huh?"

Uncle Herb had to restrain himself from calling Peter and CJ back to the house, though CJ looked completely safe and content in her section of Josh's garage. It was obvious to Herb that Peter enjoyed Josh's company, and Herb's instincts about Josh were positive despite the hippie look, but that twinge of fear Herb felt when he took the kids down Slocin Road had returned. Josh looked squeamish using the nail gun and was visibly surprised at the kickback of the circular saw. Obviously he was not a carpenter by trade. Herb had to remind himself that he was the kids' chaperone, not their party director on a cruise ship.

But then Josh looked as if he was getting comfortable. *BAM! BAM! BAM!* After nailing another board to Peter's vertical piece of wood, opposite the first horizontal board, they dragged the ladder a few feet down and repeated the process. Soon they had five of these creations, looking like a column of half opened umbrellas.

Josh put the nail gun back in the case, and Herb started breathing easier.

Peter admired their work as he followed Josh back down the driveway to where they started. Whatever it was they were building, they were doing it quickly.

"Do you build a lot of things, Josh?"

"I think I built a birdhouse in Boy Scouts a long time ago before they threw me out," Josh said, matter-of-factly.

Peter again looked over their work. This was some leap from a birdhouse. It spanned half of the driveway, longer than a pickup truck but shorter than a school bus.

Josh climbed the ladder again. He asked Peter to grab his drill and a fastener from a bucket on the driveway. Josh held one of the black pieces of metal to the sky.

"They don't make 'em like these anymore, young Peter. Pure, corrosion-resistant, galvanized iron, hot-dipped in molten zinc. I bought them off an old wreck from a shipyard in Greenport."

Peter realized the opportunity to ask was now in front of him. He hoped Josh wouldn't laugh at Peter like he did to the guy delivering the wood.

"What are you building, Josh?"

Josh lowered his drill gun and smiled. "I was wondering when you'd ask."

Peter gazed down the column of letter Ts. "What is it?"

Josh scratched his cheek and placed the drill gun on a ladder rung. "Do you believe in God, young Peter?"

"What?" Peter said, though he heard the question perfectly clearly.

Josh waited a beat and then repeated his question.

"Yeah," Peter said, in an eye-darting, murky-sounding sort of way. It wasn't that he didn't believe in God, but the point-blank question rattled Peter, threw him off-kilter. No one ever asked him this question directly, not even in the short time he had attended Sunday school.

"Do you believe God talks to people?"

Peter shifted the weight from one foot to the other. He did believe in God, but his image of God was this distant, all-powerful, school principal type who made and enforced all the rules from a high and unreachable office in a cloud. He was the one who decided who stayed and who was suspended indefinitely. You never heard his voice, even over a P.A. system. Josh had this very serious look on his face, and he was waiting patiently on Peter's answer. His expression motivated Peter to say the answer he thought Josh wanted to hear.

"I guess so."

Josh nodded and looked at Peter with evaluating eyes. Peter felt like the face of a clock again. Josh had opened him up and was now tinkering inside, searching for the real answer.

"I'll just come out and tell you, young Peter. You can decide if I'm crazy or not."

Peter thought of the young woman who'd peeled out in front of Josh's house a couple days ago. Had he just told her about the project?

"God told me to build an ark," Josh said plainly.

Peter looked over to his house just to make sure Uncle Herb was still outside watching. "Like Noah?" he asked. He couldn't think of anything else to say.

Peter made a mental note to refresh his memory on the story of Noah. Without knowing the particulars, Peter was confident Noah's Ark was longer than a half of Josh's driveway. Josh's ark would be one of the smallest boats in the local marina.

"What about all the animals?" Peter asked.

Josh waved off the question off, smiling. "Everyone asks the same question. The animals, the animals. The animals weren't part of our conversation, young Peter! I can only go on what I was told, there was no follow-up Q&A. I decided to handle it like Kevin Costner does in that baseball movie. I'll build it, and whoever comes, comes. I'm hoping the answers to the questions will show themselves."

Peter squeezed his lips together and pictured every boat he'd ever seen before (he'd never seen an authentic ark). Not one matched the look of Josh's six letter Ts.

"It doesn't really look like an ark to me, Josh," Peter said carefully.

The features of Josh's face softened. "Well, I told you I've only built a birdhouse. We've just started."

Josh fished into his jeans and pulled out his pack of cigarettes. The sun had started its descent and now hung over the golf course behind Josh's house. Josh pointed. "This sun is like how I felt about my ex-girlfriend: never leaves."

"I should go check on CJ. We should probably be going home soon," Peter said. There was something about darkness and Josh that still didn't mix well with Peter. Plus he had a lot to chew over in his mind.

Josh lit his cigarette, studying Peter. "You still don't see it, young Peter."

"No, it's just that my mother will be coming home soon and—"

Peter started walking to the garage to get CJ.

Josh held his hand in the air. "Wait, wait, wait. This will help."

Josh dropped to his knees, and, with cigarette still in mouth, did a headstand on the driveway. CJ would have been impressed, but the strange behavior only resurrected the image of the menacing guy praying and walking the street at night in Peter.

"I have to go," Peter said.

"Look, young Peter! Look at it through my eyes."

Peter only saw the column of letter Ts, now connected by two long boards that ran the length of the fixtures.

Josh mouthed to him, "It's upside down."

Peter tilted his head and the picture clicked. *It's upside down,* Peter told himself. *We're building the boat upside down.*

Josh collapsed from his headstand position when he started to clap. "It's easier to secure the planks to the hull this way," he said, getting to his feet and examining his cigarette that snapped in two during the fall. "I think I read that in a book somewhere."

Over macaroni and cheese again at the dinner table, Peter's mother laid it on him and CJ. "I don't want you two going over there anymore."

"Why?" Peter said, thinking this was greatly unfair. Crazy or not, his afternoon with Josh was the most fun day he'd had the entire summer, maybe since moving into the Creek. The smell of fresh cut wood and sweat, his muscles tired from hard work, had made his post-seizures symptoms and pity fest disappear into the air like sawdust. There was something cool about the work, tough even. He liked placing a pencil behind his ear, and even deliberated taking his shirt off like Josh, but then came to his senses. His pale, hairless chest would have made him look like a recently hatched chicken compared to Josh.

"I'm your mother. Do you need another reason?"

"Yes," CJ said, defiantly matching her stare.

Uncle Herb shifted in his wheelchair. Despite his responsibilities during the day when Abby was at work, Uncle Herb felt he didn't have a say in the matter. He was still a guest in this house and would never do anything to undermine his sister's authority, though the repeated glances from Peter and CJ were killing him.

Abby glared at her daughter. "Because I said so. How's that? Anyway, I've decided to put you in camp for two weeks, Missy. You'll love it. I ran into Suzie's mom in the supermarket, and she said Suzie never wants to come home from camp. A new session starts on Monday. How does that sound?"

CJ dragged peas around her plate with a spoon. "Horrible."

"There are a lot of kids who would love to go to summer camp but don't have the opportunity."

"Give them my spot," CJ said.

Abby picked up her plate and went to the sink. "I can't believe I'm raising such brats."

"But I can't go to camp until the project is finished," CJ pleaded.

Abby turned and faced the table. "What project?"

Knowing she let a secret slip, CJ looked at Peter and Uncle Herb for some support. Peter scowled at her.

"What project?" Abby demanded.

CJ started shoveling peas in her mouth as if they were marshmallows. Peter's spoonful of peas hung suspended in the air, waiting to see who would break first.

"What project?!"

Then Uncle Herb started coughing, lightly at first but progressing harder as time went on.

"Herb, you okay?" Abby said. She rushed in front of the wheelchair. "Are you choking, Herb?"

Peter sat motionless in the seat next to Uncle Herb. He was the one feeding him, and the last bite had seemed to go down fine.

Uncle Herb cleared his throat and nodded. He asked for water. Peter handed his mother the glass, and she held the straw as Uncle Herb sipped. He nodded again, and Abby wiped his mouth with the bib around his neck.

"You're okay?"

Herb nodded and said he wanted to lie down. Abby motioned for Peter to follow. Herb avoided eye contact the entire time they changed him into his pajamas, even as Peter lifted him by his armpits into bed. Abby rubbed his cheek, and Peter stayed at the foot of his bed.

"I'll check on you in a couple minutes," Abby said.

Peter said good night and started to follow his mother out, but Herb called him back.

"Pita."

Herb's head struggled to rise from the pillow. Peter leaned in to cut the distance. Then Peter saw his uncle smile and wink at him.

"Ew-id-ud-aday," he said. *You did good today.*

Peter went back and helped his mother clean the kitchen. Abby cleared the dishes from the table while Peter rinsed and loaded. They worked in silence, until Abby came up from behind Peter and put an arm around his shoulders.

"That was pretty scary, huh?"

Peter nodded. He didn't want his voice to betray him.

"I know you're close with him, probably even more now. I just want you to know he's fine, nothing to be too alarmed about. This has happened before."

Peter nodded again, but he didn't agree with his mother; he certainly would have remembered if his uncle had previously faked choking to cover for his niece and nephew.

Nighttime Reading

Peter flipped through the *Children's Illustrated Bible* in bed. He'd found it on his bookshelf and had to wipe the layer of dust from the book jacket. The title page was inscribed: *To Peter—Love, Uncle Herb* in a handwriting reminiscent of CJ's, only with accurate spelling and letters facing the correct way.

Peter had forgotten all about the book and wasn't sure when Uncle Herb had even given him the gift. It must have been when Peter was very young. Peter lowered his gooseneck night-light to get a better look at the picture of Noah's Ark. Josh would have needed a part of the golf course to build a replica of Noah's handiwork, not to mention a couple of construction crews. The Bible explained that the Ark was four hundred and fifty feet long, seventy-five feet wide and forty-five feet high with three levels. Peter wondered if Josh knew these dimensions.

Peter closed the book and turned off the light. He recalled the last part of a conversation he'd had with Josh before he and CJ ran home.

"How long will this take to build?" Peter had asked.

"Faster than you'd think. I'm working under a strict deadline here, young Peter."

"It will rain soon?"

"More than rain, young Peter. Not your ordinary drizzle, my friend."

Peter turned on his side and looked out the window. For the first time since he'd moved to the Creek, Peter went to bed with the shades open. He could hear Josh rustling around, and he saw a faint light coming from the direction of his house. Josh had set up portable lights to work in the dark. For more light, he'd strung up tiny, white Christmas lights up and down the driveway, which hung from rods made of scrap wood.

Peter fell back in bed and stared at the ceiling. He came up with two lists in his head. For the first list, he tried to work his way through chronologically:

Reasons Why Josh Is Probably Crazy
A List by Peter Grady.
1. He jumps in the middle of races to cross the finish line.
2. Ex-girlfriend rushes away.
3. He swims naked at golf course ponds at night.
4. He's building an ark because God told him to.
5. He asks his twelve-year old neighbor to help with this ark.

Peter stopped there, but there was still the mysterious event that Mrs. Keeme alluded to: the trouble Josh got into while away. That might have to be added at a later date if Peter could find out more details. It would take some investigating.

Peter started to form his other list: "Reasons Why Josh Is NOT Crazy—A list by Peter Grady." He yawned several minutes into constructing this list, still stuck on number one. The list stayed untouched until sleep crept up slowly from behind Peter and clobbered him.

Day 64

Uncle Herb stopped his wheelchair at the doorway to Peter's room and studied his sleeping nephew. Peter was lying on top of the lone rumpled sheet in only his underwear, his hair matted to his head. Peter had zombied through his morning chores, and Abby had ordered him back to bed before she left for work. Peter hadn't fought the idea. Herb wanted to check in on his nephew.

A week from today, Herb's summer vacation would end, and he'd head back to his group home and work. The ticking started. He missed his coworkers in the mailroom, many middle-aged like Herb, but unlike Herb, they possessed the mental capacity of children. The staff workers who ran the agency programs treated Herb well, and many were patient enough to engage in conversations with him. Even friendships had developed over the years. Herb thought it was a decent enough life considering his circumstances.

All that changed in the last six days. He felt different lately, anxious almost, but he couldn't pinpoint the root of his apprehension. He doubted he had a sixth sense, like a dog who can detect a medical emergency in his owner from the slightest change in breathing, or the rats who could foretell a sinking ship before the crewmen, but Herb couldn't shake the feeling. He blamed it on nerves, blamed it on worrying about the kids, and his responsibility to watch them. He was also bothered by the seemingly cracking foundation of his sister's marriage. Nick hadn't come home since that last argument with Abby. Was he traveling again the last few days? He was gone the entire weekend, and Abby hadn't even mentioned his name. Who conducts business on a Sunday? Deep down, Herb told himself, he was ready to do whatever he could to protect Peter and CJ—a willing, though broken, servant in the master plan.

Peter groaned and turned over in his bed. Herb dropped his hand on the wheelchair's control knob and started to reverse the wheels when he heard CJ sprinting down the hallway. CJ's inner gearshift had only two speeds: park and full.

She stopped behind Herb's chair, and he felt her quick and shallow breaths on his neck, then the top plastic layer of her lasso rub against his arm as she squeezed by his wheelchair and into Peter's room.

"What are you doing, Uncle Herb?" she whispered.

"Ukin a teeta." *Looking at Peter.*

CJ looked over to the bed, then cocked an eyebrow and tilted her head toward her uncle as if she was about to let him in on a deep secret. "He's sleeping, Uncle Herb."

Herb agreed with her.

CJ hovered until the silence and inertia became too unbearable for her, squeezing past the wheelchair again and into the hallway. She started climbing up the back of Herb's wheelchair, using the oversized rear tires as footings. His body sank in the wheelchair under her weighted grip on his shoulders. A thick, sweet smell drifted under Herb's nose, reminding him of a bakery. He turned his head back, almost inhaling a mouthful of CJ's golden curls.

"Ew eatin mar-male-oh again?" *You eating marshmallows again?*

"Only two. Mom hid them behind the cereal." She grunted as she balanced her legs and stood straight up.

"Ta-da!" she shouted, her mouth barely clearing the dome of Herb's head.

Peter jumped up, startled, his arms frozen forward as if he was carrying a heavy tray.

Uncle Herb sighed.

"CJ," Peter moaned and crashed back down to the bed. He hoisted the sweat-soaked sheet over his head.

Herb motioned to CJ, and she jumped off the back of the wheelchair and took off down the hallway. Herb maneuvered the wheelchair in reverse out of the doorway. He sat parked in the hall and watched as his groggy nephew rose and headed for his desk. Peter glanced out the window, then removed the cap to his orange Magic Marker, unaware he was being watched. *Such a diligent boy,* Herb thought, *it was time to circle the calendar. Another day without rain.*

* * *

Uncle Herb watched as CJ "put on a show" for him, dancing around the living room imitating the dancers from some teen television show. In a heartbeat, he would trade years of life for the ability to dance with CJ.

Herb's playful and private motto was "don't diss the abilities." It had a youthful, urban feel that he liked, though he couldn't stand the rap music of today. He liked the message behind his motto though: don't focus on the disability, accentuate the positive. But at times it was hard not to dwell on the negative, on how he limited the kids. Sometimes he felt like a dragging anchor.

Earlier Peter had looked out the window for Josh, but the entire street was quiet. Peter sprawled out on the couch and stared up at the ceiling. Usually Peter acted as CJ's television censor, and a teenybopper show like this would never have lasted long, but Peter barely seemed to notice the television.

Herb wheeled up to the couch and asked Peter if he wanted to go play at a friend's house. He figured he and CJ could manage. It was a long sentence for Uncle Herb; he found short bursts to be the easiest way to converse.

Both Peter and CJ stared at him incredulously. Then Peter's eyes returned to the ceiling.

"Peter doesn't have any friends in Willow Creek," CJ stated bluntly, as if she was reading from the community fact sheet. She shook her head slowly, like a person conveying a sad truth in life that could not be changed, only accepted.

Peter glared at CJ. "I do too, CJ. You just don't know any of them. They're older than you."

CJ stared blankly at Peter then turned to Uncle Herb. With less exaggeration this time, she shook her head again, confirming her earlier statement.

Peter noticed and jumped off the couch, storming past Uncle Herb to the hallway until the high pitch sound of small dogs barking stopped him in his tracks. The dogs sounded excited and agitated, as if they were chasing a waning scent.

CJ leaped onto the couch and pointed out the window. "Look, Peter! It's Mr. Terry's dogs. They're loose!"

Herb buzzed over to the screen door where he could get a better look. The matching, furry, white dogs were scampering down the sidewalk on the opposite side of the street, their tiny legs in overdrive.

"Let's save them!" CJ yelled as she jumped down from the couch, sidestepping Uncle Herb and pushing open the front door, never breaking stride.

Peter followed, squinting and shielding his eyes from the sun as he tried to keep pace with his little sister. He could feel the hot driveway through his socks.

"Don't run into the street," he told CJ, but it was an unnecessary warning. The dogs had already crossed the street, and were angling straight for them.

CJ and Peter stopped running.

"They're friendly dogs, *right?*" CJ asked.

"I think so," Peter said. He couldn't remember their names, but he'd pet them several times on their walks with Mr. Terry. They seemed sociable and accustomed to the amount of attention Mr. Terry showered upon them.

The dogs ran side by side. Their paws skimmed the ground; their legs paddled through the air at a furious rate. Peter knew all about rabies, how good dogs can turn bad. As the dogs headed straight for him and CJ, the prospect of punting them like a football as an act of self-defense occurred to Peter, but he hoped it wouldn't get to that. Mr. Terry wouldn't be happy with his dogs being kicked, even if they'd gone crazy. He looked over and saw Uncle Herb nudging his wheelchair past the front door and down the stone pathway to the driveway.

Peter stiffened as the dogs came closer, and he felt CJ clutch the side of his shorts, but then the dogs parted and ran right around them, not even stopping for a sniff. Peter and CJ turned to watch them go.

Uncle Herb stopped right in front of them. "Hee-hay!" he yelled, and the rise in his voice startled both Peter and CJ.

Never run off again, he added, and the kids could see the anger in his eyes.

CJ bowed her head. "I'm sorry, Uncle Herb," she murmured.

Peter's eyes widened. *For a day that started off boring, things had certainly changed in a hurry,* he thought. First the dogs running wild, then an immediate apology offered by CJ, something their mother had been trying to get since CJ started talking.

The incessant barking never faded because the dogs had stopped next door. They were circling Josh's ark now, going faster than the seconds hand on a clock.

CJ looked up at Uncle Herb. After sensing that everything was okay between the two, she smiled and asked, "Why are they barking? Is someone inside the ark?"

The skeleton of the upside-down boat was more recognizable now that Josh had started securing the planks to the frame. Peter thought Josh was moving fast with the ark for someone who had only built a birdhouse. Peter dropped to his knees to check for legs underneath the boat. Nobody was there. He wondered if Josh had worked through the night and was sleeping now. It was noticeably cooler at night, which provided better working conditions.

Uncle Herb stopped at the edge of the driveway. He watched the dogs circle with mild curiosity. The dogs seemed frenzied and out of whack but considering the current weather situation, Herb didn't dwell on it. The heat can make animals do funny things.

A shout came from down the block. "Truman! Capote! You get over here right now!"

Mr. Terry was making his way down his lawn, utilizing a combination of jogging and speed walking. Peter never had trouble spotting Mr. Terry; he was the most colorful dresser in the Creek. Today he sported a half-buttoned, orange Hawaiian shirt with blue flowers on it, and matching blue shorts that hung over his knees, an outfit that most of the creek's residents, including Peter's father, wouldn't be caught dead in.

Mr. Terry's sense of urgency made Peter take another step further away from the dogs, though their attention remained solely focused on Josh's boat. In size, the dogs were hardly intimidating, but Peter knew not to mess with animals, especially agitated ones—they were just as unpredictable as people.

CJ sat on the grass between the yards and watched the yapping dogs lap the boat as if she were at a NASCAR race. Mr. Terry stopped next to Peter and shook his head. His round shoulders temporarily shadowed Peter from the blinding sun.

"I don't know what got into these two. They're like mini-Cujos," he said, his words separated between gulps for breath.

"They're acting weird," CJ said.

"I know, darling. But aren't we all in this godforsaken heat?"

CJ shrugged. "I guess so."

Peter stole glances into the windows of Josh's house, looking for signs of life. Nothing.

Mr. Terry stepped down to Josh's driveway and entered the dogs' path. He lunged for one, but the dog easily slid past him. On their next pass, he grabbed one, either Truman or Capote (Peter couldn't tell them apart), by the backside. The dog squirmed and fought like a hooked marlin. Then Mr. Terry quickly pulled back one of his hands and let the dog free. "Ow, Truman, you bitch!" he yelled and shook his hand in the air.

A laugh came from behind them. Mr. James was walking toward them, taking it all in.

"He bit me!" Mr. Terry told him.

CJ stood. "Do you need a Band-Aid?"

Mr. James inspected Mr. Terry's finger and, with his back to the kids, quickly kissed Mr. Terry's finger. "You'll live. Let them run. Tire 'em out."

Mr. James turned and smiled at Peter and CJ. There was something genuine about his smile that Peter liked; there was no fakeness behind it, unlike the smiles adults typically gave children. *A supermarket smile,* Peter had labeled it. Mr. James looked over Peter's head and waved to Uncle Herb.

Peter had forgotten his uncle was on the driveway, blocked from joining them because of the slightly uphill grass divider between properties. Peter started walking over to him, and Mr. James followed.

"I'm James," he said over Peter's shoulders to Uncle Herb. "The injured party over there is Terry. We live across the street."

Uncle Herb nodded. "Erb."

"Uncle Herb is staying with us while he's on his summer vacation from work," Peter added delicately. This was a complicated situation to Peter. He didn't want Uncle Herb to think that Peter felt he had to speak for him, but he also wanted to keep the conversation flowing and knew Uncle Herb preferred to speak little in front of unfamiliar people. Unlike Mr. Terry, who seemed like he lived to talk.

The complexity of the situation seemed to have little bearing on Mr. James. He inspected the grass below him, wiped something away, and sat at the edge of the driveway next to Uncle Herb. Peter didn't know why, but this relaxed him.

"You're Abby's brother, right? Enjoying this heat?"

Uncle Herb said he wasn't.

Mr. James laughed. "I hear you. It's hot as hell."

Peter squirmed at Mr. James' word usage in front of Uncle Herb.

Mr. Terry came over and pointed back at the boat. CJ was chasing the dogs, though she was having a hard time keeping up with their pace. "Is it cocktail hour yet?"

"It's about that time," Mr. James said, smiling as he watched CJ round the boat. She was lagging behind, wiping sweat from her forehead.

"You can thank us later, Peter," Mr Terry said.

Peter had no idea what he was talking about, but once Uncle Herb and Mr. James started to laugh, he did too. His thoughts were occupied with wondering if Truman and Capote knew something they all didn't, and were vying for a good seat on the ark next to Josh.

A Visitor

"What is going on out there?"

Peter's mother was leaning on the kitchen counter and looking out the bay window that aimed at Josh's house. The laughter drifted in through the window screen, carrying the smell of burning charcoal and grilled hamburgers. The sinking sun had softened the colors of everything in the house. Lately, this was Peter's favorite part of the day—one of the few moments when the sun was still present but didn't have you in a headlock.

Peter looked out the window next to his mother. Mr. James and Mr. Terry were sitting in lawn chairs at the bottom of Josh's driveway, a foldout table between them holding a glass pitcher half-filled with a greenish-yellow liquid and a container of ice. Josh was standing in front of them in his usual dirty jeans and T-shirt, drinking out of a brown bottle and motioning with his arms as he spoke. Mr. Terry interrupted frequently, bouncing in his chair and holding his hands to his chest as he laughed. Mr. James nodded in contained amusement. Josh had dragged out his grill and periodically turned to roll a hotdog or flip a burger. Truman and Capote were no longer barking and running but still circled the boat slowly like guards.

"Smells good," Peter said, hinting that their neighbor's idea of dinner was a lot more thrilling than the broccoli and mac and cheese in their kitchen. His mother didn't catch on.

"It's a strange pairing, Josh and them," she said as she diced the broccoli for Uncle Herb. "To each his own, I guess."

She called everyone to the table. Uncle Herb was already sitting there patiently. CJ peeked out the window before she sat down. "I want a hotdog too."

"Maybe tomorrow," Abby said, placing the bowl of macaroni on the center of the table.

"That's what you always say."

Abby closed her eyes and exhaled through clenched teeth. "I'm getting tired of that lip, missy," she said.

CJ didn't look at her as she took her seat across the table from Uncle Herb. "You always say that too."

Uncle Herb shifted slightly in his chair to get CJ's attention. In their short but concentrated time together, Uncle Herb found that CJ was keenly aware of him at all times. It was impressive, if not mystifying, considering her age and the fact she tended to march to the beat of her own drum. She picked up on his little move immediately. He smiled at her and motioned with his head, a gesture suggesting CJ should move on from the little squabble. Herb felt that Abby was not in a good place right now; things were on her mind. He wanted CJ far away from that place.

Peter grabbed four glasses from the cabinet and a container of cranberry juice from the fridge. He placed them in the center of the kitchen table and sat at the head of the table, which was not really the head since the table was a perfect square, but it was the side where his father usually sat, so Peter considered it the head. Uncle Herb had taken Peter's regular place. It was the most accessible side for a wheelchair and a reminder of how long his father had been absent. Uncle Herb had been at the house for over a week, and they had yet needed to make room for five at the table. It was becoming commonplace that his father wasn't around.

Peter dragged his chair across the laminate floor, a fake plank style designed to give the appearance of hardwood floors, and parked next to Uncle Herb. He scooped a small mountain of mac and cheese from the bowl and dropped it on the plate in front of him, then started equally distributing spoonfuls between his mouth and his uncle's. Only the sounds of forks scraping plates tapped the silence until Abby said, "I want you kids to go to bed without a fuss tonight. I have to go out for a while."

Uncle Herb waited to swallow before glancing at his sister. She didn't look up from her plate. Something sat wrong with him. Maybe it was the way she hadn't changed out of her work clothes the second she walked in the door like she usually did, or the way she casually mentioned that she was going out without giving details, or maybe it was just this edginess she had to her tonight. Whatever it was, it tweaked him in an unsettling sort of way.

Peter held a fork of broccoli bits at Uncle Herb's closed mouth. "Uncle Herb?"

Herb looked at him and smiled. "Sawee."

Suddenly a deep voice bellowed from the front door. "Hello, anyone home?"

A large man opened the screen door and walked in. He was dressed in a full suit and walked with his chest puffed out as if to make sure his growing midsection would never be the first body part to enter a room. Peter knew exactly who it was. Kenneth Kassel Sr. had the same permanent sneer as his son, only with more lines in his face, and his skin was a rusty orange.

Peter's mother smiled, and Peter felt instant resentment toward her. Didn't she realize who this man helped create?

"Oh, hi, Kenneth," she said, wiping her hands on a napkin. "Good to see you."

The teeth of Chipper's father were too white and too straight. He apologized for dropping in like this, but he was in the neighborhood—a stale joke of Creek residents. When you live within gates, you were always in the neighborhood.

"I just came by to tell you that right after we spoke, I gave Lori Keeme a call, and she said she was upset with the lack of potential buyers for her house. She thought she'd have offers to sift through by now," he said, looking more at the furniture and ornamental pieces in the house than the people in front of him. He made no attempt to acknowledge anyone but Abby, nor showed any desire to do so. "It was rather serendipitous. So naturally I asked her if she'd mind if you took over representation. She thought that was a fine idea. You'll have to work out the details with the realtors."

Abby's face lit up. "No problem, thanks a lot, Kenneth."

Her warmness towards Chipper's dad made Peter want to choke on his broccoli. He had no idea what they were talking about, but Peter was nauseous over how nice his mother was to Chipper's dad. He'd told her many times about Chipper's tormenting ways, but now she chose to ignore it. Shouldn't feuds carry over the generations?

CJ was frowning at both her mother and Mr. Kassel. Peter wondered if her dislike for the man in front of her was instinctual or stemmed from a history of watching her brother get bullied. Peter knew his own ill feelings were rooted more from a deep and muddled pool of general raw emotion: fear, humiliation, a forecast of physical harm. All brought on by this man's son.

If Mr. Kassel sensed CJ's hostility, he didn't let on. He nodded as Abby thanked him, soaking it all in like an actor standing on the edge of the stage to a round of applause.

Peter shoveled a spoonful of broccoli bits off the plate for Uncle Herb, who opened his mouth naturally as the spoon neared. Herb's eyes traveled between everyone in the room. Peter wondered what was going on in his uncle's mind, but he knew it was fruitless to guess. Uncle Herb contemplated at a deeper level than most.

Before he became a successful businessman, Mr. Kassel was once a hotshot city lawyer who years ago had represented a famous actress, landing his face on television and in the newspapers for a few months. Peter didn't know what part of law he specialized in, but by the way Mr. Kassel spoke, he seemed to specialize in, well, everything. He'd stopped practicing law, probably because it interfered with his golf game. Peter often saw him around Willow Creek, mostly starting or finishing a round of golf, or hanging around the clubhouse bar or office. To Peter, being on the Willow Creek board of directors was like being in the popular clique in school.

Kenneth Kassel Sr.'s eyes ambled over to the bay window and the laughter coming from outside. He looked ready to give his summation before the jury. "Just an FYI, Abby. I understand from the last realtor that she had several problems with the occupant. Stupid stuff, like 'for sale' signs disappearing in the middle of the night, but also things that might slow down the selling process, such as the inside of the place being an absolute pigsty: clothes and pizza boxes all over the place. Not to mention that albatross in the driveway, which pisses me off. I mentioned it to Mrs. Keeme, but she was not hearing it. Apparently, Bernie is preparing to give her a fight in court—"

"I'll talk to him," Abby said.

Then it dawned on Peter what they were talking about. Anger flooded him. "You can't sell Josh's house, Mom!"

Abby raised her hand like a traffic guard to Peter. She turned to Mr. Kassel. "I'll take care of it," she assured him.

"You can't sell Josh's house. He lives there," CJ said.

"If I don't, someone else will, guys," Abby said.

Peter understood the logic, yet he still felt his mother had betrayed him.

Kenneth Kassel Sr. showed mild annoyance at the interruptions. "What I was saying, if it makes it easier for you to do your job, there are certain contract guidelines that would give us a course of action if we think it would expedite the sale—"

"You can't throw Josh out now!" Peter yelled, thinking Josh would never get the chance to finish his ark.

"I'll take care of it," Abby repeated, her hand still in the air and facing Peter.

Mr. Kassel pursed his lips into a toothless smile. "I knew you were the right person for the job. Call me tomorrow, and we'll work out the details on our end."

He turned and started to leave when CJ mumbled, "Don't let the door hit you in the ass on the way out."

If there was any food in Peter's mouth at that moment, it would have fallen to the floor. He looked over at Uncle Herb thinking he might have misheard or imagined the whole thing, but Herb's mouth was open too, revealing the chewed broccoli matter at the back of his tongue.

Mr. Kassel kept walking. Peter thought there might have been a small chance that he hadn't heard, but as he pushed on the screen door to leave, he looked back and smiled with his perfect, sparkling, and symmetrical teeth and said, "Cute kid."

He didn't mean it.

The screen door barely shut before Abby jumped up from the table and grabbed CJ by the wrist without saying a word. She pulled her from the table with such force that it knocked CJ's tiara off her head and to the floor. CJ didn't fight as her mother dragged her down the hallway to the bedrooms, but neither did she help to maintain her mother's angry pace. Peter and Herb watched in suspended silence.

Before she was yanked inside of her own room, CJ braced herself with stiff arms against the door frame and pushed, resisting her mother's force long enough to make eye contact with Peter. Then she was gone.

Night

Peter sat at the foot of Uncle Herb's bed, clipping his uncle's toenails. He'd noticed the need after helping his mother transfer Uncle Herb from wheelchair to bed. A burning sensation had tingled up the inside part of his arm and then a long and thin red scratch appeared, courtesy of Uncle Herb's big toe.

Peter hadn't realized how much of toenail clipping was done on feel. It was much more difficult to do on someone else than yourself. He was trying to be careful, but before each snip Uncle Herb's face knotted with anxiety.

The evening brought a slight breeze and a respite from the heat. After hearing CJ's muffled sobs from her bedroom, all Peter wanted to listen to now was the soothing chirps of some birds outside. But his mother's rattling around the bathroom, and the whine of her hair dryer trounced nature.

"Hee-hay, okay?" Uncle Herb asked, as if he read Peter's mind.

Peter snipped and dropped a toenail clipping into a paper cup on the floor. "Her door's closed. I'll check on her later," Peter said, meaning after his mother left.

He sized up the next toe, gently slipping the clippers over the nail and squeezed, quick and forceful. This seemed to work best. The nail stabbed out from his toe, still attached at the corner.

"Mr. Kassel really wants Josh out of here, huh?" Peter said.

Uncle Herb just looked at him.

"You don't think Josh is bad, right?"

Uncle Herb shook his head no. Peter wanted to talk; he wanted to fill his brain with other things and push out what inhabited his thoughts. Uncle Herb, however, seemed preoccupied with the task at hand, fixated on Peter's tweezer-like fingers separating the sliver from the toenail.

Abby had spanked CJ before, but there was something different about it this time. For one, Peter thought it went on for too long. Way longer than past spankings. As usual, CJ had put up a stubborn, silent front, not revealing pain on her face or through her mouth. *Maybe her show of defiance was counterproductive,* Peter thought. *Maybe if she'd cried from the first slap, the spanking would have been over a lot quicker.* When it was happening, Peter was sitting on the couch in the living room, trying to ignore it, but as the smacks came faster and harder, he found himself pleading to her in a whisper, "Cry, CJ. Cry already. She'll stop."

The smack that did it reverberated through the house, and CJ let out her first sound: a tiny yelp, like a puppy whose tail was stepped on. Once she'd crossed that threshold and her vow of silence was broken, her yelp melted into a long and pained wail. Peter hurt for her.

The hair blower stopped, and footsteps sounded from down the hall. Peter was glad his back was to the door. He didn't turn around, but he knew his mother was standing there, a faint smell of perfume drifted into the room.

"I'm going," she said. Her voice sounded flat, void of emotion.

Peter didn't turn around.

"Hell-oooo," she said, this time her voice sharpened.

"When is Dad coming home?" Peter said, and he didn't know why. He wasn't even thinking of his father.

She snorted. "I know what you are doing, Peter."

And then Peter realized what bothered him most about CJ's spanking. It wasn't done as a form of discipline. It was like a release of anger, of frustration, or whatever his mother had pent up inside her. She did more than punish CJ.

"Well, your father should be home soon. Then you can tell him what a bad mother you have. It's not easy, Peter."

"Yeah, and it's not easy being CJ right now either," Peter said. He didn't know where this anger came from. Peter had never spoken to his mother like this before. He was always the good child.

"Pita," Uncle Herb said quietly.

Peter looked at his Uncle, surprised. He couldn't believe he was taking his mother's side on this.

"Call my cell if you need me. Don't stay up late," Abby said, walking away.

Peter listened to the door shut and the car start, then drive off into the distance. He finished Uncle Herb's toenails in silence, with a little less patience. He dropped the last of the big pieces in the paper cup below, then slapped at the sheets with his hands to knock the small shavings off the bed. Uncle Herb stared at Peter the entire time, but Peter wouldn't meet his eyes.

"You're all set, Uncle Herb. Night." Peter stood and started walking to the door.

"Pita, ew o-k?"

Peter turned to see his uncle smiling at him. It wasn't an apology smile or an I-told-you-so smile. It was just Uncle Herb's plain, old smile.

"I'm okay, Uncle Herb. I'm just gonna check on CJ. I'll be back to put a CD on for you."

The fan and lights were off in CJ's room. It was dark and quiet. Only the crickets spoke. CJ was in her pajamas, lying on her bed facing the wall. Her coiled lasso rested on her stomach. She traced the wall slowly with a finger.

"Are you sleeping, CJ?" Peter whispered. He knew it was a stupid question. No one traces the wall in their sleep, but he didn't know what else to say.

CJ stopped tracing and wiped her nose with the back of her hand. She didn't answer him. Peter stepped closer but stood near the door. He'd leave if she wanted him to. He thought about all the times he couldn't get rid of her, how she shadowed him or was always in his way, like a basketball player defending his hoop.

"Maybe Josh will be out tomorrow, and we can help him. You can finish painting the door."

CJ pulled the lasso close to her chest, as if it was her teddy bear. She sniffled and asked, "Is she gone?"

Peter turned his head, half expecting to see his mother at the door or hear her car pulling back into the driveway, but the hallway was dark and empty.

"Yeah, she's gone."

CJ closed her eyes. "Good."

* * *

Peter stared at the ceiling in bed. Images of people tumbled in his mind. He thought of CJ, Uncle Herb, his parents, Josh, Mr. James and Mr. Terry, and Mr. Kassel and that awful offspring of his. He thought of the changes that were coming, that loomed and approached slowly like thunderclouds. Uncle Herb was going back to his life, Josh was leaving his house, and school would start in less than two weeks.

He wondered if he'd ever stop drawing orange dots on his calendar, when his dad would stop traveling so much. He remembered a day, back in the old house, when his dad walked in and shook the rain from his jacket, looking happy, like he used to, not exhausted, angry, or preoccupied. He'd hug or kiss Peter and CJ on the head and give their mother a playful hug or a kiss on the lips. It was that feeling that Peter missed most. Nothing big, no trip to Disney World or anything like that, just the typical day where everyone is home, and that's the exact place where everyone wants to be.

Peter shifted his body to look out the open window. Josh's Christmas lights shone through the August night. He hoped to fall asleep before the sun rose.

PART II

Day 65

It might have been because an eight-foot gate surrounded the entire development, but within Willow Creek Landing there were more natural boundaries than fencing, such as the neat rows of miniature poplar trees (with each tree planted equal distance apart) distinguishing property lines. The design gave the community a simulated, zoo-like quality.

Peter biked out of his driveway and rode down Ranch Road, pounding down on the pedals for speed. Out of habit, he glanced behind looking for CJ, temporarily forgetting that he left the house early and alone. If CJ was back to herself, she'd be disappointed. She loved biking into town, but Peter knew it would be too hard to do his research with one eye on CJ the whole time.

He cut right at the pavilion and headed to the front gates, smelling fried eggs and bacon coming from the general store inside the pavilion. He made a wide turn around the guard house, alertly spotting the raven's beak of Brutus's tattoo sticking out of the booth and steered his bike a safe distance past.

The peacefulness of the early morning ended abruptly at the gates of Willow Creek—morning rush hour on Slocin Road. Peter cautiously took the turn onto the shoulder and made a mad dash for Trent Lane, the side street that started the maze of back roads into town. Cars whizzed by, filling his shirt and shorts with bursts of air. Peter tightened his grip on the handlebars. He pedaled fast and measured, his eyes focused on the road ahead, and made sure he had control of the bike at all times. He knew what one accidental swerve meant—he would be road pizza.

He cut sharply onto the side road, and his breathing resumed a normal pattern. These back roads were considered the "T" section of town: an older development with high ranches and colonials, and residents who probably despised the Willow Creek Landing community. What used to be woods behind their development were now McMansions and McRanches and a gated, private golf course.

He turned left on Twilight Drive, and then a quick ride to Terrence Street. *This isn't such a bad trip once you made it past Slocin,* Peter thought. Maybe he'd meet some boys from school who lived around here. He'd come to terms with the fact that he'd never make a friend in Willow Creek as long as Chipper had a stranglehold on the entire population under age fifteen.

Peter hit Main Street and slowed in front of the plate glass window of Handley's Drug Store, looking to make one pit stop before the library. He scanned the aisles for any sign of Chipper and his cronies. When he was sure the area was secure, he hopped off his bike and entered.

On the bottom shelf of the magazine rack, below the glossy publications of monster trucks and chiseled men and women, Mr. Handley kept a small collection of comic books. Peter wondered why he'd never thought of this before. He fingered the titles until he found the one he was looking for. Admiring his luck, he jogged to the counter with comic book in hand.

Mr. Handley greeted him with a friendly smile. "Do you have anything to pick up, Peter?"

Peter slid the comic book across the countertop. "Not today, Mr. Handley. Just this." Mr. Handley studied the cover after ringing up the comic book. He held a finger to his forehead. "Let me guess here. This is not for you," he said, pausing for effect, "but for the fair-haired child who follows you around like a puppy."

Peter nodded, slightly embarrassed.

"You're a good big brother, Peter. All my brothers ever gave me were bruises." Mr. Handley handed the comic over to Peter and winked at him.

He'd worn his knapsack for this purpose, so he wouldn't ruin the comic book by handling it too much. Usually he'd leave the knapsack home because it was like wearing another layer in this heat. Deep down he hoped to find something interesting enough to print at the library, making the knapsack necessary, but he didn't want to raise his hopes up too high.

The morning sun hung in the sky as Peter carefully placed the comic into his knapsack. He mounted his bike and pedaled past the hardware store, art gallery, and Starbucks, where customers sat outside, hidden from the sun by umbrellas and sipped their iced coffees and cappuccinos.

The library was on the outskirts of Main Street, separated from the string of stores by a small park. Across from the library was the Sleepy Beagle Pub, the favorite restaurant of Peter's father, an old tavern poorly lit with dark, wood booths where the backs are so high that you can only hear the murmurs of the diners behind you. Peter liked the waffle fries there.

He turned into the library's parking lot and pulled into the bike rack. His shirt was pasted to his back with sweat. The automatic doors to the library opened and a burst of cold air enveloped Peter. He shivered from the extreme and sudden change in temperature.

The main floor was more packed than Peter ever saw it, especially so early in the morning, with people floating down the long passageways of books. Peter wondered how much the air conditioner had to do with the crowd using this public place as an oasis.

He made his way downstairs to the computer room and sat in one of the open cubby holes. He turned the computer on and waited for it to load, his eyes darting around the room for familiar faces. If Peter had a phone, he could have done his research in the privacy of his own home, but his parents said they would buy him one next year (they said that the last two years). And with his computer broken (another thing his Dad said he would take care of "this weekend"), Peter's computer access was restricted when he couldn't borrow one of his parents' laptops. But Peter wouldn't want them to see what he was about to Google anyway.

He clicked the keyboard a couple times, entered his name and library card ID, and found himself on the library homepage. He went to Google, and before typing in anything else, he looked around the room one more time. He typed *Josh Keeme*. Peter tapped enter and on the screen appeared:

We did not find results for: "Josh Keeme." Try the suggestions below or type a new query above.

Peter frowned. He knew there was a strong possibility that the search would turn up nothing.

Peter leaned back in his chair and scratched his face, deep in thought. The librarian looked over from her desk across the room, but Peter avoided her eyes. You can't ask for help when you're being a snoop.

He typed in *Joshua Keeme* and hit the enter button.

The search found two results.

Peter straightened himself and moved his face closer to the screen. The first was from a small newspaper, the *Hagerstown Gazette*. The headline read: "University Student Arrested for Punching Police Horse." In the description blurb, Peter saw the name Joshua Keeme in bold. He clicked on the headline to go to the website.

It was a dated newspaper police blotter, more than a year old. Peter scanned the sentences. Hagerstown seemed like a relatively safe place, the first two crimes were a noise ordinance violation and vandalism, someone who spray-painted *Food stinks!* next to the sign of a downtown café. Halfway down the page, Peter saw the police horse story.

At the Hagerstown Music Festival, Hagerstown University student Joshua Keeme, age twenty, who authorities said punched a police horse, pleaded no contest to disorderly conduct Wednesday and was fined $250 and ordered to perform twenty hours of community service. Police say that Keeme, a second-year chemistry major, seemed agitated and aggressive before punching the horse outside of the festival's entrance, where police were helping with crowd control. Keeme denied that he punched the horse, saying he put his hand out and the animal's head ran into it. Witnesses stated that Keeme was agitated and acting strangely, stating that the horse had spoken to him.

Oh no, Peter thought. He read the story over and over, wishing there were more details. He estimated the age was right. What were the chances this *wasn't* Josh? How many Joshua Keeme's in their twenties can there be? Peter figured he could find out easily enough by asking Josh some questions, like where he went to college.

Peter clicked back to the search page and clicked on the second result. This too was a paper from Hagerstown, but from the design of it, crazy scripted headlines, lots of colors and sketch drawings, it looked like something created in a bedroom. Peter didn't have to look hard to find Josh's name. The front-page title read "Horseplay at Hagerfest!" The article read as if the writer was standing next to you in conversation.

I'm sure we're all in consensus that the Unabombers absolutely rocked out the Hagerstown Music Festival last weekend, but for those of you who thought the rap-metal band was the main attraction during the weekend long festival—not so fast. That title goes to our very own perpetual senior Joshua Keeme, who found himself locked up in the Hagerstown one-cell jailhouse on Sunday night after punching a police horse. You read it right, Hagers and Haggards, punching a police horse. Rumor has it he was a little out of his mind that night. Uh, yeah. Anyway, now we know what the chemistry major is making in the lab all those long hours. We just want to know how we can get our hands on some.

This account was not as fact-based as the newspaper, but Peter read it a second time anyway. He decided against printing anything. He could always come back and look it up again. He stood and tossed his backpack onto his shoulder, looking around the library. He was in no rush to leave the air-conditioned environment. It was close to ten o'clock now, probably ten degrees hotter outside than when he entered the building.

Even though he was excited about giving CJ the comic book, there was something freeing to being alone. So he walked up and down the aisles, scanning the book titles. Right at the time he was thinking that he should do this more often, a voice hissed from between two shelves of books.

"Fish out of water."

A set of eyes peered over a row of books from the adjoining aisle. Peter felt a sharp pinch in his chest. Chipper reached through the opening and grabbed a hold of the front of Peter's shirt.

"Howdy, Nemo. Come here. I missed you."

Peter's body slammed against the wall of books as Chipper tried to pull him through the narrow opening of the bookshelf. Peter heard stifled laughing and knew Chipper's goons were there too, giggling from the other side. Peter felt more hands on him, clawing and pulling.

"Stop," Peter said in a muted voice, his mouth pressed against the spine of a book.

Books started falling to the floor, and Peter felt the whole unit start to sway. A hand slapped at the back of his head and his cheek several times. Peter felt his feet leave the ground, and he knew he was in trouble, the only comfort coming from the notion if the entire bookcase fell, it would crash down on Chipper's skull.

"Peter, there you are, I've been looking all over you," a voice called from down the aisle.

Peter landed on his feet and stumbled, pulling his shirt down over his stomach. Mr. Terry was standing at the end of the aisle, a pile of books in one arm. He waved Peter over with his free hand.

Thankfully, Chipper couldn't get a full view of Peter's face, filled with surprise and relief. Peter combed his hair in place with his fingers and wiped dust from his cheek. Mr. Terry put his arm on his shoulder. Peter glanced over into the next aisle as they started to walk away together. Chipper and his goons huddled in a triangle trying to look innocent while concealing their laughter.

Mr. Terry stopped. "Hey, boys. There's a mess of books in the next aisle. We're in a rush, so can you do us a favor and pick them up? Thanks."

They started walking again, but not before Peter saw a look of rage cross Chipper's face.

On line to check out the books, Mr. Terry tilted his head down toward Peter and whispered out of the corner of his mouth, "You okay?"

Peter nodded, embarrassed that his neighbor had to witness one of his poundings. Mr. Terry had a musky smell to him, not bad just strong. It was like a combination of sweat and cinnamon.

"You need a lift home?"

"No, I have my bike."

"I could throw it in the trunk. No problem."

"No, I'm okay. Thanks, Mr. Terry," Peter said, trying to convey that he appreciated more than the ride offer.

Mr. Terry appraised Peter then smiled. "You better go then. I'll hold them off if I have to."

Peter took off, thinking that was the best adult advice he'd received in a while.

The ride home from the library wasn't quite as much fun for Peter as the ride there. He knew that Chipper wouldn't be happy that his sadistic acts kept getting interrupted. Chipper liked seeing things through to completion—must be the Boy Scout in him. Figuring Chipper would take Main Street right to Slocin, Peter took the back roads again, turning around every so often anyway, expecting to see Chipper and the goons on his tail. He missed colliding with a parked car on Tremont Street by inches. It felt like a foxhunt to Peter. Unfortunately, he was the fox.

By the time Peter reached the gates of Willow Creek Landing, the back of his neck felt like someone had held a match to it. Brutus was now standing outside the booth, and Peter had the feeling that he'd been watching him bike up since he'd turned off Slocin. He hugged the curb farthest from the booth and put a little extra push behind each pedal, but then Brutus stepped into the middle of the street and held his hand out for Peter to stop.

Peter's flight instinct told him to hop the curb and make a dash for it, but just as he did every time with Chipper, Peter froze and surrendered. He almost fell off the bike trying to stop it so quickly.

"I live here. 50 Ranch Street. My name is Peter Grady." He would have offered his social security number if he knew it by heart.

Peter was amazed at the size of the hand in front of him. It could have easily palmed his entire face. He couldn't think of any reason why Brutus would stop him. It's not like he didn't know Peter lived in the Creek, he'd passed him several times with and without his parents. A car pulled in behind Peter, and he was thankful for the company.

Brutus turned his head and waved Peter through. Peter didn't waste any time, making sure to thank him first for . . . Peter didn't know what for. Maybe those dark sunglasses are also prescription glasses and Brutus needed his eyes re-evaluated. Peter didn't care, as long as he was leaving. He looked back once quickly and saw that Brutus had stopped the unfamiliar car and was looking at the license plate.

Brutus went back to the booth and grabbed his clipboard with the visitor sign-in sheet attached. He slowly walked around to the driver's side and waited silently for the visitor to get the hint and roll down the window. Brutus didn't talk through glass.

As he waited, he glanced down Ranch Street. The boy on the bike was already out of sight. Brutus was glad. The Boy Scout boys had come in minutes earlier and were looking for this boy. Brutus didn't speak often but always listened. He could tell it wasn't for a birthday party. The boys had parked their bikes outside the general store entrance, and Brutus had held the kid on the bike until he was sure the others had entered the pavilion.

Brutus had done his good deed for the month.

The Giant Pine

The giant pine tree in Peter's front yard, a symbol and reminder of the predevelopment days, lifted majestically into the sky. It dwarfed the landscaper-planted trees that decorated the community like ornaments.

It was also Peter's favorite place to read.

But now he stood at the trunk, shuffling his feet, and casting glances at the nearest limb, six feet above the ground. Whenever he climbed the tree, the effort was enormous, involving a running leap and a fierce grip. Pulling his weight up was another story entirely. Success rarely came before three tries.

"How did you make it to the first limb?" he wanted to know.

CJ stared out at the golf course. She sat on one of the fatter limbs, midway up the tree, and higher than the limb where Peter commonly stopped, any higher tested his comfort level too much. CJ was a good ten feet in the air with her knees curled up into her chest.

"Lasso," she whispered. "I threw one end over and climbed up with my legs."

Peter was impressed. "Can I come up with you?"

"No."

Peter nodded. He sat on one of the large protruding roots and scooped a handful of rocks. He tossed one rock at a time.

"I'm not going to camp, Peter."

"You might like it, CJ. Mom thinks you will."

"I won't."

Peter picked up another handful of rocks and shielded his eyes as he looked up at his sister. "I have something for you."

CJ wanted to act indifferent and she fought to avert her eyes from Peter as he dug through his backpack.

Peter held the comic book to the sky. "It's a Wonder Woman comic book. I got it at Handley's."

CJ examined the cover from the safety of her limb.

"I'll make you a deal," Peter said. "It's yours if you promise to try camp tomorrow without giving Mom a hard time." He didn't want CJ trying their mother's patience again.

CJ broke off a small branch. She dropped it and watched the plummet. "I want to stay here," she said, then added, "with you."

Peter was thinking of a reply, when CJ pointed behind Peter.

"Why are there so many animals around?" she asked.

Peter hadn't noticed. He squinted to the sky, following two or three different groups of birds circling overhead. Two brown rabbits nibbled brown grass in the area between their house and Josh's. Squirrels bounded through the yard, which was not at all unusual, but they seemed to have invited every one of their friends and relatives.

A maroon van crawled up the street, slowing in front of each house and coming to a stop in front of Josh's. Two young men dressed in work jeans and stained, saggy T-shirts got out. They spoke Spanish to each other in machine-gun-like bursts. One wore a red bandana, pirate-like, on his head. He nodded in the direction of the ark, and his friend shook his head and laughed.

A shirtless Josh met them on the middle of the lawn. They stood in a triangle and shook hands. The distance they kept from each other and the stoic look on their faces gave the impression they were not familiar with each other. Josh spoke, and the others nodded. He added something else, and they nodded again. The bandanna guy pointed to the ark and spread his arms wide. Josh shrugged then dug into his front pocket and handed the bandanna guy a roll of dollars.

"Why is Josh giving them money?" CJ asked.

Peter didn't notice Josh receive anything in return. Bandanna guy tapped his buddy in the shoulder with his knuckles, and they headed back to their car and left.

Peter stood and wiped his pants. Chipper's library attack had temporarily put Peter's investigative research on the backburner of his mind. "I have to talk to Josh, CJ."

"About what?"

The image of a woozy police horse formed in Peter's mind.

"I'll be right back."

"I'm not going to camp, Peter."

"I'll be right back."

Peter started walking over, but CJ called him again. She nodded toward the Wonder Woman comic book still in his hand.

"Will you go to camp tomorrow without a fuss?"

She gave a noncommittal nod and lowered one end of the lasso to the ground. Peter rolled the comic and looped the lasso end around it, then tugged the lasso once. The comic book rose.

As Peter walked over to Josh, his mother's car pulled into their driveway. Through the windshield glare, Peter saw her waving hello to him as she spoke into her phone.

Josh was now cutting a long board on a table saw, the wood dust flying into his protective goggles. Peter didn't want to distract him, so he waited until the table stopped buzzing.

"Hello, young Peter," Josh said, removing his goggles. Peter noticed dark purple pools under Josh's eyes.

Peter stole a glance over at his mother. He didn't want to start asking Josh questions if she had plans to interrupt. She was still sitting in the car, yapping on the phone, probably to a client. This could be a short visit from his mother. She usually stopped home throughout the workday to check in and help toilet Uncle Herb if necessary. Sometimes she ate lunch with them.

Josh wiped sawdust out of his matted hair. "You look troubled, young Peter."

Peter tried to think of a way to word his question. Blurting out point blank, "Did you ever punch a police horse?" was a little too forward.

"Did you like going to college, Josh?"

"Why do you ask? Are you thinking about skipping high school?"

Josh laughed after saying this, but Peter liked the idea. He thought of all the abuse from Chipper he'd avoid.

A car door slammed, and Peter's mother was at the rear of the car still talking into her phone while lifting a bulky "For Sale" sign from the trunk. She dropped the phone to her shoulder and impatiently said, "Peter, where are CJ and Herb?"

"Uncle Herb is inside. CJ's there," Peter said, pointing high into the pine tree.

Josh's face changed as he watched the "For Sale" sign come out of the car. Peter thought maybe now was not a great time to be asking Josh a question of a sensitive nature.

But Peter's curiosity was getting the best of him. He decided to take the long way there. "Josh, how old are you again?"

Josh's attention turned back to Peter and his expression softened a bit. "Twenty-three."

"Where did you go to college?"

"A small school upstate. I'm still a couple courses short of graduating. Listen, young Peter. Don't try to grow up too fast. It's not all it's cracked up to be."

Two men in a golf cart drove past and stopped in front of Abby, engaging her in small talk about the weather. She asked them about the upcoming community golf tournament, which seemed to be another big deal around Willow Creek. Peter wondered if Josh would crash that party too.

"Golfins," Josh muttered and went back to his work.

Peter watched as the driver of the golf cart leaned in and whispered to Abby. He motioned to the sign in Abby's hand, and Peter could have sworn they all looked over in his direction. Then the passenger of the golf cart said something, and they all laughed.

"Peter, can you hold this up for me?" Josh said, eyeballing the board he'd cut to the frame of the boat. If it bothered Josh that the golfers were talking about him, he sure didn't let on. "Golfins," he'd called them. Peter warmed to the term immediately. The golfins said goodbye to Abby and took one last look over at the ark. The driver shook his head in an exaggerated, disapproving fashion. Josh regarded the golfins in the complete opposite fashion, as if he was unaware of their existence.

Josh nailed the board to the frame of the ark with a hammer.

"What happened to the nail gun?" Peter asked.

"It jammed, and I couldn't fix it. It's okay. That thing made me a little uneasy anyway."

Josh dropped the hammer on the grass, yet the sound of hammering continued. Peter hadn't noticed his mother walk across

Josh's lawn and plant the "For Sale" sign in the front of his yard. She pounded it further into the ground with a mallet. A wave of shame and anger washed over Peter as his last name glowered from the sign in bold letters.

Abby dropped the mallet to the grass and wiped her hands together, proud of her handiwork. She walked over to where Josh and Peter were standing and watching her.

"The last agent said the sign she put out mysteriously disappeared," Abby said, looking Josh directly in the eyes.

"I didn't notice," Josh answered.

"Probably some mischievous kids. You know how they are in the summer with so much idle time."

"Was it you?" Josh accused Peter.

"No!" Peter shouted, his face reddened instantly from the indictment. Then he noticed that thin smile forming at the corner of Josh's mouth.

"Of course it wasn't, Peter," Abby said.

Josh's smile disappeared, replaced with the flat face of boredom.

Peter had no idea what anyone would want with a sign. Maybe Chipper and his fellow Boy Scouts stole the sign for their next merit badge: how to make lethal weapons out of modes of advertising.

"Anyway, with school starting soon I'm *sure* we won't have any problems with this sign," Abby said.

"I sure hope so," Josh said, in a rather unenthusiastic voice.

Peter wanted his mother to leave. She seemed to zap energy out of Josh by the second.

Abby flashed a smile as though some misunderstanding was cleared up. She said in a perky voice, "Did your mother tell you I was selling the house now? Well, assisting in the sale of the house."

"Haven't spoken to her. The home phone was disconnected. My phone was under my ex-girlfriend's plan. That was cancelled along with me. I guess Mom hasn't had time to stop by between court visits," Josh said.

Josh walked over and unplugged the table saw, then connected his circular saw to the extension cord. Peter sensed the conversation was over. He hoped that his mother had taken the hint. Apparently she had.

"Let's go eat lunch," she said to Peter.

"I'll be there in a bit," Peter said. Despite interruptions from his mother and the golfins, Peter remembered the purpose of his visit to Josh—police horse.

Abby appeared reluctant to leave but did so anyway, not before reminding Peter that "a bit" was indeed a short amount of time.

Peter lingered as Josh worked, holding the board for cuts and helping to find the pencil that Josh always misplaced. Josh worked at a steady and intense pace, stopping only now and then to wipe sweat from his brow. Then he hammered his thumb.

"Ouch! Damn it, damn it," Josh cried, holding his hand and dancing around the lawn until he fell to his knees.

Peter wondered if his mother had anything to do with Josh losing his concentration. Then he got a better look at Josh's hand. He looked like he was wearing nail polish, the tips of several fingers were a purplish black.

Josh must have seen the look on Peter's face. His pained expression softened, and he started to laugh. "What can I tell you? I suck with a hammer. I told you I only ever built a birdhouse."

CJ climbed down from the tree and sprinted toward them, the comic book in her clutches.

"Peter, I have a question!" she shouted.

At the edge of Josh's driveway, CJ abruptly changed directions and ran into his garage. "You didn't finish painting my door," her voice echoed outside.

"I wouldn't dare," Josh answered as she reappeared.

CJ tried to hide the pleased look on her face. She pointed to the comic and asked Peter, "Why do they call it the Lasso of Truth?"

"Because if Wonder Woman wrapped someone up in her lasso, the lasso forced them to tell the truth."

CJ looked at the comic, wide-eyed. "Will my lasso do that?"

Peter looked at Josh then answered, "I think you have to practice it a lot first."

Josh's eyebrows rose. He was impressed with Peter's answer.

"When are you going to finish the door, CJ? There's not much time left," Josh said.

It struck Peter as odd at how calm and confident Josh was

about the flood coming. If Peter felt as strongly as Josh about the looming disaster, he wouldn't be able to eat or sleep.

CJ's head dropped. She kicked at loose pieces of gravel in the driveway. "I don't know if I can finish, Josh. My mother is sending me to camp tomorrow."

Josh's eyes narrowed. "Well, I'll tell you what. We'll hold off on the door as long as we can, and maybe you'll find some spare time to do it. Otherwise we might just put up what you finished."

"But I'm not even close to done."

"It'll be good enough. Trust me. No worries."

CJ had a bounce in her step, more than usual, as she ran back to the house, possibly to test her lasso's truth capabilities on Uncle Herb. Peter lingered. He knew time was wasting and his mother would call through the window any second. Josh tested the circular saw with a light squeeze of the trigger and grabbed his safety goggles, pointing with his chin to where Peter should clasp down the board.

Then Peter heard a menacing laugh that instantly registered in the cavern of his chest. Chipper and the goons were coming up the street. They wore football jerseys and carried their shoulder pads. They walked slow and lopsided, undoubtedly returning from practice. The library incident was only this morning. Peter wondered where Chipper even found the energy to torment kids. He also thought it interesting how they were coming from the dead-end direction of Ranch Road. There must be a hole in the fence and shortcut through the Pine Barrens, avoiding all of Slocin Road. He made a mental note to explore this further. When they noticed Peter on Josh's lawn, they huddled closer together with Chipper at the center.

Josh was focused on the cut as the circular saw wheezed its way through the wood. Peter couldn't hear anything over the saw, but the recollection of Chipper's sharp laugh rattled around his head. It was like Pavlov's dog, which Peter had learned about in school last year. Peter associated Chipper's menacing laugh with a beating, and for good reason—usually after Peter heard it, a beating followed shortly thereafter.

CJ stopped in the middle of their lawn, halfway between the door and Peter. For a second she stood motionless, as if she were deliberating her next step. In his mind, Peter urged her to go inside the house. The mental telepathy didn't work. CJ remained still, her back to Peter and facing an approaching Chipper.

Josh finished the cut and put the saw down. He took the piece to the ark while Peter stayed behind at the makeshift workbench: two plastic horses underneath a square piece of plywood.

Chipper and the goons reached the edge of Peter's lawn just as Chipper's voice enveloped Peter.

"Howdy," he said to CJ.

Deep down Peter knew they wouldn't do anything with Josh around. But CJ was standing on the lawn by herself, and Peter felt this pressure to protect her, not that they would do anything worse than make fun of her, call her some names. But she was his little sister. His legs felt like wet cement as he walked around the workbench and headed to CJ. He kept his head down and his legs moving. It was painfully apparent to Peter that the closer he got to CJ, the further he was from Josh.

"Nemo." It was a chorus now.

He stopped at CJ's back and spoke into her neck, shielded from the eyes of Chipper and the goons. "Let's go inside, CJ."

She turned around, and Peter expected to see a face filled with fear and anxiety, but only saw defiance.

"C'mon let's go inside, CJ." Peter whispered again, looking somewhere below her eyes. CJ's lips trembled and her body stiffened. Then she said, "No."

"CJ," Peter said with as much authority as he could muster. He looked over her shoulder. Chipper and his gang had stopped at the curb in front of the house. They dropped their shoulder pads to the street and watched this interaction with full amusement.

"C'mon," he said, trying to sound persuasive despite his begging and pleading tone. Josh's sawing sounded like it was a hundred miles away. Peter shifted on his feet.

"Are you hiding behind your little sister, Nemo? How cute."

CJ had a frozen look to her stance, but her eyes were flooded with emotion, as though she couldn't have moved even if she wanted to. Peter's throat tightened, and his face flushed, and he felt the hot wetness forming in his eyes.

"Is little Nemo going to cry? We haven't even done anything yet," Chipper said, in a weepy, sarcastic voice.

"Little Wonder Woman is braver than her brother," said one of the goons.

Peter looked quickly at the one who spoke. Up until this moment, he never distinguished the two. Now he would.

Chipper started laughing.

Peter couldn't read CJ, which wasn't normal. Usually she told him instantly whatever she felt, whether happy, hungry, or bored. She was like a doll in that way—squeeze her stomach or touch her arm, and she'd speak to you. But now she acted somewhere between a person bracing herself for an approaching storm and the actual storm itself.

"CJ, come on," Peter said, through gritted teeth. His shame was finding new heights.

"No."

Peter felt his shirt sticking to his heavy chest. He wiped his forehead and the side of his face. He felt dizzy. He craved Dramamine. He whispered "please" to CJ, trying to ignore the snickers. Peter could hear the desperation in his own voice. He knew he was shattering his pride, but it was a feeling he was getting used to. This was all about damage control. There was nothing more in the world that he wanted to do than go inside, sit next to Uncle Herb and turn on the television. He yearned for safety.

"No," CJ said.

In an act of desperation, Peter grabbed her arm and tried to pull her toward the house. CJ thrashed and her tiara fell off her head and onto the grass. Peter let go of his grip.

CJ's body started to shake, and her face turned burgundy red as she picked up her tiara. Peter had never been forceful with her; they didn't even play wrestle. She stared at him with her fists clenched as Chipper and the goons catcalled and howled.

"You do that again, Peter, and I'll knock your head off. I mean it." Her voice shook as she spoke.

Chipper fell laughing over the curb onto the lawn, making sure anyone on the block who might be watching knew how funny he thought this was. Peter looked back for Josh, but he had disappeared behind the ark's frame, carrying a plank. His head started to spin, and his knees felt like putty, and he feared a seizure coming on, but in a way, he almost welcomed one to get out of this situation. But then a voice called for Peter, not from the clouds like he'd originally thought, but from the screen door of his house.

"Pita, Hee-hay."

Peter closed his eyes and walked toward Uncle Herb's voice, fighting the sickness that rushed through his body. He tried to walk casually and hoped CJ was close behind, but he wasn't going to fight her anymore. She'd listen to Uncle Herb, and Chipper wouldn't do anything in front of an adult to ruin his Boy Scout image. After a few seconds, CJ's shadow trailed his dark silhouette.

The front door was miles away.

In the living room, CJ burst past Peter, passing Uncle Herb without a word and went straight to her room. She closed her door. Peter avoided Uncle Herb's eyes and dropped on the couch. His mother had missed everything, sitting at the kitchen table and talking on her phone again. Peter stared at the blank TV screen until Uncle Herb parked in front of him and asked him if something was wrong with CJ.

Peter thought about telling him that maybe she'd finally realized her brother was a wimp, a frightened kitten, a fish out of water. Maybe the shame and fallen image of her brother was too much for her to stomach.

He wanted to tell his Uncle that maybe he was glad. Maybe CJ would be out of his hair now. Maybe she'd stop following him around, and the pressure to entertain and watch her would be off him. He had enough problems of his own to worry about. This was too much, he wanted to shout.

But all he ended up saying was, "I don't know, Uncle Herb."

Day 66

The house was quiet. Peter was marking his calendar with an orange dot and a blue dot as Uncle Herb watched a morning news program in the living room. CJ had left early for camp without a fight—barely made a peep. She didn't say a word to Peter. When he heard his mother's car pull out of the driveway, Peter felt the sensation of losing something and not knowing where to find it.

His mother returned shortly after dropping CJ off; the camp was held at the elementary school behind the library. Peter tipped his shade back and watched as his mother stepped out of the car with the phone to her ear again. Since she'd started working again, that phone was like an earring.

Peter sighed and headed to the living room.

"Uk-a-tiss," said Uncle Herb, motioning to the television. *Look at this.*

Peter flopped down on the couch. A spirited weatherman was pointing to a computerized map behind him, where a big green arrow was heading from the ocean to the East Coast of the United States.

"And with that," said Mr. Very Happy Weatherman, "look for heavy and steady rain, with possible thunderstorms within the next twenty-four to forty-eight hours, if you can believe it, folks. And there is a front behind it too. We can be in for a real storm. At the top of the hour I'll have the ten-day forecast."

Abby walked in and stopped at the door, watching the television. "Yeah, I heard on the radio a couple minutes ago. Everybody is going crazy. Finally, right? A big storm. It's feast or famine around here."

The camera panned to two female newscasters, one young and the other middle-aged, sitting at a large desk. They applauded and thanked the weatherman, as if he had a hand in bringing the rain.

"When it rains, it pours," the older newscaster said, and all three laughed heartily, with the weatherman now walking back into the picture and tapping the desk with a pencil in front of the younger newscaster. Once they got their excitement under control, the older newscaster said, "After the break, an update on the California wildfires."

Peter stood and went to the window in the kitchen. Josh's ark didn't look ready to float in the next twenty-four to forty-eight hours. Actually, Peter doubted if the ark would ever be seaworthy. It looked more like a storage crate than anything.

"Maybe this heat will finally break now," Abby said, entering the kitchen.

Peter didn't answer, wondering if Josh knew about the weather forecast.

"You okay, Peter? You're awfully quiet lately. So is your sister. I can't believe how easily she went to camp."

"I'm fine, Mom." Peter considered telling his mother that in a roundabout way, his cowardly ways might have had something to do with CJ's attitude reversal toward camp, but decided against it.

"What is he building over there, anyway?" Abby asked. "I can't figure it out. Yesterday I asked him. I said, 'Heaven knows what you're building over there. All he did was smirk and say, 'Exactly'."

Peter grabbed a box of cereal from the cupboard and a quart of milk from the fridge. Abby placed the three orange vials next to his bowl at the table. Some dessert.

"Crap, I keep forgetting to call that doctor James told me about. Peter, will you call me at work today to remind me? We really should schedule an appointment soon," Abby said. "I'm such a horrible mom."

For a second, Peter wondered if she truly meant that. If she did think she was horrible mom, and wanted to get better, wouldn't she practice it more? Like shooting a basketball—keep working at it until you start getting some into the basket. "Sure," Peter said, but he didn't commit the task to memory. His brain felt overloaded with the things spinning around in his head, a washing machine where everything was sudsy and unclear.

Abby sat down across from Peter as he shoveled the first spoonful of cereal into his mouth. "Are you sure you're okay? You're not acting yourself."

Peter nodded.

Abby stared at him for a beat longer, then said, "I was thinking, honey. Uncle Herb goes back to work next Monday, and you don't start school until a week after that."

She didn't need to remind him. Chipper sightings did more than an adequate job.

"Do you think you will be fine here for a couple days by yourself? I hate to do it, but I'm crazy busy at work. Did I tell you I might close on my first house today? Well, assist in closing. I really need to get my license. I also have two other leads—"

Her voice drifted off, and Peter wondered and hoped that one of those leads was not for the house next door.

"I'll stop in during the day like I do now with Uncle Herb, and I'll try not to make any late afternoon appointments, but sometimes those are the only times the clients can see the house. You'll be okay, right?"

"Yeah, Mom."

"I knew you would. I have to go. I'll try to make it home for dinner, but I left money on the counter for takeout. I'll call. If you and Uncle Herb want to go for a stroll, we could use milk from the general store," she said. She stood and kissed the top of Peter's head. She grabbed her briefcase and phone and rushed out the door to her car.

Peter pushed his bowl away. He looked up and saw Uncle Herb staring at him from the living room.

"Ucks-ike-e-n-ew," Uncle Herb said. *Looks like me and you.*

Peter swigged from a glass of orange juice, leaving some at the bottom to wash away the taste of his medication. Uncle Herb made a funny face at him, one that tried to convey toughness and intimidation. Peter thought about trying to return the look but knew he couldn't even fake tough; he was the opposite of tough. He was Play-Doh.

Uncle Herb's face broke into a crooked smile with the corner of his bottom lip sinking down as if a fishhook was stuck in it.

Peter smiled and reached for the nearest orange vial.

* * *

Peter spent the rest of the morning organizing his room and reading *The Three Musketeers* in front of his fan. He was plodding along slowly through the book and was at the part when d'Artagnan duels Athos after being challenged by all three Musketeers separately. How come these guys were never afraid? They had to be, at least a little! They fought with swords—much more frightening than Chipper's fists and caveman bullying tactics. Peter tossed the book on the floor, thinking at least he could be grateful for the little things in life, such as the change in society that made it unacceptable for people like Chipper to walk around with swords at their hip.

Peter's mother had called minutes before from the office. She'd officially helped sell her first house. Peter tried to match her enthusiasm but found it hard to muster any excitement, especially after his mother asked him to pick up CJ at camp, because her coworkers wanted to take her out for a celebration—"Happy hour," she said. Peter sensed that happy hour would turn into happy hours, and he'd be ordering pizza for dinner again. Now it was lunchtime, and he had no idea what to make for himself and Uncle Herb. He headed down the hall for the kitchen, passing Uncle Herb in the living room. Herb's Bible lay opened on his lap, but his eyes were fixed on the Weather Channel. Peter looked instinctively out the front screen door. The sky was pale and cloudless. He'd have to see a raindrop to believe.

"What do you want for lunch, Uncle Herb?"

Uncle Herb shrugged and smiled, as though he'd happily eat grass if Peter prepared it.

In the kitchen Peter stopped abruptly at the sight outside the bay window. More than two dozen Canadian geese stood on Josh's lawn. Some walked in circuitous routes, knocking into one another like amusement park bumper cars, while others pecked at the brown grass.

It was an odd sight indeed. Peter knew the geese antagonized the golf course groundskeepers to the point that they had hired a company to rid themselves of the pests. Peter saw the trucks driving around once in a while. He couldn't remember the name of the company, Geese-R-Us or something to that effect, but their slogan stuck in Peter's mind: *Their goose is cooked.* It was a small operation with a couple of dogs trained to patrol the golf course and chase the geese off the greens and fairway. Usually they flew over to the safe haven of the Pine Barrens or a local park or ball field, only to return later. But rarely did the geese convene in the Creek's residential section.

Peter's stomach grumbled. He opened the fridge to barren shelves. There was bread and peanut butter and jelly, but the milk had run out at breakfast. Water or juice with PB&J just didn't work for Peter.

"Uncle Herb, I think I'll run up to the general store and get some milk," he yelled. This would give him a good excuse to take a closer peek at the geese and maybe see if Josh was around.

Uncle Herb looked up from the television. The California wildfires had taken a turn for the worse after a sudden change in the wind. *Fighting Mother Nature was a volatile and futile battle sometimes,* Uncle Herb thought. It was interesting to watch, but his vacation was almost over. He could watch as much television as he wanted when he was back in his group home.

He asked Peter if he could come, scanning carefully for any hint of Peter not wanting him to tag along. With CJ not at home, Peter could finally enjoy some alone time.

"Sure," Peter said.

Uncle Herb smiled at the simple, quick and natural reply. The last thing he wanted was to be a nuisance.

Outside the temperature was in the midnineties and the air was dry and stifling. Peter lifted his head. The heat had burnt the color out of the white sky.

"It doesn't look like rain's coming," Peter noted.

Uncle Herb's attention was further below, specifically on the geese bumping around Josh's lawn.

"Crazy, huh?" Peter said, and they started toward the sidewalk. Herb followed closely behind, careful not to run over Peter's heels. The geese were distracting his driving.

Herb held no particular affection or dislike for geese, but as they neared the flock, he could see a sort of bustling grace to them, not as much as when they were in flight but still a noticeable beauty.

The geese took notice of them. One started honking which led to a chorus, either a thoughtful warning to the others or a menacing gesture aimed at Herb and his nephew.

"Uncle Herb, you don't think they're here for the ark, do you?" Peter said, quietly, as if he didn't want to the geese to hear.

Herb considered cracking a joke here, one of a biblical nature, maybe along the lines of the geese missing the memo on pairings only. The problem was, as always, delivery. By the time he spit it out, Peter would have struggled to understand not only the words but the tone. Inflection and timing is required for humor, and Herb knew he failed miserably at both.

Herb smiled but didn't say anything.

In a way, Herb thought his challenges stopped him from accidentally pushing his knowledge and opinions on his impressionable nephew—which was not exactly a bad thing. He believed young kids too often had to face the harshness of reality and give up on the magical enchantment of adolescence. Usually, so-called responsible adults were at the root of the problem. The longer he lived, Herb realized, science and fact were overhyped, and the aura of mystery and magic were short changed.

With his eyes, Peter pressed Herb for an answer.

"May-be," Herb said slowly.

Josh and his ark were a tricky situation. He wanted Peter to reach his own conclusions. Herb admired Josh's conviction and gave him a lot of credit for acting upon it, but Herb knew the Bible. There was no flood coming again. God was pretty black and white on that.

Peter pursed his lips and looked beyond Herb's head at the geese. Herb could picture the mental scale weighing in his nephew's mind. On one side is Josh the crazy neighbor, and the other side is the second coming of Noah. It was probably enough to drive a twelve-year-old insane.

"It's amazing that all he ever built besides this was a birdhouse," Peter said, taking in the ark behind the geese.

Herb silently agreed and cited some scripture for his nephew: *All things are possible for one who believes.*

"And Josh sure believes," Peter said, turning around and heading toward the general store. Herb waited until Peter took a few steps, and then with a crumpled fist nudged the wheelchair's joystick forward. He hoped Josh wouldn't be crushed in the end.

The General Store

Herb wished he'd worn a hat. The lopsided sunburn he'd received at the beginning of his visit had finally evened out. The sun now punished his near-naked scalp. It was close to noon, and since passing the geese, they hadn't seen a living creature on the street. It was like the sun had set a curfew.

They reached the pavilion, or the clubhouse as some of the residents called it—the modern-looking, two-story square building considered the hub of the Willow Creek world. All the residential streets extended from the clubhouse center like bicycle spokes.

Herb had never been inside the pavilion, but he remembered the brochures Abby had shown him before they moved in. The place was more like a hotel than a clubhouse with its catering facility, gym, bar, lounge area, pro shop and general store.

Herb followed Peter into the air-conditioned lobby. A huge chandelier hung from the ceiling. A marble stairway curled around a rock garden with waterfall to the second level. To the left was a lounge area with tables, leather chairs, couches, and a long mahogany bar. Open French doors led to a patio overlooking the golf course.

It was very beautiful, but Herb felt out of his element. If money had a smell, he was breathing it in right now.

To his right, Herb saw the one step in front of the general store, handicapped inaccessible. He told Peter he'd wait in the lobby.

"I'll be fast," Peter said, and broke off into a jog.

Herb sat parked in the middle of the lobby, listening to the waterfall and watching the bustling people. He caught pieces of conversations: tee times, stocks and insurance, and, of course, the recent weather report calling for rain. Men in their solid-colored sleeveless windbreakers and women with their cotton skirts and matching visors paid little mind to Herb and moved around him as though he was a statue set there to complement the rock garden.

In the back corners of the lobby were the separate locker rooms, men's and women's. Voices came to Herb in waves as the swinging doors opened and shut. Two white-haired men walked out of the locker room huddled together in conversation. They stopped at the entrance, and one of the guys leaned against the swinging door, preventing it from closing.

Then Herb heard Nick's laugh.

It came from deep within the locker room. There was no mistaking his brother-in-law's penetrating laugh, so loud and sharp. Herb's wheelchair crawled in the direction of the men's locker room. When the two older men figured their conversation reached a point where they could resume walking and talking at the same time, Herb blocked the closing door with his front tire.

A voice booming with bass traveled through the cavernous locker room, but the distance and lack of pitch made it difficult to pick up anything more than patches of the conversation. The place smelled like a giant deodorant stick. Herb lowered his head and tilted his ear to the voice. He inched further into the locker room, but the door was heavy, and he worried about his ability to escape quickly if the door closed entirely.

Some more laughter, and this time Herb couldn't distinguish Nick from the others. Doubt started to creep into Herb until he heard someone say:

"Ark, my ass. That thing would hold water like a toilet."

The laughs came in force, and Nick's was again at the forefront. That was enough assurance for Herb, but if he had needed more, the clincher followed immediately when Nick spoke up:

"I told you, I live in the fruits and nuts section of Willow Creek. The taxes should be lower over there."

Nick's line drew a roar of laughter, including Nick's, who was always prone to enjoy his own punch lines.

Herb knew he needed to get out of there and fast. Seeing Nick would only make a muddled situation worse, especially if Peter ran into him. He'd want to know why his father was not away on business.

"Can I help you?" a voice said from behind him.

Herb curved his head around to get a one-eyed view of an attractive, middle-aged woman hunched over and looking at him. She flashed expensive gold jewelry underneath her casual polo shirt. She thought he was stuck in the doorway.

Herb rushed a "no, thank you," but he knew the words dropped out of his mouth in a jumbled, indecipherable mess. He heard locker doors slam and voices started to grow closer. He had to go. There was no time to humor a Good Samaritan when his nephew's feelings were on the line.

He rushed to pull his wheelchair from the doorway, but his front tire clipped against the edge of the door. Now he *was* stuck. *The irony,* he thought.

He concentrated as hard as he could, now sensing that there were more eyes than those of the woman on his back.

"Are you sure I can't help you?"

Herb slowly moved the wheelchair's controller forward, then angled it back, freeing his chair from the door. He heard the footsteps shuffling along the locker room carpet. Soon the bodies attached to the voices would appear from around the corner. He craned his neck to look behind him. The well-intentioned woman stood in his path, leaning over and nodding her head.

"Let me help you," she said, assertively.

She moved forward as Herb started to steer backward, and they collided, one of the wheelchair's push bars jammed into her side.

"Ooomph!" she said.

A man appeared from around the lockers. He looked strangely at Herb and the doubled-over woman. Precious seconds were draining away.

"Skoo-e," Herb said to the woman. *Excuse me.*

"What?"

"Skooz-e." Herb felt his frustration level rising.

"I—I don't understand," the woman said. She moved closer, further inhibiting Herb's escape.

"Mooo-ve!" Herb shouted. Spittle rocketed through the air.

The woman jumped back, clearing a space for Herb to turn his wheelchair around. Now he faced a group of people, all wearing the same aghast expression.

Peter appeared at the step in front of the general store. He studied the silent crowd then looked at his uncle.

"Is—is everything okay, Uncle Herb?"

Herb shoved the wheelchair's joystick forward with the back of his hand and sped to the exit. As he had hoped, Peter fell dutifully in tow without saying a word. Herb felt the eyes of the crowd and heard the murmurings. He felt bad for Peter, who was probably wilting under the gaze of all these adults. He stared straight at the exit.

By now, Nick was certainly one of the spectators. Herb waited for Peter's name to be called, but he wasn't entirely surprised when it wasn't.

The automated doors opened, and the heat forced its way into the air-conditioned lobby. Herb pushed through into the sunlight, thankful when the doors closed behind them.

Day Camp

Peter was fifteen minutes early to pick up CJ from camp. He'd taken the fastest route, Slocin Road straight into town, because he wanted to stop at the supermarket and buy a small bag of marshmallows for CJ—a peace offering. A short, chain-link fence enclosed the playground where all the campers were running around fueled on sugar cookies and fruit juice. Peter lingered outside of the fence. The elementary school already looked smaller to him. In a couple of weeks, he'd be bussing down the road to the middle school and seventh grade.

He scanned the playground's climbing towers, slides, and swings for CJ. Kids ran together in clumps, changing direction on whim, and stopping only to laugh or shout over one another at the top of their lungs. He leaned over the fence, as though the extra inches would help. How hard could it be to find CJ? She would be the one wearing a sparkling outfit and gripping a lasso. He finally spotted her in the back corner of the playground, a fair distance away from the swarms of kids. She was standing alone, using a jump rope to tie a complex series of knots along the fence.

The image bothered Peter. He'd wanted to find her playing with the other kids, maybe even acting as a group leader. This was like staring at a reflection of himself in school. He hoped that CJ had *chosen* to stay on the perimeter, a decision she made on her own, because for some reason having the choice made a huge difference. At school, Peter felt relegated to outside the circles, as if this invisible and collective force from all the other kids pushed him to the back like a body fighting sickness. Once he found his customary place in the shadows, away from the moment, the world regained its balance.

Peter felt anger and envy as he watched the other children bounce around without a care or an unhappy thought in their heads. Then a boy shouted "Cricket!" from his knees in the tall grass along the fence, and the games of chase and hide-and-seek paused. There was a mad rush to circle the boy and get a closer look at the cricket. With cupped hands, the boy fought off aggressive grabbing as he shielded his body and elbowed his way through the crowd. The kids followed him, begging for a better look or a chance to hold the cricket. Peter watched with a curious detachment, until he saw the boy was making his way toward CJ. He stopped in front of her and opened his hands slightly for CJ to peek inside.

"Do you want it?" the boy asked CJ.

CJ looked away. "No," she said, softly.

Several of the boys and girls shrieked from behind the boy, placing dibs on the cricket, but the boy kept his hands in front of CJ, giving her ample time to change her mind. When she didn't, the boy barely glanced back before cocking his arm and throwing the cricket as far as he could over the playground's fence.

On the bike ride home, Peter asked CJ about the boy and the cricket. It was difficult having a conversation with CJ sitting directly behind him on the seat and speaking into his back while he peddled and kept his eyes on the road, but CJ wasn't haven't any of it anyway. She didn't respond the first time he asked or the follow up attempt. On the third try, she said, "Please leave me alone."

This did not sit well with Peter—this wasn't at all like his sister. She always wanted to talk to him, to be around him. He was always the one telling *her* to leave *him* alone. What was most concerning was that she used the word *please*.

Peter kept trying to look back at her, but then the bike would swerve, and they would almost hit a mailbox or fall off the curb entirely. It wasn't until they had passed the gated entrance into Willow Creek Landing that she spoke.

"I heard them talking about me, Peter. In camp."

"Okay."

"They said no one wants to play with me, because I'm weird."

They turned left at the Pavilion onto Ranch Street.

"Kids are mean sometimes, CJ. Trust me. I know."

CJ rubbed her face against Peter's back. Peter knew that she wasn't wiping away sweat. She told him that the boy only gave her the cricket because he felt sorry for her, since no one would play with her.

"I have no friends, Peter. I say that about you, but you used to have friends. I never did."

"What about that girl Penny? Or Jenny?"

"They stopped being my friend. Because I was weird."

As they pulled into their driveway, Peter said very delicately, "CJ, maybe you shouldn't dress as Wonder Woman every day. Maybe leave your lasso home some days."

CJ jumped off the back of the bike as soon as it stopped. She wiped her eyes with her forearm. "No," she said firmly, and ran into the house.

Peter watched the screen door close. He hoped that there was more to the boy and cricket story. He hoped that the boy was some sort of savant—that he'd picked up on something very quickly that the other kids didn't, something that even took Peter a long time to understand: that CJ was special and deserved to be treated that way.

The Giant Shoe Box

After they went inside, CJ told her brother she hated camp and was never going back. Peter thought he could create a quick and concrete list of reasons why she was wrong, starting and stopping at Mom, but decided against it. Nevertheless, buying the marshmallows had been a good idea; he and CJ were on good footing again and she told him what had happened that day.

The camp counselors had taken CJ's lasso away and returned it to her only under the condition they never see the thing again. Peter guessed prying the lasso out of CJ's fingers hadn't been the most enjoyable activity of the day. Between marshmallows, CJ casually mentioned some of the older girls made fun of her Wonder Woman costume, but Peter sensed she didn't want to talk about it. She didn't bring up the boy and the cricket, and Peter didn't reveal he'd witnessed the scene, though the boy's actions were still on his mind.

Looking out the window Peter saw that the geese had split and Josh was outside holding a paintbrush and coating the seams of the ark with a dark, thick liquid. The ark was no longer upside down. Peter wondered who Josh had asked for assistance.

The sky was a gray blanket, and the lack of a blazing sun made the temperature bearable. The dry heat that scratched at the back of your throat was replaced with a heavy, humid air.

"I have to find my rain boots. I want to puddle jump, unless Josh wants to give us a ride in his ark," CJ said. Obviously the gravity of the situation, if Josh was correct, was lost on CJ.

The siblings went outside.

"That doesn't look like the ark in your Bible," CJ whispered.

Peter silently agreed. Josh's ark looked like a giant shoebox without a lid. He couldn't be finished yet. For one, there was no top. If it rained, for forty days and nights no less, the thing would fill up like a bathtub. Also, a gaping hole appeared in the side where CJ's painted door should have been.

As though he could read their thoughts, Josh patted the boat in a "good dog" fashion and ran his fingers along the hull. Peter felt the awkwardness of intruding on a private moment.

"How did you flip the boat around?" Peter asked.

Josh spun slowly, not startled or embarrassed in the least as if he knew they were there. His tan had darkened, and his beard was fuller. He looked a lot older than the mysterious guy who'd ruined the Creek's road race. Josh smiled.

"Young Peter. Wonder Woman. What do you think?"

Josh's voice was soft and wavy, and his eyes lacked their usual sharpness. He sipped from a green bottle and smiled. Peter and CJ held their position in the middle of the street and smiled approvingly at the ark.

Josh asked, "Did you see the geese before? They've moved on, probably looking for one last chance to annoy their golfin brethren. They'll be back."

"Did you have friends help you with the boat?" Peter wanted to know. It dawned on him that Josh had never mentioned a friend or family member that he was close to.

"No, no. I paid some landscapers to help me."

That explains the Spanish-speaking guys from a week ago, Peter thought.

"Are you done, Josh?" Peter asked, though he knew the answer. He just wanted to know why Josh wasn't running around frantically given the approaching storm.

"Not yet, but it's almost complete. Pretty impressive, isn't it?"

Not yet, Peter thought. It was pretty big, all right, definitely bigger than a birdhouse. But as far as buoyancy, Peter wasn't so sure the thing would stay above water longer than you could say, "Where are the life preservers?"

"I have to say, I'm pretty proud of it. I never really finished anything before. Nothing of this magnitude, at least. Goes to show you, all you need is a little spirit." Josh laughed aloud and flipped his empty bottle onto a pile of scrap wood.

"Remember that first day, Peter? I'm glad I didn't cut off any of my digits. Look, it's solid as a rock," Josh said, and with that he hit the hull with a closed fist.

The two boards underneath the plank he struck loosened and separated slightly. They stood in silence, staring at the open crease.

"Ooops," Josh said. He paused, "Well, I guess it's good that this happened now. I haven't finished sealing yet."

Peter and CJ looked at Josh, worried.

"You know it's supposed to rain soon," CJ said, painfully. "Maybe today even."

"I heard it might hold off until tomorrow," Peter offered, but to him the rain was a moot point. If one animal larger than a squirrel tried to enter the ark, Peter would bet the thing would fold, collapse, and flatten until it resembled a coaster.

"It won't rain today," Josh said, and the sudden confident manner in which he spoke caught Peter off guard. Did Josh not see what just happened? How could he be feeling good about anything? A sprinkle would do irreparable damage.

Peter looked uncomfortably at the sky. "It doesn't look too good out."

"The ark will be ready." Josh said the words with such conviction that Peter almost believed him. He didn't know if he wanted to believe him or not.

"I should probably repair these boards," Josh added. He patted Peter on the shoulder. "I guess I'm stronger than I look."

Peter forced a smile. "We should be getting home. Uncle Herb might be worried." On their front lawn, CJ leaned into Peter. "I hope it doesn't rain tonight. That might drive Josh crazy."

Peter wondered how far of a drive that really was.

Cocktail Hour

When the sun slowly drips down the sky and the heat starts to subside, it's typically time for Creek residents to make their way outside and do their chores. For Peter's neighbors, Mr. Terry and Mr. James, this time of day meant only one thing: cocktail hour.

Peter sat in a beach chair as he watched Mr. James go through the ritual of organizing the chairs and portable table on the lawn, as Mr. Terry, the official "drinks coordinator," prepared their cocktails inside.

"Usually I'd bring the drink ingredients outside with me, along with a pitcher of ice, glasses and a snack all on one tray, Peter," Mr. Terry told him. "But today's drink is the dirty martini, and to bring out the gin, vermouth, olive juice, cocktail shaker, strainer, ice, and garnish is way too much of a production, even for me."

Peter laughed, because Mr. Terry did. He didn't care that he had never heard of half the things Mr. Terry listed; Peter usually had trouble following Mr. Terry's conversations because Terry always spoke so fast and quickly jumped from subject to subject. Peter liked his neighbor, because he felt like Mr. Terry enjoyed talking to him.

"And don't mind Mr. J over here," Mr. Terry said, nodding to Mr. James as he handed him a v-shaped glass. "After all these years, I know to give him some space after a long day of work. It's not easy looking at feet all day."

Mr. James accepted his drink silently but smiled at Peter. He sipped his drink, then stared into the glass while Peter watched Mr. Terry study him, looking for a subtle sign of an opinion.

"What do you think?" Mr. Terry finally asked.

"Tanqueray?"

"Bombay."

Mr. James shook his head approvingly. "Very smooth, earthy from the olive brine. You have outdone yourself once again, Ter."

Mr. Terry beamed. "I must admit, I've become quite the mixologist."

Diagonally across the street, Josh was busy tacking a fabric to the outside of his ark. The three of them watched Josh quietly.

"I must say, since he started his project, Josh has added to the entertainment during cocktail hour," Mr. James eventually said.

Mr. Terry wiggled his beach chair deeper into the dying grass. "We should move to a place with a front porch."

Mr. James laughed. "You were the one who wanted to come here."

"Yeah, well, I thought it would be good for when we're older, with the pavilion right there for simple shopping and eating out, plus I figured I could get around on one of those golf carts once I'm too old to drive and my knees give out from being so fat. It's the closest I'll ever come to assisted living."

Peter saw CJ walk out of their house across the street and whip her lasso into the air. He warned CJ to be careful with her lasso because he was coming over. He started walking over to her, giving the adults some privacy but they were speaking loud enough that he could still hear their conversation from his lawn.

"Stop, Terry. You're depressing me," Mr. James said.

"No, I'm serious. We don't fit in here. We can move back into the city for a couple of years or go east into wine country. You can start up the business again out there. Imagine the feet problems those vineyard workers have."

Mr. James laughed as Peter warned CJ again. She ignored him.

Mr. Terry continued, "We can always move back here when we're ready. I greatly exaggerated the report of my own death. I'm nowhere near it. I'm not ready for assisted living."

"We might not get this house back."

"So what? We'll get another one. Maybe on Victorian Row this time?"

CJ cracked the lasso again, and Peter gave up, heading back to the adults.

Mr. James chuckled and smiled at Peter as he sat down next to him. "I like where we are, Terry. More every day."

Mr. Terry looked at Peter and nodded, but waved his partner off. "You're impossible sometimes. Then I guess you won't mind that the fabric Josh is using to waterproof his ark is your contribution to the project."

"What?" Mr. James tilted forward in his chair and squinted his eyes to get a better look at the ark.

"Yup. That's the linen tablecloths your mother gave us, what was that, eight Christmases out of ten?" Mr. Terry said.

"You're kidding me? You gave him all of them?"

"How much linen does she think we need? We had enough to cover the entire ark, luckily for Josh," Mr. Terry added, gamely.

Mr. James finished his drink and laughed. "One more round. And leave my mother alone."

Looking For Hoob

A rust-spotted Sedan pulled slowly up Ranch Street as Mr. James put away the cocktail hour chairs. A dark-skinned, middle-aged woman whose head barely cleared the steering wheel rolled down her window and impatiently waved James over. She looked mildly annoyed, as if she was the one being disturbed, so Mr. James chose to let her wait as he rearranged the chairs in the garage.

He ignored the car's uneven idling. Then the woman punched her horn with two angry bursts, and Mr. James fought the urge to reorganize another corner of the garage, but then Mr. Terry jumped out the front door like an eager valet.

"I'm looking for Hoobie!" Maria yelled, while Mr. Terry was still halfway across the lawn. He looked around the yard and spotted Mr. James loitering in the garage. He smiled and said, "Sounds dirty."

Mr. James muttered under his breath and exited the garage. Before he could reach the car, he knew who she was looking for. Mr. Terry was having fun with it though. "Who is Hoo-Bee? Is he like a rapper? James, does the board even accept rappers into Willow Creek Landing?"

It was clear to Mr. James that the woman's tolerance level for Terry's bantering was short. Her grip strangled the steering wheel. He noticed she was sitting on a large cushion.

"You're looking for Herb?" he asked, not wanting her to drive off, or maybe over, Terry.

"Yes," she said shortly. "That's what I tell Bob Hope over here."

Mr. Terry stepped aside. "Bob Hope? Ouch."

"May I ask who you are?" Mr. James asked, politely yet firmly.

Maria shot him a look. "What, you the FBI?"

"Just a friend."

One of the Creek's security golf carts turned down Ranch and sped in their direction. Maria noticed the flashing, yellow light in her rearview mirror. She let out a string of heavy Spanish and reluctantly placed her car into park.

Brutus stepped out of the cart. He wore his sunglasses even though there was no sign of sun. There was the sound of crickets chirping aggressively—two males must have been in proximity to one another. Maria stuck her head out the window to face the approaching Brutus.

"Ma'am, did you not see the guard house and me standing in front of the guard house?"

"I ask what you want," she answered defensively.

"And I asked you to roll down your window." Brutus emphasized each word.

"Gimme a break. I'm an old lady. It's getting dark. You could be a carjacker. You don't look like my pastor or anything."

Brutus' lips thinned. Mr. James and Mr. Terry watched the scene play out with great curiosity and admiration for the brave woman. This was the most they'd ever seen Brutus have to work. Usually he could just point silently and make people obedient.

"Ma'am, I have to ask you to come back with me. We have strict policies regarding visitors. Past five o'clock, if you're not on the guest list, we need to call down the individual you're requesting to see—"

Mr. Terry stepped forward. "I'm sorry about that, we should have told her about the protocol. It's her first time visiting. I'll gladly come down and sign her out. I hope we didn't trouble you too much—um, I'm sorry, what did you say your name was again?"

It wasn't the first time Mr. Terry tried to coax his real name out of Brutus. Brutus didn't answer.

The strings of Christmas lights in Josh's yard blinked on, and Josh walked out of his garage holding a paint can in one hand and a beer can in the other.

"It's an oil-based waterproof paint," Mr. Terry said, not because anyone asked or seemed interested but born from his yearning to be informative when he could. "Two coats over the layer of linen should seal it. James' mother donated the linen."

Brutus' head tilted ever so slightly in the direction of Mr. Terry before returning to Maria. "Ma'am?"

Across the street, the front screen door opened, and Uncle Herb wheeled out and waved, his stiff fingers pointing in several directions. Peter and CJ followed him out.

A smile softened Maria's rigid features. She pushed open the car door. Brutus had to step back to avoid being hit. She stood, reaching the curve of Brutus' bicep, and walked past him without saying a word. There was a slight shake of his head and a small release of air from his pursed lips. It was his largest public display of emotion to date.

"Ma'am, next time please roll down your window and sign in," he said.

Maria kept walking toward Herb. She turned her head to say, "Next time tell me what you want, and I will."

Brutus walked back to his golf cart. He shifted into reverse, and the golf cart beeped. He looked once more at the woman, now hugging the guy in the wheelchair, before pressing the accelerator.

Brutus doesn't talk through glass, he answered her silently.

Maria

Maria didn't like it when she found out Herb was left alone with the kids. And he was in charge! Peter was thankful she had no clue to the number of times this had happened, or for the length of time.

"Tomorrow, I get agency van and come pick you up, Hoobie. Come home where you belong, and I take good care of you," she had said, repeatedly.

Uncle Herb was appreciative of her concern but declined each time. He said he was having a great time.

They were sitting in a circle on Peter's driveway. Mr. Terry had brought out the cocktail hour chairs again and even offered to make Maria one of his famous margaritas, but Maria passed. Josh's Christmas lights dimly lit their circle and the strong fumes from his paint permeated the air.

"It's nighttime, and Mrs. Grady still not here," Maria said, not bothering to hide her disgust. "What did you eat for dinner?"

Peter felt it was his sole responsibility to prove to Maria that his Uncle was in good hands. "I'm just about to order pizza," he said.

Maria slapped her hand against her forehead.

"We're right next door, Maria. Peter knows he can come over any time if he needs a hand," Mr. James said.

Maria looked far from impressed. CJ was the only one not sitting or accommodating Maria. She was trying to whip a lightning bug out of the air. Maria yelled, "You better not be jumping all over your uncle like he a piece of furniture."

CJ stared at her, then flicked her wrist gently. The lasso dropped softly in a line pointing straight at Maria. The message was sent.

"Oh, little girl. You are so lucky you not my child."

CJ flicked the lasso back behind her. "You're lucky you're not my mother."

Maria glared at CJ, but she'd turned her back to her.

"Would you like to stay for dinner, Maria?" Peter asked.

"No, I have to get home. I'm working a double tomorrow."

Peter was relieved. He had no idea what time his mother was coming home.

Maria stood and kissed Herb on the forehead. "You call me soon. I don't like this not hearing from you. I pick you up any time you want. You still have almost a week left. Too long, right?"

Uncle Herb only thanked her and promised he'd call.

"Herb is very lucky to have someone like you," Mr. James said, standing to say goodbye.

Mr. Terry grinned. "Yeah, he never told us he had a spitfire like you on the side. No wonder we don't see him around here more often. Go Hoobie."

Maria ignored them. She patted Herb on the shoulder and walked away without saying a word to anyone else. Suddenly, she stopped and pointed at Josh's house.

"This place reminds me of my old neighborhood. Cheap lights and trash all over the front lawn."

Mr. Terry howled with laughter. "Get back before the rain starts, Maria."

Maria looked at the sky. She muttered, "Rain."

Pizza Again

The microwave beeped, and Peter walked over to get the bowl of carrots. Herb watched his nephew's movements as he methodically chewed his pizza square. Stopping in front of the kitchen window, Peter said, "It's dark out there. Josh turned out the Christmas lights."

CJ was sitting next to Herb at the table, staring down her nose at the slice of pizza dangling from her mouth. She took a big bite and said with her mouth full, "Josh said it won't rain today, Uncle Herb."

"He weda-man ow," Herb teased.

Peter placed the carrots on the table, then spooned out portions for all three of them. "No, he's not a weatherman. I think God told him, or I think he thinks God told him, or—you know what I mean."

Uncle Herb grinned.

CJ stopped chewing and a serious look crossed her face. "Do you think God spoke to Josh, Uncle Herb?"

This is where it gets complicated in dealing with children, Herb thought. *How much do you tell? How much do you hold back?*

"Uncle Herb?" Peter said. He too was waiting for an answer.

"Haybe," Uncle Herb said. Heck, who was he to doubt? Maybe God *did* speak to Josh. He wouldn't cast the first stone. Maybe God said *hark* and Josh heard *ark*. Who was he to doubt or pass judgment?

The noncommittal "maybe" seemed to be enough for CJ and Peter, rooters for the Josh-is-not-a-crackpot team. Herb felt relieved. This chaperoning job was a tight-wire act.

Things fell back into routine after that. CJ wondered why a perfectly good pizza dinner had to be ruined with carrots while Peter read *The Three Musketeers* and Herb chewed deliberately on his cut-up pizza squares. The carrots were Herb's idea. For the second night in a row, Abby got stuck at work and didn't have anything prepared for dinner. The kids didn't mind ordering pizza again, but Herb thought adding a vegetable would bring some nutritional balance, even if he'd have to sweeten the pot by allowing some marshmallows for dessert.

Peter closed his book and pointed to the muted television where there was video of the California wildfires.

"Wow, two-hundred-and-fifty homes have burned down. They can't put this thing out," Peter said.

"Stop, drop, and roll," CJ said, as was her way whenever the subject of fire came up.

The phone rang and Peter rose from the table.

"Maybe it's Dad. He hasn't called in a couple days," CJ said.

Nick. Herb sighed quietly, *another subject to mentally sashay around.*

Herb stared at the fire on TV. He looked up to see an ashen Peter holding the phone loosely away from his ear.

"Who?" Herb asked.

Peter hadn't said anything after hello.

"Who is it, Peter?" CJ said.

"Ang-up, Pita," Herb said. His voice was surprisingly clear and level.

Peter remained frozen.

"Pita!"

Peter forced the phone back into the receiver and stood staring at the cord, as if it had betrayed him.

"It wasn't Dad?" CJ asked though she didn't have to.

Peter shook his head no. He returned to the table and started clearing the dishes in silence.

Late Night List Making

All the people who call me on the phone and how I feel about it, plus one reason why I'm not in a rush to get an iPhone—A List by Peter Grady.
1. Dad—to say his business trip is going well (don't care about his business, but it's good when he talks about other things).
2. Mom—to say she is held up at work and won't be home at the time she said she would (don't care about her reasons, but care about dinner and the extra chores I now have).
3. All my friends (would be a plus, and I would care very much, if it was true).
4. Chipper—to say he is planning to fillet me like a fish before school starts (care very much, but not in the nice care type of way).

Peter sat in his bed, leaning against the bedpost underneath his gooseneck reading light and doodling around his newest list. Chipper's phone call at dinner wasn't the source of his insomnia (he'd actually fallen asleep surprisingly easily) but rather a nightmare Peter just had. In it, he was surrounded by dark, toxic-smelling clouds created by some vague-yet-complete devastation. Behind the clouds Peter could hear the shouts and screams of voices, but they were unfamiliar and unfriendly.

The dream had startled him awake, and now he was experiencing the dreaded aftereffects of a nightmare. The combination was a lethal one: all alone, middle of the night, and the feeling of being smothered by this heavy blanket of gloom, one weaved from the basement of your own mind where dark, deep fears bubbled.

Thankfully, the fallout wasn't as bad as usual, because Peter had indirect company. The Christmas lights were back on, and Peter heard Josh working outside. If he strained his neck to look out his window, he could see Josh's silhouette walking up and down the driveway between the ark and the garage. It had a calming effect on Peter.

Josh was softly singing "Amazing Grace," but Peter could hear the song perfectly through the still night. He sang only the first two lines, stopping at the "wretch like me" part, and then hummed the rest, slipping in a couple *des* and *das* until it was time to start all over again with the lyrics he knew.

After putting CJ to bed, Peter had stayed up with Uncle Herb to watch the Weather Channel. Uncle Herb shook his head in disbelief as the chance of precipitation in their area was downgraded; the approaching storm had drifted off to sea. Peter smiled.

Before the weather report switched from national to local coverage, Uncle Herb asked Peter again who'd called during dinner. He said the phone call was a telemarketer, but Peter could tell his uncle wasn't buying the story yet chose not to press.

Of course the call from Chipper had spooked Peter at first. But in hindsight, Peter was surprised it took so long for Chipper to add this form of terrorism to his repertoire. The Willow Creek Landing Membership Committee made it easy, providing all residents with *CreekLife*. A four-color, glossy periodical, *CreekLife* printed event photos and happenings, listed golf course etiquette, general store hours and catering capabilities, as well as names, addresses, and phone numbers of all the residents, in case you needed a late replacement for your golf foursome or something.

Chipper's telethreat was of the garden variety—nothing he hadn't told Peter before in person. Chipper was more action than talk anyway, more bite than bark. The distance of the phone diluted the fear.

Peter dropped his notepad to the floor and tried to close his eyes when he realized Josh's singing had stopped. He looked out the window to Josh's house and saw pure black—the driveway and holiday lights were out, not even a moon in the sky. Only the streetlight shed orange warmth on the street.

Suddenly Peter yearned to hear Josh's singing. It was too quiet, too dark. This is why they have music in elevators and dentist offices. His clock read 11:53, but Peter never felt more awake. His mother snored lightly from her bedroom. She'd come home after everyone was in bed. Peter guessed she went out with some coworkers. She always snored after drinking a couple glasses of wine.

"Can't sleep?" a voice said from the window.

Peter almost jumped out of his skin.

Josh was peering in through the screen, smiling.

Peter took a deep breath, a poor attempt to regulate his breathing. "You scared me." An awkward silence followed, forcing Peter to ask, "What are you doing?"

"Standing outside your window."

"Why?"

"I'm about to go for a boat ride."

"Not on the ark," Peter said. He immediately regretted the way the words left his mouth, as though a bowling ball had a better shot at floating.

"No, no, no. I'm borrowing a boat. Practice."

Peter looked at the clock. "At this time of night?"

"Sure."

Peter thought about Josh leaving now. He'd be all alone again until he fell asleep, if he could. He weighed his options in his mind and, ignoring his logical side, asked, "Can I come?"

SNEAK

Josh said he'd meet Peter out front in ten minutes. Peter turned out his light and dressed quietly in the dark. He put on jeans thinking there might be some wind on the water. He couldn't remember the last time he slid on pants—probably during school before summer started, right before the drought started. He thought about bringing a sweater but decided against it. He didn't want to go overboard, a statement you could take several ways.

Peter wasn't worried about waking his mother. She sounded like she was sawing wood in her bedroom. She must have had that extra glass of wine. CJ could sleep through a marching band. Peter tiptoed quietly past their rooms. Uncle Herb was a different matter, however. Peter drifted to the far wall and listened. Nothing. He skulked an inch forward when he heard his name called.

"Pita."

His name wasn't posed as a question. Uncle Herb knew who was in the hall.

"Hey, Uncle Herb." Peter tried to sound casual and sleepy. He didn't walk over to the door. How would he explain being fully dressed at this time of night?

"Can-ew-elp-e?" *Can you help me?*

Peter bit his lip as he tried to think fast. He stopped at the door and showed his head in the doorway, keeping the jeans and shirt in the hall. He could see Uncle Herb's faintly shadowed face staring at the doorway.

"Do you have to go the bathroom?"

"No," Uncle Herb said. He asked Peter to help him into his wheelchair.

Peter poked his head further into the room. "You know the time, Uncle Herb? It's not morning yet."

Uncle Herb said he knew.

"You want to get up now?"

Uncle Herb said he did.

Peter's brow furrowed. "Now?"

Yes, now. Uncle Herb's eyes were fixated on Peter, freezing him in the doorway, and his words were adamant and came out of his mouth in steely bursts. He moved his head on the pillow, and raised his fingers crooked in the air. He told his nephew he was coming with him.

Hecksher Park

All his life, people had cared for Herb. Since he was a teenager, his goal was to gain independence. In adulthood, as people his age were getting married and adding dependents, he was still striving for a measure of autonomy that most people took for granted, like learning to brush your teeth without poking out your eyeball. The electric toothbrush helped with that one.

His decision to join Peter rather than forbid him was not spontaneous. He'd heard Peter talk to Josh. Some of Peter's whispers were hard to decipher, but Josh's deep voice rolled down the muggy hallway. When he'd heard Peter's footsteps in the hallway, he knew something was up. Not bad detective work—sleepless nights can have a payoff.

His sister would have commanded Peter back to bed and then unleashed "Hurricane Abby" upon Josh's house, which would have been totally warranted. No matter how he felt about Josh, sneaking a boy out on a boat in the middle of the night is, at best, poor judgment. Yet Herb felt his choices were limited. Herb knew he couldn't enforce a lockdown, so the next best alternative was insisting on his presence. Peter could just as easy climb out his own window, though Herb didn't like to think Peter would ever defy him like that. He would make Josh turn the boat around at the first sight of danger. Hopefully he was dealing with a young man who could be reasoned with.

As they waited outside, Peter seemed concerned about Josh's reaction, but, as Josh pulled up in an official Willow Creek truck with a trailer carrying a seventeen-foot motorboat, Josh looked almost relieved to see Herb perched next to Peter at the bottom of the driveway, as if he was having second thoughts himself.

They quietly loaded Uncle Herb into the seat, and Josh lifted Herb's wheelchair into the truck's bed. They drove slowly past the dark, quiet houses of Ranch Street. Peter steadied himself in the middle of the bench seat; his arm locked with Uncle Herb's to keep him from sliding downward.

Josh looked over and smiled as they passed the guardhouse. Brutus was inside reading a magazine. He didn't look up. Peter was disappointed. Brutus without his sunglasses was a rare sight, and Peter hoped to get a glimpse of the color of his eyes. He'd once made a list guessing the color. Coal-black won.

Slocin Road was deserted—the first time Peter had seen it this way.

"How did you get this truck, Josh?"

Herb was wondering the same thing, but thought some things were better left unknown.

Josh smiled into the windshield. "My man back there. We have a deal. I don't make his life difficult by swimming in hole number eleven or disrupting community events anymore, and he slips me some insider information at times, such as the groundskeepers leave the keys to the truck under the seat."

"Brutus? You're friends with Brutus?"

"I wouldn't exactly say friends."

Peter was highly skeptical that Brutus even had acquaintances. He was about to follow up with another Brutus question when Uncle Herb asked a question of his own. Josh had trouble understanding it and looked at Peter for help.

"He wants to know what will happen if the police pull us over."

Josh looked over at Uncle Herb and gave an assuring nod. "I have a driver's license, and the registration is in the glove compartment made out to Willow Creek. It will take a little fancy talking but no big deal. But, I don't know how I'll explain you guys. You might have to go to jail."

"Very funny," Peter said.

Uncle Herb smiled and returned to looking out the window. It was not often he went for drives in the middle of the night. Never was more accurate.

Peter told Josh the weather experts downgraded the chance of rain. Josh smiled and winked. They traveled in silence on Sunrise Highway. Few cars were on the road. The air rushed in through the open windows and smelled clean. Josh pulled off at the Hecksher Park exit and onto a narrow, pine tree-lined straight away that led to a large, wooden dock. Tall, fluorescent lights ascended into the sky and illuminated the dock, but it was difficult to differentiate between the water and the sky. It was as if the dock was a diving board at the end of the world. It didn't give Peter a good feeling.

"The water's calm," Josh said.

Trucks and SUVs with empty trailers were parked in the corner of the lot. Josh turned the truck around and backed the trailer down an asphalt path descending toward the water. He stopped before the trailer wheels hit the water. The air turned salty.

"Time for you guys to get in," Josh said. He unstrapped Herb's wheelchair from the truck's bed and carried it over to the boat. Peter craned his neck to watch as he held his uncle upright with a little help from the seat belt and passenger door.

It wasn't the most comfortable ride for Herb; he'd grown accustomed to handicap accessible vans where he could remain in his wheelchair. This was old school for him, things his parents had to do for him before technology found a way to improve quality of life for the disabled. He felt watery in the truck, as though any second he would drain to the floor.

Josh came around to the passenger window, smiling as if he had a good secret about the world that only he knew. "Ready, dude?"

Herb laughed to himself. No one ever called him dude before. *Okay*.

Josh stuck his arm through the window and leaned Herb's body into Peter as he opened the door. Herb could feel Peter's grip around him tighten. Then Josh lifted him out of the truck. Herb felt like Josh barely struggled as he made his way to the boat, as if he was carrying a cooler for a day on the water.

Josh turned his head and called, "Follow me, young Peter."

Peter jumped out of the truck. When he reached Josh, he was standing at the side of the boat, deliberating over something, with Herb still in his arms.

"Young Peter, this might prove precarious."

With the added height of the trailer, it was a good six feet to climb over the boat, impossible for Josh to do with Herb in his arms.

"It's lower at the back, near the engine," Peter remarked.

Josh chewed on the predicament. "Impressive observation, young Peter."

Josh carried Herb over to the back then deliberated again. "Okay. Uncle Herb, tell me if you're comfortable with this."

Uncle Herb nodded but refused to look at him. He felt ridiculous in this position, like a damsel in distress, and looking into Josh's eyes would just add to the humiliation.

Josh said, "I can prop you first on the trailer, then lift you on the edge of the boat. Then Peter can hold you on top while I climb aboard, and then we'll put you in the wheelchair from there."

Herb looked at the distance from the top of the boat to the ground, then said, "Hut-dus-uh-rack-ullll-feer-ike."

Josh was studying Herb's lip as he spoke. When Herb finished, Josh continued to look at his lips, then to Peter, then back to Herb.

"I'm sorry," Josh said.

Peter was smiling. "He asked, 'what does a cracked skull feel like?'"

Josh grinned and nodded in agreement. "Yeah, maybe that's not the best plan."

Peter mentioned, "Josh, what if we lower the boat into the water first, then put Uncle Herb in from the dock?"

Josh took a few seconds to revise the plan in his mind. "Young Peter, you are a genius."

Peter felt his cheeks warm.

"Go, go, go! This fine gentleman in my arms does not lighten by the moment," Josh shouted.

Peter was confused. He didn't move.

"My hands are full at the moment, young Peter. You drive. I trust you. Of course, it's not my truck to worry about. Yet I trust you still." Josh was acting weird, very excited.

"I can't drive this truck, Josh."

"I'll guide you," Josh said.

They went back to the driver's side. Peter's feet barely reached the brake. Josh walked him through starting the ignition, applying the brake, R meaning reverse, and then slowly releasing the brake and guiding the boat into the water.

"A little more, little more, that's it. More," Josh said, as he stood a safe distance away. Herb couldn't bear to look until he heard the truck's brakes squeal to a stop. Before he knew it, he was seated safely in his wheelchair in the back of the boat.

The boat engine started right away, and Josh unhooked the rope lines from the dock. They puttered into the bay, leaving little wake. Peter locked Herb's wheels and sat on a bench next to him as Josh steered slowly into the bay, promising not to open up the throttle.

Josh kept the boat at a moderate speed, and no one spoke as Josh cut the engine in the middle of the wide-open water and let the gentle rhythm of the waves sway the boat. The salty air washed over them. Josh left Peter in charge of the wheel and went to the bow and sat cross-legged. He opened his arms and held his hands to the sky, then let them fall to his side. They sat in silence. Pulleys clanging on the masts of sailboat at the marinas could be heard in the distance. Stray seagulls flew through the air. Peter stared at the mesmerizing, blinking red light of a faraway buoy. He was amazed how there was nothing going on, yet there was so much to see. He felt no anxiousness, no pressure, just the calmness of the water below him. Peter lost all sense of time. Dark shadows of homes and buildings began to take form on land as the sky went from a black to dark purple.

Then Josh turned his head and spoke. "Young Peter, those three boys—they bully you."

It was more of a statement than a question. For a second, Peter wondered how Josh knew. Did he pay more attention than he let on when Chipper appeared at the house? Did Mr. Terry tell him about the library incident? He realized that it didn't matter, but his peacefulness vanished at the mere thought of Chipper.

"Mostly the one boy. The other two just follow him."

Josh told him to let the boat float for a bit and join him on the bow.

Herb had used this ideal setting for his morning prayers, and the tranquility of praying outside had put him in a deeply meditative, state but now he was alert as he watched Peter carefully navigate his way to the bow, holding his hands out just in case the rhythm of the sea knocked him off balance. Josh was standing at the tip of the bow, his eyes focused on Peter, beckoning him to come further until they were in a grasp's reach.

"For the record, I do not condone violence in any way, but I'm a firm believer in self-defense," Josh said, looking over Peter's shoulder in the direction of Uncle Herb. "Do you mind, Herb, if I show Peter the proper way to throw a punch?"

One pink-and-orange stream streaked the sky. Herb could see enough of Peter's face and the way that his body jerked with anticipation that this was something his nephew wanted. How could he not say yes? Even though it was not a response he hoped his nephew would ever use in a situation, Herb approved of any action that might nurture confidence and self-esteem in his nephew.

Josh proved to be an able and thorough teacher. Herb was impressed that, before having Peter throw an imaginary punch, Josh explained how to hold his fist so he wouldn't inflict pain on himself, where to aim, and how to follow through. Peter's first punches were tentative and awkward, but with each repetition, his competence and confidence grew.

As Josh modeled and Peter followed, backlit by the colors of the sunrise, Herb thought they looked like mythological creatures fighting in the sky. He couldn't stop watching Peter. It was the happiest Herb had seen him since his vacation started. *You are a gift, my nephew*, he thought. *You don't even know*. He realized in all his forty-two years, he had never experienced a sunrise.

Peter must have felt Herb's eyes. He looked over and smiled.

When the lesson was complete, and they all decided they better return home, Josh stood and took his shirt off. "I'll be right back," he said, and dove into the water.

Herb watched the multiple pink-and-orange streaks turning the darkened sky into a beautiful shade of red. *God's artwork*, Herb thought. *Josh was right about it not raining yet, but what was that sailor's lore? "Red skies at night, sailor's delight; red skies in the morning, sailors take warning?"*

He didn't want to waste time thinking about the day ahead. He stared at the sky and tried to burn this moment into his memory. He wanted it to leave a scar.

Day 67

Peter woke to his mother's voice coming from somewhere outside his bedroom. His skin felt dry, and he could taste salt on his lips. The boat ride seemed like a fuzzy dream.

He rolled over and looked out the window to another overcast day. Funny—from the sunrise they had seen, Peter figured the day would be clear.

He started getting dressed. His mother's voice sounded sharp. He could tell she was at a point where Peter always had the sense to back off. The stack was about to blow. He figured CJ was giving her a hard time about going to camp. Then he heard Uncle Herb speaking, and a pit formed in his stomach.

He was pretty sure they had gotten away with it. His mother was still snoring when they walked in the door. Peter wondered if he'd left some incriminating evidence. He thought he'd covered his tracks pretty well.

He edged closer to the door and heard his mother clearly. "I don't really have time to talk about this right now. He's a grown man. I need to get CJ to camp," she said. Then she yelled for CJ to turn off the television and put her shoes on.

Who was she talking about? Peter thought. Surely not him—twelve and a half is not a grown man. His father? Josh?

Peter quickly pulled his shorts on and made sure the jeans from last night were safely folded in his closet when his mother appeared in the doorway.

"You're up, good."

Peter felt her eyes studying him as he yanked his socks over his feet.

"You feeling okay, Peter? You look tired."

"I didn't sleep so well."

"Me too. It must have been the anticipation of this rain. Did you hear? The storm moved further over the ocean. We might not even get rain now. These weather people know nothing."

Apparently not as much as Josh, Peter thought.

"I have to drop CJ off. I'll call you from work. I want you guys to drink a lot of water today. I'm worried you guys are dehydrated. Uncle Herb didn't even have to go the bathroom this morning."

Peter nodded without looking at his mother. The image crossed his mind of Uncle Herb peeing over the side of the boat while Peter and Josh held him by his arms.

After breakfast, Peter lounged on the couch in front of the television while Uncle Herb nodded off in his wheelchair, his Bible teetering on his knee. Peter must have dozed off too, because when he opened his eyes, CJ was sitting at the end of the couch, watching some random talk show.

He rubbed his eyes. Feeling disoriented, he asked, "What time is it, CJ?"

"I don't know." CJ was one of those kids who turned into a zombie in front of the television, no matter what the show.

"What are you doing home? Where's Mom?"

"I don't know," she said, not taking her eyes off the new weight-loss scheme being explained by some skinny lady on a puffy couch.

Peter searched for the remote and pointed it angrily at the television. The screen went black. "CJ, I'm talking to you."

"I don't know!" she shouted.

The phone rang, and Peter stormed off to the kitchen to answer it. He should have guessed—the caller was from CJ's camp. She identified herself as Lisa, camp director. Apparently CJ hadn't shown up today, and they were doing their routine call. They wanted to talk to one of CJ's parents.

"They're not here right now," Peter said slowly, trying to think ahead to the next question.

Lisa asked whom she was speaking to. Then asked for the reason CJ was absent.

"Uh, she's sick."

Uncle Herb's eyes opened slowly, and he looked at CJ oddly for a second, then his eyes closed again.

CJ had picked up on who was on the line. She stood and shook her head furiously and silently mouthed, "I hate camp."

"Okay. Maybe, but she's really sick," he said into the phone and hung up. He pointed at CJ then to the kitchen. CJ followed him reluctantly.

Peter did his best to whisper so he wouldn't wake Uncle Herb. "They wanted to know if you'll be back tomorrow."

"So?"

"You're going to be in a lot of trouble if Mom finds out."

"So?"

"How did you get home?"

"The back roads."

Peter was speechless—that was a good two miles. He pushed it to the back of his mind, not wanting to think about the potential danger CJ could have faced. He'd seen a lot of those movies on Lifetime with his mother. It wasn't a safe or smart thing to do.

He said the first thing that popped in his head after that. "You are so lucky Dad is not home."

CJ shrugged and rolled her eyes, her way of saying *as if*.

"You walked all the way home?"

"I ran a lot of it." There was a hint of pride in the statement.

A circular saw whined outside. Through the bay window, Peter saw Josh carrying a piece of plywood up a ladder.

"I told you I wasn't going back to camp, Peter. I hate it."

Peter held his hands up in surrender. He was too tired to fight. "I'm going outside."

CJ didn't ask to join him; she simply did.

The sky was the color of old chalk, and the air felt heavy and sticky, not the attic-like dryness that Peter had grown accustomed to over the past several weeks. Peter walked across the front lawn to Josh's house, with CJ on his heels.

Josh was standing on the ladder, securing the plywood to the top of the ark. The roof was a simple inverted "V," the sides of a triangle, angling up to a peak no higher than fifteen feet. The roof was the final piece and provided a more complete picture in Peter's mind. The ark definitely did not possess the magnitude of Noah's creation. If Josh was the savior of all the animal species, the giraffe was in a lot of trouble.

Three wood columns supported the roof: one on the inside of each end of the ark and one directly in the middle. With the finished product in sight, the ark didn't look nearly as spacious as it once did, nor did it project as a vessel of sturdiness. The whole thing looked a bit wobbly.

A thought popped into Peter's head, one he had considered earlier but at the time seemed too far away to take seriously: who was Josh planning on taking with him? There was no way Josh could fit more than a couple of people and animals comfortably. Would he go alone if no animals made reservations?

Josh, however, didn't seem ready to field questions at this time. As soon as he finished nailing the roof section, he scurried down the ladder to cut another piece. He was moving around faster than Peter had ever seen.

Peter stopped walking, thinking maybe he shouldn't bother Josh. He clearly looked like he was working under a deadline. Then Josh saw them standing on the brown and stale grass and waved them over.

"You look busy," Peter said.

"The rain is coming, Peter. I received word. CJ, how fast can you finish your painting?"

"Fast," CJ said, and sprinted off to the garage.

Peter looked up to the sky. Maybe it was his mind playing tricks, but the sky did seem a shade darker since he'd walked out the front door.

"When is it coming?" Peter asked.

Josh penciled out his measured cut marks and looked around the ground for his circular saw. He had a frenzied look on his face. He looked at Peter, his face flushed. "Tonight, young Peter. The rain comes tonight."

Josh's excitement made Peter's heart beat a little faster. Peter heard CJ rattling around in the garage as Josh readied to make his cut. Instinctively, Peter held the end of the board to prevent the wood from splintering. Josh looked up at Peter and smiled. "You have done really well, young Peter. An assistant of the highest quality."

Peter felt his face redden.

He helped Josh lift the cut piece of plywood to the roof of the ark, then stood back from the ladder. Once this piece was secured, one side of the roof would be complete.

It took a few minutes, and Peter used the time to try to sort his thoughts. First of all, he liked Josh—one of the few people who took any interest in him. Well, Chipper had an interest in him, but not in a feel-good sense. If Josh was wrong about the flood, he'd be upset. But if he was right, then there were a whole lot of people in trouble very soon, Peter concluded.

A movement from the driveway near the garage caught Peter's eye. A tuxedo cat and a marble-gray tabby were sitting side by side, watching him.

"Josh, who are you taking on the ark?" Peter needed to know. He couldn't wait.

Josh paused before answering. He looked down at Peter from the ladder. "You know, the way I see it is this: I look at myself as the caterer, the one who makes the stuff. I didn't create the invitation list. I'm just here to serve. It's one of those things that I figured I won't have to search for the answer. It will show itself. He works in mysterious ways, you know." Then Josh pointed to the cats and smiled. "Maybe them."

Peter was listening so intently to Josh's answer that he didn't notice another spectator had joined the cats until he heard a long, throaty cough come from the bottom of the driveway. It was one of those coughs that you knew when the person finally finished, there was an urge to spit.

An old woman was leaning forward over a metal walker, a wide-brimmed, yellow sun hat covered her face and most of her bony shoulders. She wore thick, round glasses over well-formed wrinkles and sun spots.

"Damn pollen," she muttered.

Josh placed his hammer on the roof, looking slightly annoyed at the distraction. "Can I help you?"

The old woman shuffled up the driveway past the cats, the legs and squeaky wheels of the walker making twice the noise of her feet clad in worn cotton slippers.

She stopped next to Peter and caught her breath. She smelled like mothballs and stared at Peter through the thick glasses, giving the impression that she was looking at him through a jar. Her head tilted up in the direction of Josh on the ladder.

"So, I guess it's crunch time, boys," she said; her voice was deep and raspy. She was wearing a long, floral jacket much too warm for the weather, and she fumbled in one of the deep pockets until she found what she was looking for. She pulled out a pack of cigarettes and slowly put one to her mouth.

Josh climbed down the ladder and sighed. "Maybe it's more than pollen that's affecting your cough," he said.

"Shut up," she said, without looking up. She lit the cigarette skillfully.

Josh looked at Peter and raised his eyebrows. He stood in front of the woman and smiled.

"I'm Josh, and this is young Peter."

"I know your names. You think people aren't talking about you? It's not like you're planting a tomato garden over here," she said, a trail of smoke leaving her mouth and curling into the air. She shook her head. "My mind is good, unlike my poor husband. Every day is new to him. He's like an eighty-year-old infant."

Peter looked to Josh. He planned on leaving the entire conversation up to him.

"I assume you live here?" Josh asked.

"Not by choice. My husband's idea—wanted to be near the grandkids and to golf all day. Well, he's gone. St. Joe's Nursing Home. People kept finding him roaming the golf course. Probably thought he lost a ball instead of his marbles. I couldn't take care of him anymore. And the kids and grandkids can't be bothered. I don't live here—I'm stuck here."

Josh nodded. On some level, Peter could relate too. He kicked a pebble across the driveway.

CJ came out of the garage, probably at the sound of an unusual voice, and made her way to the sitting cats.

The old woman pointed to the ark with her cigarette. "I didn't think you had it in you. Marge lives two houses down. We'd watch sometimes while we drank tea in her living room. We're not nosy bodies; I'm not, can't speak for her, but you run out of things to talk about after a while, especially with Marge. At first you looked like you couldn't buy a clue."

Josh smiled at this.

The old woman continued, "It was harmless fun at first. But at the club we heard you were building Noah's Ark, and Marge and all her bridge friends thought you were blasphemous. And the husbands said you're some drug-crazed lunatic."

Peter looked up at Josh to see if he was getting angry, but he seemed amused with all of it. CJ was petting the cats while keeping one eye on the smoking lady.

"Henry wasn't like that, when he was still Henry. He was kind and gentle. Never liked to speak bad about anyone. I was always the one to stir the pot. I got sick of listening to those guys. I told them if they had any guts, they would come over and say it to your face. They just went back to sipping their gin."

"I guess I should thank you for sticking up for me."

"Oh, horseshit." The old lady lobbed her half-smoked cigarette over the driveway onto the lawn. It smoldered on the dry grass. "I just have a little devil in me, that's all. You should get your hair cut. Even Marge started feeling bad for you after a while—she thinks you're setting yourself up for a fall. She wanted to come over here and read some Bible verse to you, but every time she worked up the nerve, you were walking around half naked. Don't you own any shirts?"

Josh looked down at his bare chest.

The old lady cleared her throat. "Yeah, well, I told Marge I'd come down today. 'Better late than never,' I told her. She wants me to read a Bible verse to you. I told her she talked about it so many goddamn times I had the thing memorized, which is something else since I haven't set foot in a church in years."

Josh smiled gently.

The old lady cleared her throat again and started, her voice gruff yet clear. "Genesis 9:11. 'Never again will all life be destroyed by the waters of a flood; never again will there be a flood to destroy the earth.'"

She finished and nodded her head emphatically. "Not bad for an old heathen like me," she added.

"Thank you," Josh said, and then waved to the house the old lady had pointed out earlier. "Thank you, Marge," he shouted.

The old, smoking lady grabbed a hold of her walker and turned it back down the driveway. "At least she'll be off my back now."

"I'm glad," Josh said.

The old lady wasn't in a rush to leave. She turned back to Josh. "Whatever happens, at least you have a boat out of the deal. If you can call it that."

Josh nodded and waved goodbye, but the old lady stood there as if she was waiting for a bus. Eventually, she shrugged and mumbled something, then started hobbling down the driveway. She stopped one last time as she reached the street. "Might not be a flood, but the rain is definitely coming. My knees haven't hurt like this in months."

Josh watched as she made her way back to Marge's house. Peter was staring at him, looking for some sort of reaction to help make him understand what was going through Josh's head.

After standing there in silence for several seconds, Peter asked, "Did you know about that verse, Josh?"

Josh shrugged. "Nah. I'm not that strong of a reader."

He patted Peter on the head as he passed and said, "Time to get back to work."

CJ called for them. She was holding the two cats in the air by their tails, their front paws thrashing the air in an attempt to grip pavement. "Look!" she shouted. "One boy and one girl."

Lunchtime

CJ was glad to cut out of camp. She told Uncle Herb this several times as he sat across from his niece during lunch, admiring her as she slowly peeled apart her peanut butter and jelly sandwich, licked one side, then the other. It was like watching a painter at work; there was passion, creativity, meticulousness, and a spiritual nature to the entire experience. Uncle Herb could think of nothing he enjoyed or appreciated more.

As he watched her, Herb could almost taste the peanut butter. The last time he enjoyed peanut butter, he was around Peter's age, concluding then that the trouble outweighed the benefits. He didn't have the muscle control in his mouth that peanut butter required. Herb remembered tears of relief welling in his eyes after one clump had finally dropped on its own accord from the roof of his mouth.

Herb looked across the table at Peter. Little, dark saucers sat underneath his eyes, and his skin was a sickly white. Even Herb himself had a tan, now on both sides of his face.

"CJ, Mom told you not to eat your sandwich like that. It's too messy," Peter said.

Herb appraised his nephew. He had an edge to him since coming in from Josh's house. Herb questioned himself—was he watching the kids close enough?

"So?" CJ said. She continued licking the insides of the sandwich. She kept the bread so close to her mouth that a dot of jelly appeared on her nose.

"So don't do it."

CJ opened her eyes long enough to stare at her brother in defiance, then went back to her sandwich.

"CJ!"

Uncle Herb intervened. He nodded slowly. "Pita, o-k."

"If I have to be her babysitter every day, she should have to listen to me!" Peter shouted, and stormed away from the table.

Herb watched his nephew run to his room, and suddenly he felt like a fifteen-year-old boy again.

It had been a Friday night, but it wasn't Herb running to his bedroom. He wished it *was* him—but it was Abby. Jon O'Leary had asked her on a date. He was good looking, popular, a talented soccer player. She used to tell Herb everything, and Jon was a constant subject. Their mother had suggested to Abby that maybe it would be nice to bring her brother along considering he'd be mainstreaming into the public school system next year (though he was three years older than Abby). *A good opportunity to meet people*, she'd said. Herb didn't want to go. He knew this date was important to Abby. He knew the drag he'd be on her. *No one* wants to bring their brother around, but Abby felt the pressure of having a disabled brother. Herb knew that even back then. He remembered how her face flushed and her eyes welled. He tried to get out of going to help his sister, but their mother wasn't hearing any of it, thinking he was just being shy. It was a no-win situation for Abby, and Herb felt for her. The night wasn't a total disaster, but Jon O'Leary never called Abby again.

CJ finished her sandwich, and Uncle Herb told her to clean up. She dragged the stepstool to the sink and turned on the faucet.

Uncle Herb wanted the best for his sister. She deserved it. But the longer he stayed in Willow Creek, the less he saw signs of the old Abby. This morning, he'd brought up hearing Nick's voice in the clubhouse. She wasn't shocked, and this stunned Herb. She knew. She tried to cover by saying he was only in town for a short meeting and then off to Texas again. He was busy and under a tremendous amount of stress. The business was growing. *But at what price*, Herb wanted to shout. But then Herb put it all together. Nick was staying at a friend's, spending a lot of time in the clubhouse nearby, and Abby wasn't too upset. That was not a good sign.

He felt a moist hand on his arm.

"What's the matter, Uncle Herb?" CJ asked.

He smiled and shook his head. He was always amazed at the perception of children. He wanted to coddle her, comfort her, and offer her a shield of protection. To tell her there was an infinite blue sky in her future. How do you do that when you see dark clouds forming overhead?

Uncle Herb pressed the joystick of his wheelchair, and the chair nudged forward. She laughed, startled. That always got her. He looked at her and winked, and she followed him as he buzzed down the hallway to Peter's room.

Dusk

For the third night in a row, Peter, CJ, and Uncle Herb had pizza for dinner. The delivery guy looked past Peter after handing him the box as though trying to uncover some great secret to report to the authorities. Peter told him his parents often worked late. He tipped him extra, and the guy shrugged and walked away.

Peter groaned as he flicked the last piece of crust onto the paper plate. After his mother had called to tell them she'd be home late, they were low on options. Who knew how to cook?

A warm breeze circulated through the house. Peter didn't have much of an appetite, so he wrapped the remaining slices in aluminum foil and dropped them on a refrigerator shelf. He was always the last to finish eating, after preparing food for Uncle Herb and helping CJ with whatever she needed.

Herb rolled in front of the television, which was already on and showing an emergency worker feeding a baby deer with a baby bottle. On the West Coast, the California wildfires were chasing all the wildlife from their homes.

Tension had filled the afternoon. Peter felt exhausted. He didn't apologize to Uncle Herb or CJ, nor did they seem to expect him to. Peter had felt this tightness inside his body since Josh told him the rain was at hand. The Weather Channel confirmed Josh's belief, stating the rain would come sometime after nine p.m.

What if Josh is right, Peter thought. Would he wake up tomorrow floating down the street in his bed? No one else seemed to take Josh seriously. According to the old smoking lady yesterday, everyone knew he was building an ark. If people thought it was for real, they'd be lining up down the block trying to get a ticket aboard. Peter glanced out the kitchen window just to make sure this wasn't the case.

Josh was all alone on his driveway, fiddling with a fishing pole.

Peter hoped his mother would come home soon, so he wouldn't have to toilet Uncle Herb and get CJ ready for bed by himself. He wanted to go to sleep early and get this night over with.

Rain

Peter slept curled against the wall, fully dressed and dreaming. In his dream, columns of rain assaulted the asphalt street and cement walkways of Willow Creek Landing. The droplets hit the hard surfaces in a deafening rush. Streams formed at curbsides, filling every heat-induced crack and gap in its way. No pothole was too large. The grass and soil drank, unquenchable.

He woke to a voice whispering his name.

"Young Peter, the time is near."

Peter rolled over and looked at the clock on his nightstand. 11:37. He rubbed his eyes. The sounds from his dream were absent—rain pounding pavement, patches of rumbling thunder, lightning fracturing the sky. Only the soft chirp of a lone cricket dotted the night.

"That bed is not flood-proof, my friend. It's time to act," said the voice from outside.

Peter moved into a sitting position and rubbed his eyes. He could make out Josh's silhouette at the window. He flicked his reading light on and could see Josh sporting a canary-yellow raincoat, the hood masking most of his eyes but not his beard and open-mouthed smile.

The air smelled clean, detergent-like.

Josh pointed through the screen at Peter. "Fully dressed? So you think I might not be certifiably insane, huh?"

"No, well, I fell asleep reading . . ."

Josh's smile widened. "It's okay, young Peter. No time to explain. There is nothing wrong with hedging your bets."

"Has it even started drizzling yet?"

"There will be no drizzling, young Peter. Nope. It will fall upon us out of chutes. Golfins will float helplessly down the street like fallen leaves."

Peter suddenly felt a pit form in his stomach. He didn't like the image Josh had conjured, of capable people being rendered completely powerless, no matter how poorly the golfins treated or ignored him. He looked closer at Josh. His wide smile had tapered into a grin, and his eyes looked glassy and unfocused.

"You really think so?" Peter asked.

Josh snorted and threw his hands into the air. "I have no idea, young Peter. I was just being dramatic, taking a little creative license to highlight what some might think of as poetic justice."

Peter had no idea what Josh was talking about. For a second, he wondered if *Josh* knew what Josh was talking about.

"Did you come here to say goodbye then?" Peter asked.

Josh pressed his face against the screen. "Goodbye? Hell no! Did you really think I'd leave my trusted assistant behind?"

Peter tried to suppress a smile.

"But I need to tie down some tarps to the ark, to protect against the worst of the rain," Josh said. "Do you think you can help? I tried, but it's awful to do by myself."

"Yeah, sure," Peter said, but something else was bothering him.

Josh turned around to leave when Peter called his name. "Who else is coming on the ark?"

The tip of Josh's yellow hood grazed across the window screen. "Well, I'm saving some room for guests who didn't make personal reservations with me."

Peter pictured elephants and giraffes stomping through the gates of Willow Creek. Boy, would they be disappointed when they caught sight of Josh's ark. But then he imagined CJ trying to get Uncle Herb in his wheelchair as water flooded around her ankles, and he knew he couldn't leave without them.

"I don't really know, Peter. Who'd you have in mind?" Josh nodded into the screen. "Maybe at least a devoted uncle and a little girl with lasso expertise?"

Peter nodded.

"Of course. We'll make room for them even if we have to stand for forty straight days and nights. Are you skilled with a fishing pole?"

"No."

Josh let out a small sigh. "Well, that makes two of us. We'll learn. We'll wake the others once we feel the first drop of rain."

Peter felt a sense of relief. "What can I bring?"

"I have the necessities. Just give me a hand with the tarps. Then we will have faith with the rest. You know where I'll be." And then Josh disappeared.

Peter sat for a moment at the end of his bed. He'd prepared himself just in case Josh did ask him. He was already dressed in his cargo pants with a lot of pockets. But there was a big difference between preparation and actually going through with something. Without waking CJ and Uncle Herb, he tiptoed through the dark into the kitchen and filled one of his side pockets with his orange medication vials. He inhaled a slice of pizza by the light of the refrigerator, then quietly rummaged through the closet for his raincoat. He hadn't seen it in months.

What should he fill his other pockets with? Toothbrush? Pocketknife? Flashlight? Cheese sticks and individually packaged beef jerky? Peter thought that Chipper the Boy Scout would probably be better suited for this. He felt his heart starting to beat faster; the days of anticipation were gone. Now there was immediacy to his every move despite his constant glancing out windows revealing no signs of rain.

Peter stood facing the front door for several seconds, then turned and walked down the hallway to CJ's room. Her leg was draped over the bed sheet, her arms resting on her chest in full baby-vampire mode. The red-and-blue outfit, tiara and lasso lay neatly on the rug in front of her bed. Then he stopped in front of Uncle Herb's room and heard his gentle breathing patterns. He was asleep. Peter couldn't hear anything coming from his parents' room, but he checked anyway. The bed was made and empty.

When he pushed opened the front screen door, Peter didn't know what to expect as he looked over at Josh's driveway: possibly horses trotting around the ark or monkeys hanging off the roof. But the entire block looked no different than any other night, except for a small light coming from the center of Josh's ark.

The medication vials rattled in his pockets as Peter walked

across the lawn. A ladder was leaning on the side of the ark, and Peter climbed it and looked down at Josh. He was sitting on top of a case of bottled water and whittling a stick with a pocketknife. He seemed calm, content. A battery-operated camping lantern hung crookedly in the air suspended by a rope tied to the roof. Cases of canned vegetables and packaged goods sat under a plastic tarp. Peter noticed a whole case of fudge-striped cookies.

"Perfect timing, young Peter. The only competition for space right now is from these guys." Josh leaned over and pointed behind him with the stick. The two cats from earlier were sleeping on the floor.

Josh looked ghostlike in the pale, fluorescent light, his teeth glowing. Peter stayed where he was on top of the ladder.

"I'm glad I thought of the tarps. This roof will serve as little protection against a driving rain. The only thing is, it's muggy already. It will get really hot in here if we hang all the tarps. Maybe we'll just do one side for now."

Peter couldn't stop staring at the cases of food.

"What's the matter, young Peter?"

"It's just—I can't believe this might happen."

Josh stood and started unfolding a tarp. "We'll get through it. You're a brave man."

Peter stepped into the ark and accepted the edge of the tarp Josh handed him.

"I'm twelve," he said.

"And a half!" Josh shot back as he jumped off the side of the boat.

Josh had climbed down the ark and turned on the Christmas lights from the garage while dragging another ladder back with him. Peter held the tarp tightly to the roof as Josh secured it with a staple gun. When they were done, Peter was sweaty and thirsty. He grabbed a water bottle from inside the ark and drank, then regretted it immediately. He should have drunk from the garden hose rather than lower the ark's rations.

"It's okay," Josh said, reading Peter's face. "I have plenty, plus some iodine tablets in the first aid kit."

Peter walked over to the side of the ark that faced his house. His body felt tired but the sense of anticipation had him wired. It was like the night before Christmas or his birthday. Flood Day.

He took another sip of water. “Josh, what time is it?”

“Past midnight. I’d say around one, maybe one-thirty. You thought the rain would be here by now? I was thinking the same thing.”

Peter was looking at the empty driveway. He had no idea when the rain would finally come, but he sure thought his mother would have been home by now. As Josh moved quickly, making the final preparations, Peter formulating his own plan. When the rain comes, how will he convince Josh to not only take a little girl who thinks she is Wonder Woman and a guy in a wheelchair, but the woman who is trying to sell his house?

PART III

Day 68

Peter woke to the sound of chirping birds. Disoriented, his eyes came into full focus on a small puddle of water inches from his nose. His wet shirt stuck to his shivering body. He was lying on the floor of the ark. He didn't get that feeling of buoyancy as if they were floating.

From the floor, he could see the roof of Josh's house. The ark was still in the driveway.

He rose to his knees and found the source of the puddle. The water bottle he had been drinking from last night now rested on its side, empty.

Patches of pink spotted the light-blue sky. Peter placed the time around dawn. He stood and looked out beyond the ark. Everything—the cars, the trees, grass, the houses, driveways—was all intact and looked as dry and dull as it had for the last several weeks. All that was missing was the clean, washed look after a fresh rain, when everything looked brand new.

"Go home, Peter," a low voice said from behind him.

Peter turned, trying to hide his initial startled reaction. Josh sat huddled in the bow, his back leaning against the hull and his knees drawn to his chest.

"I must have fallen asleep," Peter said.

"I was planning on waking you when the rain started," Josh said, then shook his head.

"It never rained at all?"

Josh didn't answer. He appeared to have withdrawn to a remote place, far away. The cats were gone.

Peter wanted to say something. He couldn't help but feel a sense of relief as though a tough choice had been made for him, and he was happy with the result. He thought Josh might have felt relief too, but he didn't look comforted in any way. It could have been exhaustion, but then Josh's eyes sharpened as though he'd returned from wherever he'd been and was mad that Peter was still standing there.

"The last thing I need is your mother freaking out and calling the cops. Go!"

Josh had never used a harsh tone with Peter, and Peter left awkwardly without saying goodbye, more hurt than insulted, surprised but not all that much. Deep down he'd wondered why Josh was so friendly and open to his companionship in the first place. Why should he be different from anyone else? Peter almost tripped out of the boat, trying to get out as fast as he could.

His mother's car was back in the driveway, and he found her sleeping fully clothed on top of her made bed. At least he wouldn't get in trouble for staying out all night. He went quietly to his room with the knowledge that she'd come home in the middle of the night and hadn't even checked on him. That hurt almost more than getting in trouble.

He peeled his clothes off and went to bed.

The Sound of a Black Dot

CJ sat at the edge of the kitchen table, her legs dangling above the faux-wood floor and moving to the speed of a dance song coming from Herb's portable radio above the sink. She tapped the air to the beat with the same spoon she was using to feed her uncle cereal, completely unaware of the milk spitting from the utensil. Herb turned his head to shield his face.

"I like this song, Uncle Herb. Do you?"

Uncle Herb shook his head in agreement. Actually, the song sounded like a cat dying, but Herb felt refreshed this morning. He slept great, completely uninterrupted until morning—a rarity.

That was more than he could say for everyone else in the house. They all looked like the walking dead this morning. They had their secret mission, "Project No Camp," working to a tee. CJ told Herb she hid behind a shrub at the school, until Peter appeared on his bike to take her home. Herb was slightly uncomfortable with the whole plan, but he chose to pick his battles.

Peter went straight to bed after walking in the door. Herb was disappointed. He couldn't help thinking of Josh next door, and how he was handling the nonflood. Maybe Josh had taken it as a false alarm. Herb would have to wait for a report when Peter woke.

"Train, airplane, or car?" CJ asked.

He answered train.

To Herb, being fed by his niece was like a hidden pleasure in life. Over the years, hundreds of hands had fed him, but none like his niece's, with every loaded spoonful traveling via various modes of transportation. Maybe his parents had done something similar with him when he was young, but he couldn't recall, and he was pretty sure he didn't appreciate it like he did now. Herb smiled as the spoon chugged through the air to the sound of *cha-cha-cha-cha-cha-CHOO-CHOO*.

A loud thump came from down the hall, stopping the train in its tracks. Herb and CJ turned their heads in unison.

CJ called, "We're in the kitchen, Peter." She turned back to Herb. "Plane or car this time?"

But Herb was staring past CJ, past the kitchen entrance and down the hallway leading to the bedrooms. He heard a tapping noise—not drips, but a constant rhythm of light knocks. He couldn't place the abnormal sound.

"Pita?"

Herb nodded to CJ, but she had already hopped off the table to follow the sound. Uncle Herb guided his wheelchair around the kitchen table and into the living room by the time CJ yelled his name.

No, Herb thought.

He reached the straightaway of the hallway and tried to gun his chair, but his gnarled fingers slipped over the knob. He kept the chair moving forward with his forearm.

Peter lay sprawled on the floor of his room, his head buried under the frame of the bed. Only his pale, gray pajamas showed. The knocking noise was Peter's head banging against one of the bed's wooden legs. A trail of blood ran down Peter's neck.

Call for help, Uncle Herb told his niece.

CJ had backed herself in the corner of the room, frozen. She held her half-closed hands in front of her face like a boxer. She didn't move.

"Hee-Hay!"

CJ looked at Uncle Herb strangely. He felt a pool of saliva forming in the corner of his mouth. He tried to muster a soothing tone as he told her again to call for help.

She ran out of the room, and Herb cursed his lack of clear instructions when he heard her shouting, "Josh!"

He should have been more specific.

Herb's own body started shaking. This was *his* nightmare: a set of circumstances you always push into the back of your mind in fear that by letting them come to the forefront, they just might materialize.

Herb tried to clear his head. There was a phone in Abby's

room. He had given up on dialing phones years ago out of frustration. If he could somehow miraculously dial 911 without frustrating attempts like 914, 92, and 912, would emergency services even understand him?

The other problem was manipulating his wheelchair out of Peter's room. Herb had pulled in too far out of panic, and with Peter's legs sticking out into the middle of the small room, a 360 turn would take a dozen minor pivots.

Herb's hand shook as he attempted a blind reverse. He hit the door frame with a bang, snapping his head back.

Slow down, he told himself. He moved forward and tried again. The sound of Peter's head hitting the post made it impossible to concentrate. In his mind, Herb tried to line the wheelchair even with the doorway at his back. He hit the steering knob and again slammed into the doorframe, this time breaking off a piece of molding. On his third attempt, he hit the other wall, spinning his chair around but not enough for him to make it out the door.

Uncle Herb cursed aloud for the first time that he could remember.

He cursed again, his head tilted, face aimed at the ceiling. He cursed his sister. He cursed her husband. He cursed the world until spittle fell onto his lap like rain. How long has it been since the first loud *thump*? Two minutes? Five minutes? The elastic V-neck of Peter's pajamas had turned a deep wet maroon.

Herb gave up on leaving the room. He inched his chair as close as he could to Peter's legs. He closed his eyes and spoke to himself. *Lean, Herb. Fall, useless body*. He squeezed his eyes tighter. *Will yourself*. Herb pushed his brain to push his body. He was a reticent cliff diver, a fearful parachutist standing at the edge of the airplane. *Fall, damn it. Fall!*

Herb landed face-first inches from Peter's chest, and his glasses pulled and stretched away from his ears. The room turned mosaic, as though he was looking through Saran Wrap. His left arm, the better arm, was stuck under his belly and bearing his weight, stopping him from receiving a full breath of air. Peter's face was mapped with blood—a gash on his nose and his forehead from the best Herb could tell. His eyes were pure white, the pupils rolling around somewhere in his head. With his right arm, Herb took aim. He tried to lift his chin for a better view, feeling like a floundering seal. He threw his arm and missed badly, his hand slapping the floor on the other side of the bed leg. His next attempt hit high on the bottom of the mattress, and Herb let his hand drip slowly down until it was safely wedged between Peter's head and the wooden leg. The thudding stopped. Peter's head tapped at Herb's hand, and the sound was strange to him, like a polite clap.

"O-hay, Pita. O-hay," Herb said, softly.

Herb looked at his hand and pleaded with it not to move, to not slide into Peter's mouth. When the strength in his neck gave out, his face hit the floor sending his glasses sprawling, and he closed his eyes, thankful for a small circulation of air coming into his mouth and nose.

Peter's tremors started to gradually decrease until nothing was left but the gentle rising of Peter's stomach. Herb heard CJ's footsteps, accompanied by a heavier pair.

"What the—" Josh whispered, upon entering the room.

"Uncle Herb?" CJ said, her voice an octave higher than normal.

Josh lifted Herb into his wheelchair and dragged Peter slowly into the middle of the room. He found Herb's glasses on the floor and placed them on Herb's face, but the frame was bent, and they dangled crookedly off his nose.

"Hank-ew," Herb barely managed. He needed to get his own breathing back under control.

Josh stood over Peter's limp body, shaking his head. "I'm sorry, young Peter," he said.

He stepped over Peter and walked out of the bedroom.

Shortly after, CJ answered the door to Mr. James and Mr. Terry.

The Cavalry

Peter sat with his eyes closed and legs up on the couch, holding an ice pack over his bandaged forehead and sipping from a glass of iced tea. His head felt like it was ready to explode. He lowered the ice pack and scanned the room, squinting from the bright sunlight that beamed in through the windows. The sun had returned in its full glory. Uncle Herb was sitting at the screen door watching CJ in the front yard.

"Where's Josh?" Peter wanted to know.

Mr. James, on his phone as he paced between the kitchen and the living room, looked up at the sound of Peter's voice. He motioned to someone in the kitchen, and seconds later Mr. Terry appeared before Peter and sat down next to him. He inspected the Band-Aids on Peter's nose and forehead.

"How is the iced tea?"

"Really good."

"Do you taste the mint?"

"Yes," Peter lied. Mr. Terry was very proud of his homemade iced tea.

"Josh had to go," Mr. Terry said. He patted Peter on the knee. "I think you gave him a good scare."

Mr. James walked into the room. An air of purpose followed him. "You're looking better already, Peter. I left messages for your mom on her phone and at the real estate agency. I told her everything is okay, but she should call us right away."

"Thanks," Peter said, also grateful that Mr. James didn't ask if his mother had called the doctor he'd recommended. Peter didn't think she had.

Mr. James walked over to where Uncle Herb was parked. "Are you okay, Herb?" Mr. James asked.

Uncle Herb just nodded, not taking his eyes off the screen. He looked over at Peter and smiled, then nudged the front screen door open and disappeared.

No one had told Peter about his uncle's heroics, only that CJ had run to get help from Josh. He'd regained total consciousness on the couch. Peter thought his uncle looked wiped out.

A soft breeze swept by Peter. It was late afternoon, and the heat wasn't stifling. "I'd like to go for a walk," he said.

Mr. James looked at him, unsure. "Really?"

"Yeah. I don't taste blood anymore." Peter had bitten his tongue and the inside of his mouth during the seizure.

"I think a walk sounds like a great idea. I'm sure Josh can use a walk too," Mr. Terry said, but then looked at Mr. James. "But maybe we should wait until Peter's mother calls."

Mr. James thought about this and then answered coolly, "I left my number."

Mr. Terry looked at Peter and raised his eyebrows. "I love it when he gets like this."

They started getting ready. "You know, Peter, it's really good you didn't swallow your tongue. You know what happens then?"

"What?"

"You start talking out your butt like me," Mr. Terry said. He clapped his hands together and laughed, despite Mr. James' look of disapproval.

Outside, Uncle Herb waited to approach CJ. He slowly drove over the walkway onto the lawn. He stopped behind her and asked if she was okay.

She didn't answer right away. She was picking at the dead grass. CJ turned and looked up at Uncle Herb. "Peter was the Wicked Witch, Uncle Herb."

Herb nodded, wondering where she was going with this. He wanted his niece to speak freely.

"He was the Wicked Witch. The witch who had the house fall on her head. Only her legs showed, and that's what Peter looked like. I could only see his legs coming from the bed."

She looked at Uncle Herb and the anguish in her face made him yearn to wrap her in his arms. *The Wizard of Oz*.

"That scared me, Uncle Herb."

He nodded this time because he understood. He could relate. "Mmeee-ew, hee-hay. Meee-ew."

Me too.

Golfin Sighting

Peter joined Mr. James in the street. He noticed for the first time that the ark tilted in the direction of Josh's house, as though the two structures were whispering to one another. Mr. Terry was standing on Josh's stoop, talking to Josh through the screen door.

"It looks like it's taking some persuasion to get Josh out of the house," Mr. James said.

"Why?" Peter asked.

Mr. James sighed. "Well, I guess when you work so hard and believe so deeply in something, there's bound to be disappointment along the way."

"You mean the ark?"

"I think the ark is a part of it, Peter. But there is a bigger picture. The ark was just part of his escape plan."

Peter looked down. "I don't understand. But now he doesn't need an escape plan."

Mr. James laughed. "When things in life aren't going the way you planned, or you're not happy where you're at, you need an escape plan. I think Josh is just really confused right now. You will understand one day."

Peter hated when adults said stuff like that. He knew about escape plans. He had to devise one regularly when dealing with Chipper.

Mr. James went on, "I can tell you from experience, and you can probably relate in your own way, it's no fun feeling like you have nowhere to turn."

Mr. Terry walked down Josh's lawn, past the ark, with Josh following slowly behind. CJ and Uncle Herb were still on the walkway in front of their house, and Mr. James called to them.

"Hey Wonder Woman, Herb, will you guys be joining us?"

"Join the fun!" Mr. Terry said, waving them over.

They fanned out, taking up most of the street and made their way down the block. Uncle Herb cruised a few steps behind the group with a silent Josh farther behind him.

CJ turned to Mr. Terry and whispered, "Why is Josh not happy?"

Mr. Terry smiled. "He's a rebel, darling. Rebels are never happy."

They decided to get some water and sandwiches at the general store. At the end of Ranch Street, as they waited to cross the street to enter the pavilion, a silver-colored SUV lugging a boat trailer came through the gates heading their way. Peter didn't recognize the vehicle, but the boat sure looked familiar. From under the sun's glare on the windshield, Chipper's menacing eyes stared out at Peter from the passenger seat.

Peter couldn't believe it was Chipper's boat they had taken for a joy ride. He hoped Chipper would never find out. At least right now Chipper would have to be on his best behavior around all the adults. Plus, he might wonder how Peter got the bandages on his face and why he wasn't a part of it somehow.

The car stopped, and the window rolled down, releasing a blast of cold air and revealing the straight and shiny white teeth of Mr. Kassel.

"You boys shooting eighteen?"

Mr. James rolled his eyes. "You know we don't golf, Kenneth."

Peter tried not to make eye contact with Chipper, but he could feel his eyes on him.

Kenneth Kassel Sr. nodded leisurely, and a smirk appeared on his face. He looked briefly in Josh's direction. "That was some monsoon last night, huh?"

A strained look appeared on Mr. James' face, as though it was taking a lot effort to take part in the conversation. "Have a nice day, Kenneth," he said through his teeth.

Kenneth Kassel's smirk turned into a full-blown smile as the car started to roll forward. Peter glanced over at Chipper and realized he'd fallen directly into another Chipper trap. Good ol' Chip was just waiting to make eye contact. He clenched his fist at Peter, as if he was squeezing juice from a lemon. Peter guessed that at some point his head would be the lemon.

Mr. Kassel didn't speed up or close the window before passing Josh. When they were face to face, Mr. Kassel stuck his head further out the window and said, "Monday," in a tone a lot less friendly than the one he'd had with Mr. James.

"Nice boat," Josh replied.

Peter watched with relief as the SUV sped into the distance. Mr. James also watched, shaking his head.

Mr. Terry came out of the pavilion with a bag in each hand, and the group headed back down Ranch Street to a cart path that cut between two homes and led to the golf course. Once there, it was a short walk across two fairways to get to the edge of the Pine Barrens.

They reached the first fairway and saw four golfers teeing off from about two hundred yards away.

"Try to track the ball after they swing," Mr. James cautioned. "If you hear them shout 'fore' or I shout duck, crouch down and cover your head. Herb, CJ, maybe you should move back a little."

Uncle Herb took note and guided his chair in reverse back onto the cart path. CJ followed him.

The first two golfers hit their balls straight but not far, landing in the center of the fairway between the two groups. The third golfer's drive traveled much farther than the first two but at a distance safe enough away from the group that they could admire the trajectory of the ball. It bounced a couple times on the fairway, then stopped on the fringe opposite where they stood. Peter watched the golfers high-five and back-slap each other. The fourth golfer studied the flag in the distance, carefully placed his ball on the tee, then practiced his stroke several times before slicing a ball that landed in one of the trees separating the holes.

Josh muttered. "And I thought I wasted my time."

After they waited for the golfers to make their second shot, moving them closer to the flag and green, the group started to cut across to the fairway to the woods in the distance. Another golf foursome pulled up in two carts to the driving tee. Peter watched as they sauntered up the small hill with their drivers in their hands.

"They're not going to hit yet, right?" Peter asked.

"They better not," Mr. James said.

Peter looked back at Uncle Herb who was having some trouble

getting through the thick high grass of the fringe. Peter retreated to help him, but by the time he reached Uncle Herb, he'd made his way onto the fairway and started to move freely again.

Josh stopped in the center of the fairway.

Peter glanced over at the golfers waiting to tee off and could tell they were all watching, leaning on their drivers or their hands on their hips. His hair stood up on his neck. He hated having eyes on him. He knew Uncle Herb was trying to move as fast as he could, but they were moving diagonally over a slight incline. The wheelchair struggled.

"Go-head, Pita," Uncle Herb said.

Peter paced alongside his Uncle, and he could sense their effort was unacceptable to the waiting golfers. CJ had walked across with Mr. James and Mr. Terry, and they were now watching safely from behind one of trees. Josh remained standing in the center of the fairway.

"Any time now, this isn't a boardwalk," one of the golfers shouted from the tee. Even two hundred yards away, the sarcastic tone was evident.

"C'mon!" another yelled.

Peter could feel himself getting hot. He pretended not to hear and fought the urge to run behind the wheelchair and help push.

Josh barely noticed when they reached him. Peter hoped Josh never looked at him the way he was staring at the golfers; he looked like he was ready to pounce. "I don't trust these golfins," he said under his breath.

Peter kept pace with his uncle. From the corner of his eye, he saw one of the golfers lean over and place a ball on a tee, getting ready to hit.

"Let's go, Josh," Mr. James said.

It was impossible to tell whether the golfer was serious about hitting the ball with Josh standing in the middle of the fairway or if he was just trying to intimidate him, but Josh didn't budge. Actually, he spread his arms and opened his palms to the sky.

This infuriated the golfers. One of the foursome, a tall, solid guy dressed in a striped, collared shirt with a navy-blue visor on his head, raised his club over his head and shook it at Josh.

"These guys aren't kidding around, Josh. C'mon," Mr. Terry said.

Peter and Uncle Herb reached the safety of the tree and Peter gave the golfers a good look. They looked to be about his father's age, all in decent shape and what seemed like matching tempers. They cawed like crows at Josh. The guy with the striped, collared shirt took a few steps in Josh's direction.

"We're all here, Josh. You can come now," Mr. Terry said.

Peter glanced up at Mr. Terry. It was one of the few times he'd seen him without a smile. Peter sensed that he was not the only one with butterflies in his stomach.

Josh looked over and saw everyone waiting for him. He dropped his arms and started to walk over at a leisurely pace, his stare never leaving the golfers.

Peter felt a sense of relief. He watched Josh saunter over. Then there was a single clap, a high-pitched whizz, and a second later a golf ball bounced in the center of the fairway, only twenty-yards short of where Josh had stood moments earlier.

The striped-shirt golfer was standing on the tee box, his body twisted and the head of his golf club at his back—the picture-perfect follow through.

Josh turned and screamed, then sprinted in the direction of the golfers. The golfers reacted and stormed down the small hill of the tee box, ready to meet Josh head-on. To Peter, it was like a civil war battle, but the only one carrying a weapon was the striped-shirt golfer who ran with his golf club at his side.

"Oh, no," Mr. Terry said under his breath as he watched Mr. James take off at an angle that would get him faster to the point of impact. Then Mr. Terry followed, his loose, orange linen shirt puffed out behind him like a colorful boat sail as he rumbled down the fairway at a less fierce speed than everyone else. It all happened so suddenly that Peter's feet felt cemented to the ground.

"Ay-ear," Uncle Herb ordered.

Peter, sick to his stomach with fear, had no problem sticking to the command. He couldn't move if he tried.

Mr. James reached Josh before the golfers did. He blindsided Josh, who was never expecting an attack from anywhere but in front of him, and the two tumbled to the grass.

Peter watched it all from a distance. As Mr. James and Josh writhed on the ground, a panting Mr. Terry reached them and stuck his hands out, crossing-guard-like, to halt the approaching golfers. The golfers had slowed on their own anyway—nothing dulled the impulse for violence more than a mad 100-yard dash, only to then see the enemy taken out by one of his own. Their confusion reached a new level when the long-haired hooligan who had baited them fell into such a hysterical fit of laughter as he rolled around the ground. He acted as if the golfers weren't even there.

Mr. Terry, seeing he had stopped the herd, doubled over to catch his breath.

Josh was still laughing as he stood and helped Mr. James to his feet.

"What are you, a closet linebacker?" Josh asked.

Mr. James lifted his shoulder and winced in pain. "You'll be getting my chiropractor's bill."

"Excuse us," Mr. Terry said, and waved the golfers off as they walked away.

There was some grumbling and some head shaking, but the golfers seemed satisfied that at least they weren't the ones limping away.

Peter was eager to move on to the Pine Barrens and put the experience behind him. It was just another moment where he could have stood brave, but he crumbled like a cookie. Even CJ had uncurled her lasso from Uncle Herb's wheelchair at one point and was prepared to defend not only herself, but her friends and family.

No wonder Chipper torments me all the time, Peter thought. *There's no risk involved. It's like fighting a guppy.* Nemo could not have been a more appropriate nickname.

As they crossed the second fairway, the trees of the Pine Barrens stood in the distance. They walked around the wide perimeter of the pond on hole number eleven, Josh's swimming hole.

The golfers continued their game. On the way up to the green to putt, one of the golf carts stopped, and the golfer with the striped collared shirt yelled, "Freaks!"

They all heard it. No one turned around. No one acknowledged it even quietly to the person next to them. But the name struck Peter as if it was shot out of a bow.

The Pine Barrens

The group reached the back fence separating Willow Creek Landing from the Pine Barrens. Josh led them to a hastily cut opening.

Mr. James raised his eyebrows. "Very convenient that you knew this was here, Josh."

Since he'd moved into the Creek, Peter had yearned to explore the Pine Barrens. There was something mystical about the twisted pine trees that rose from the hilly, dry earth. At sunset, the shadows of the pines took the shape of warriors dancing around a fire.

Some of the trees were Peter's height, others hunched over close to the ground as if stricken with osteoporosis. Even the ones that stood straight and climbed into the sky had thin branches with little foliage, offering the travelers little protection from the sweltering sun.

Mr. Terry pulled a handkerchief from his pocket and wiped his forehead. "Not exactly the majestic northwest," he said.

"About a half mile up, there's a clearing, then the pines turn larger. There will be more shade there," Josh said.

"I guess you've been here before," Mr. James said.

Josh didn't answer. After his laughing fit on the golf course, he'd resumed his brooding post-non-flood behavior.

"A half mile?" Mr. Terry sighed. He turned to Herb and stuck out his thumb. "Do you pick up hitchhikers?"

The group trekked along the marked path, kicking up clouds of dust as they went. The dry dirt made for easy cruising for Herb's wheelchair. Herb was relieved, considering he hadn't known what to expect when they'd started. This was the closest he'd been to four wheeling since he was a child and his father would push him along on all these outdoor, nonhandicapped accessible adventures, wanting his son to experience as much as he could, disability be damned.

Herb suddenly felt the familiar deep pang in his chest whenever he thought about his father. He was someone who'd never been considered the life of the party—a statue at family gatherings and neighborhood parties—but a quiet, strong, and devoted family man, an understated person whose strengths were not of the cocktail party variety, which Herb's mother often chided him for. His father was serious, solid, and reliable—characteristics that don't get you love from strangers at social events but were invaluable as a father of a disabled son.

What Herb remembered was the security he felt whenever he was around his father. Herb's father never worried about his safety, the decisions that had to be made, the follow-through; if his father said he was going to do something or go somewhere, there were no doubts. Herb knew that he was always at the forefront of his father's mind. Not occasionally, not mostly, but always. The man suffered from constant back-and-neck problems from years of lifting his son; he endured three surgeries and never once complained or acted like he'd gotten a raw deal in life. His love was unconditional.

It troubled Herb that his niece and nephew didn't have that same shield—at least not right now. Herb hoped everything would have been settled between Abby and Nick before he left. It seemed a safe bet at first; his stay was close to two weeks. But on Monday morning, three days from now, Abby would drive him back to work and his old life, and Nick was still not home or calling on his family. It would have killed his dad to be away from his children for so long. Abby shattered the theory that girls marry a guy like their father.

A bead of sweat slipped under his glasses and stung his eye. He blinked the irritation away. CJ had knotted one end of her lasso around the wheelchair's handle and made the rope move snakelike as she walked alongside Herb. He wondered if she was too young to notice the turmoil around her, or if God gave her an extra heaping of inner strength. Since crawling, she seemed independent. He remembered Abby telling him how different her children were, even as babies. Peter would wake up crying and scared in the playpen, needing his mother's companionship. CJ would wake humming or singing, content in her place, or grunting as she tried to escape the mesh playpen on her own.

Just beyond the first stand of pines, a group of deer appeared, walking slowly through a patch of brush. CJ eased her way off the path and stood on a fallen tree to get a better look. Mr. James and Mr. Terry rested against a large rock, and Peter stayed nearby, eavesdropping. Their hushed conversation seemed a lot more interesting than a pack of deer.

Mr. Terry glanced over at Josh—who had sat next to CJ on the log—to make sure he was out of earshot. He nodded to Mr. James to continue.

"They gave him until Monday to move out. I don't know what's annoying them more: Josh himself or the ark in the driveway. They think it's a monstrosity to look at and—"

Peter realized interrupting a conversation while eavesdropping was a surefire way to blow your cover but he couldn't help himself, the words shot out of his mouth like a shaken bottle of soda. "They can't do that. It's his house!" he whispered angrily.

"It's his parents' house, Peter," Mr. James corrected. He didn't seem surprised by Peter's interruption. "And apparently they gave the community board, or whatever the name is of those pompous asses that run our lovely and pretentious neighborhood, permission to enforce this legal writ of possession, which basically says Josh has to be out in forty-eight hours or the sheriff comes and takes him out."

Mr. Terry leaned over. "The board considers the home unsellable in its present state. They threatened to take Josh's parents to court, and since you figure the parents are already spending so much time in court against each other—"

"Let's limit the gossip around people under age thirteen," Mr. James said.

Mr. Terry smiled at Peter then covered his mouth.

After a brief moment of silence, Peter said, "I thought Josh was mad about the ark."

As if on cue, Josh rose from the log and swiped the dirt off the back of his jeans. He started to make his way back to the path with CJ, so Mr. James spoke softly. "I think Josh is upset and unsure about a lot of things. He might seem old to you, Peter, but compared to old farts like us—"

CJ sidestepped Josh and jumped through the knee-high brush to a spot Uncle Herb had carved out for himself to watch the deer by using his wheelchair like a lawnmower. The last of the deer disappeared into the trees.

"That was really cool, right, Uncle Herb? Josh said the deer are thirsty and heading to the river, because all the other water in here has dried up."

Uncle Herb nodded, wondering if that indeed was the case. It sounded good.

"He also said all those big trees over there burned down in the Sunrise Fires over ten years ago, but look at them now."

Uncle Herb looked up at the pines. Nature was amazing. He'd read somewhere, or saw on the news, that fire was crucial to ecosystems like the Pine Barrens. Not only could some of the plants survive fire, but they actually needed it to aid in their growth. The fire's ashes provided nutrients for the soil to promote quick recovery growth. It was amazing, really. Sometimes you have to burn it all to the ground to start again.

Almost as equally interesting to Uncle Herb was the wiry, long-haired twenty-something who now joined Peter and the rest of the group on the path. There was more to Josh than met the eye. He was not like the young people who worked at his group home, always talking on their phone, texting, taking selfies. What could they possibly have to say every minute of the day? Herb realized he was getting old, and the times were passing him by, but it all seemed like a lot of navel-gazing to him. *Maybe it's good to be young and think the world is not bigger than you,* he thought. *You sleep better.*

On the trip back home, Peter dragged behind the group. He wondered what Josh's plan was for the next forty-eight hours. Again, the thought hit him that on Monday he would lose both Uncle Herb and Josh. He kicked a stone, and it disappeared off the path. He pondered asking his mother if Uncle Herb could move in forever, if that was okay with Uncle Herb.

Next thing he realized, Mr. James was walking next to him.

"You feeling okay, Peter?"

"Yeah. I'm okay," he said, but the words came out slow and slightly slurred. The unbalanced and melting words would have worried him more but he sometimes experienced speech problems after a seizure. Usually they wouldn't linger this long, but Peter hadn't spoken much on the trip. He was in listening mode.

Mr. James nodded as though he was waiting for more, but Peter had nothing else to say aloud.

There were two great fears Peter had with his epilepsy. One was called status epilepticus, where your brain remains frozen in the state of a persistent seizure like a car that won't turn over. The other dealt with this brain surgery for epileptics where doctors purposely kept the patients awake to make sure they didn't cut into the brain fibers connected with speech. He hoped he would never require this. Peter could only imagine the conversation:

"So, how about those Yankees, Peter?"

"I like the Mets. How's it looking in there, doc?"

"Um, smaller than I anticipated. You seem a lot smarter than you actually are."

Peter had read about the procedure at a time when he was interested in researching his condition. That was an itch he sufficiently scratched that day. He decided he was better off left in the dark.

Thankfully, a question from Mr. James saved Peter from his thoughts.

"Have you ever heard of Dostoevsky, Peter? Or Charles Dickens?"

"Do they live in the Creek?"

"No. How about Julius Caesar and Alexander the Great?"

"I think so."

"Vincent van Gogh? Beethoven?"

"He plays piano, right?"

"What do your teachers do all day?"

"What do you mean?"

Mr. James shook his head. "What I'm getting at is that all these people were exceptional human beings in one way or another. They mattered, made a difference in this world. Their contributions to society are immeasurable, Peter. Do you know what they all had in common?"

Peter wanted to answer one of the questions, but he had no idea where Mr. James was going with this line of questioning, so he decided to wait him out.

"They all had seizures, every single one of them. And that is only the short list."

"Wow," Peter said. He thought he might have been even more impressed if he knew some of the people Mr. James had mentioned.

"Back in the olden days, people who had seizures were considered prophets. Maybe you're a prophet, Peter."

"I don't think so."

"Well, just in case, I'm planning on sticking close to you."

Even though Mr. James confused him most of the time, he still had a way of making Peter feel good.

"Really, what my long-winded point is—I'm sorry, I'm not too experienced with this—but you should not feel ashamed or unhappy with yourself because you're different. I've been there, and it's no fun."

"You have seizures?"

"Not exactly."

Peter saw that Mr. James was struggling to find his words. Mr. James never seemed to struggle with anything. His hair never even fell out of place. He waved his hand back-and-forth as though he wanted to erase the air. He spoke fast. "Listen, Mr. Terry said he saw some kids giving you trouble in the library the other day. What I'm trying to tell you is that since you're different, you stand out, and the bullies of the world notice you faster. But there is nothing wrong with you. You *are* different, you're special. There's the difference, if that makes any sense. I know your parents probably tell you that you're special all the time, but it can't hurt to hear it again."

Mr. James took a deep breath as if he had to pull in oxygen to replenish all the air his words pushed out. He rubbed his hand over his head.

"Anyway, bullying stunts your physical and mental growth. Those kids from the library will all grow up short and have menial jobs waiting for them in the future."

The idea of being taller than Chipper one day appealed to Peter. He pictured patting a nervous Chipper on the head.

"I was bullied. Mr. Terry was too. I'm sure even Josh and Uncle Herb have stories where they were picked on. The only one who probably doesn't here is CJ, and that's because she carries that lasso around all day," Mr. James said, smiling. "But the thing I've learned is it's not about getting knocked down. It's all about standing back up."

Peter nodded. He hoped Mr. James was finished, for his sake. He looked like he was in pain.

It was midafternoon when they returned to the Creek. The sun was at their backs, and a small wind made the return trip bearable. They walked across the golf course in the same single file formation they'd used to cross through the fence. Mr. Terry was in the front, and he started to kick his legs high in the air as if he were leading a marching band.

"It's like we're a parade!" CJ shouted.

"A parade of what?" Mr. James added, smiling.

And they all followed Mr. Terry's lead, marching happily—even Josh a little bit—until no one thought of anything else but trying to keep in step with Mr. Terry. All but Uncle Herb, who had been staring at a golfer across the pond on hole eleven. He easily recognized the confident walk and shaven head, and his eyes followed the golfer's every move. He only hoped that Peter and CJ would not take notice of their father.

Hollywood

Peter was surprised to see his mother's SUV parked in the driveway so early in the day, but then he remembered the phone calls Mr. James had made after his seizure. She was going to be angry that he wasn't home. At least they wouldn't have to order pizza for dinner again.

Mr. James also noticed the car. He asked Peter if he wanted help in explaining his whereabouts. Peter thought that might make matters worse, so he shook his head no.

Josh curled off at his house and went inside with a small goodbye. Mr. James and Mr. Terry continued to their home.

When Peter entered his house, he was surprised his mother didn't look worried or angry at all. She was lounging on the corner of the couch, still dressed in her work clothes and watching TV as they entered. A glass of red wine rested on her thigh.

"Where have you guys been?" she asked, her eyes remaining glued to a news program.

"We went for a walk," Peter said, dropping himself down on the opposite side of the couch.

CJ parked herself in front of the TV, and Uncle Herb lingered, waiting for some sort of fallout.

The Hollywood sign appeared on the screen, surrounded by smoke. In a dire voice, the newscaster said the California wildfires had spread to the Hollywood Hills, devastating several multimillion dollar homes.

"Unbelievable," Abby muttered.

Uncle Herb watched, but his thoughts were elsewhere. He couldn't get Nick out of his mind, and he felt annoyed that his sister seemed more in tune with the problems on the other side of the country than the ones under her own roof. *Stay out of it,* he told himself. *Hold your tongue.* He was leaving after the weekend. *Make sure you get an invitation back.*

The news broke for commercial Abby nudged Peter with her foot and got a good look him.

"Did you fall, Peter?"

The Band-Aid on the forehead. "Yeah, I'm okay."

"Good. And thanks for picking CJ up at camp today again, mister. I hope it's not ruining your last few days of summer."

Peter had temporarily forgotten this little white lie they were maintaining, but he noticed CJ's back stiffen at the mention of camp. He nodded, putting nothing verbal on record. He couldn't believe she hadn't mentioned his seizure yet.

"Where is your phone?"

"I forgot it in the office. I had a course for my license this morning, and then I had a couple look next door."

Her voice trailed off, and Peter knew why. She was trying to sell Josh's house and didn't want to upset him. She'd never received Mr. James's calls.

"I'm charging it now. Why? Did you call?"

"Yeah," Peter said.

Abby waited for more but nothing came. "Is camp any better, CJ?"

CJ nodded but didn't turn around to face her mother. Peter could see that she wasn't even looking at the television but at the wall.

Abby frowned. "You guys are a talkative bunch."

Uncle Herb asked her why she was home so early, and Abby groaned in frustration.

"I was supposed to show that house to a couple today," she said, pointing to Josh's house. "He promised to clean it up, but when I got there, it was an absolute pig sty. Empty beer bottles all over, dishes in the sink piled to the ceiling. He's lucky he was nowhere to be found. I was ready to kill."

Abby made careful note not to mention Josh by name. She had a feeling the kids would view *her* as the bad guy in this whole thing.

"I can't talk about it. It makes my blood boil," she added. "Anyway, I rescheduled the appointment for next week."

She purposely left off, *after Josh is gone*.

Peter looked over at her. He knew exactly who she was talking about.

Abby finished her glass of wine and placed the glass on the floor. Then she moved over to the cushion next to Peter. "I feel like I haven't seen you guys all summer. This is Uncle Herb's last weekend. Maybe we should do something fun tomorrow. How's that sound?"

"Good," Peter said. He was still in cover-up mode over the camp story. The less you say, the better off you are. Call it mother's intuition, but she turned to CJ.

"CJ, what did you do in camp today? I'm surprised you haven't brought home any crafts or artwork yet. Do we get a big boxful at the end?"

Peter wondered if his mother sensed something was amiss. Mothers are good like that, even mothers who work all the time.

"CJ?" Abby said.

CJ turned and blurted, "Peter had a seizure today!"

All Abby could muster was "What?"

"A bad one!" she added.

Abby looked from CJ to Peter to Uncle Herb. "That's why you called?"

Peter thought she might get mad but a wounded expression crossed her face. "I'm so sorry, Peter. I can't believe I forgot my phone."

Peter felt conflicting emotions, which he had a hard time separating. They had successfully avoided talking about Project No-Camp, and now here was his mother apologizing to him. He took some satisfaction in her apology for reasons he wasn't quite sure of, but maybe she *should* be sorry.

"It's okay," Peter said, but made it plain to see that it really wasn't okay. "I want to go outside for a minute."

He went to the back patio. From the look on her face, he knew he'd upset her more. And he was surprised by how little that bothered him. He wanted his old mother back and thought this might be the trick to spur her return.

For the first time since he could remember, there was a breeze strong enough to tousle his hair.

Day 69

Peter spent the morning on the couch struggling through *The Three Musketeers*. After a fast start with good sword fighting, he was mired in chapters filled with girls and love.

"How come so many books are about falling in love with girls?" he asked his mother. She was bustling around the house, cleaning and starting to pack Uncle Herb's things.

"Because that's what people want to read about," she said, placing folded clothes in an open suitcase on the floor.

"I don't," Peter mumbled and flipped a few pages ahead to the next chapter.

Abby brushed Peter's feet off the couch and sat next to him. She rubbed his knee and watched him read. Peter enjoyed the attention he was getting from his mother since the seizure.

"I was thinking," Abby said. "Tomorrow is Uncle Herb's last day. Maybe we should take him to a church around here. He'd like that."

"Okay."

"Good. I'll go tell him. I don't think he's too happy with me now."

Peter lowered the book from his face and watched his mother go down the hall to Uncle Herb's room. He knew a lot of stuff had happened last night, especially after he and CJ went to bed. That's when his parents always used to talk about important things, like planning the move to Willow Creek Landing in the first place.

CJ came into the room and shoved a paper in front of Peter's face.

"Look what I drew."

A brown, crooked boat was in the center of the page with a large, bright-yellow sun bursting from the corner. A stick figure was standing on the deck, and the boat looked ready to crumble from the weight. It was one of the most accurate depictions CJ had ever created. In the other corner of the page, CJ spelled out Josh with a big, backward "J".

"That's really good, CJ."

She smiled proudly. Abby came back into the room and looked at the drawing over CJ's shoulder. She patted CJ on the head but didn't say anything about the picture. She asked if they were hungry.

"There's nothing to eat in the house," Peter said, which was true.

Abby went into the kitchen and returned with her purse. "I don't have time to go food shopping today. If I give you money, Peter, can you run up to the general store and get us sandwiches?"

Peter said he would and asked CJ if she wanted to come. She gave an enthusiastic yes. Peter rarely invited her; she always had to ask or just tag along.

The breeze from yesterday had picked up a notch, keeping the heat manageable. At the pavilion, golf carts swarmed like bees. The golfins were out in force. Many mulled around outside, socializing and waiting for their tee times.

Peter and CJ hopped the curb and weaved in and out of the crowd. CJ, shadowing Peter's moves, missed one quick cut and bounced off the hip of a burly golfin, knocking her tiara to the cement.

"Stay close," Peter warned.

The crowd opened up right before the pavilion doors, and Peter found himself staring at Chipper and his goons sitting against the wall. Chipper sat in the middle, holding a soda and talking to one of the goons. There was no way Peter would make it through the doors undetected. He considered turning away, but the stink CJ would cause would surely gain Chipper's attention anyway. Her resistance to Peter's cowardice was almost instinctual—she never let him just run away. If he was alone, he easily could have reversed course back into the crowd, unnoticed. He drifted slowly in a direction that would lead to the door farthest from Chipper. He didn't note if CJ had spotted Chipper, but he felt her presence close behind him.

It didn't take long for Chipper to see Peter. He had a sharklike sense in picking up signals from prey in distress. He slapped one of the goons in the shoulder and nodded in Peter's direction. A Nemo sighting always energized Chipper. He pushed himself to a standing position, and Goon A and Goon B, as usual, followed suit.

"Howdy, fishy," Chipper said. He took a step toward the door, ready to block Peter's escape path.

Peter stopped. He wished he hadn't invited CJ. Without her, he could have made a mad dash for the door or back into the crowd. Or he could have sat there and taken the abuse and kept the humiliation bottled within himself. No one else would have to suffer through it. Somewhere in his brain, a voice was shouting at him to make a run for it; some survival mechanism trying to justify that they wouldn't do anything to CJ anyway. But he couldn't move. In his fantasies that took place in the sheltered environment of his room, this was the moment he stands up for himself, puffs out his chest and tells Chipper to go blow it out his ear. Or this mean streak of tough guy violence boils to the surface, and Peter would unleash a wild haymaker that would unearth Chipper from his standing position. Peter knew that would never happen. At home he never had the shiver of fear running up his spine that he felt now. His insides wilted.

"Hey Franco," Chipper said, nudging his friend. "Maybe now is a good time to practice CPR? What is it again? Ten quick punches to the chest and then five spits into the mouth?"

"That sounds about right," the taller goon, Franco, answered with a smile. "I do need the lifesaving merit badge."

They stepped toward Peter; Chipper served as the closest point of an approaching triangle of doom. Peter focused on a displaced white stone atop the blacktop.

"Let's go around back where we can be alone. Wonder Woman will be fine on her own," Chipper said, taking a step closer then reaching for Peter's shirt. "I see you have that Band-Aid on your face. Let me show you how to properly remove it."

Peter was still staring at the white stone when he heard the sound, like a kite cutting through the wind, and then a wet smack of flesh. Chipper dropped to the ground in an instant.

Peter looked up to see CJ's lasso recoiling through the air. It took a second for the action to register in Peter's mind. Chipper was reeling around the ground, holding his hands over his face. Blood poured from the slits between his fingers.

Peter looked from Chipper to CJ, his mouth wide open. The goons stared at CJ with a similar shocked expression—even CJ had a strange look on her face as she watched Chipper roll around on the ground. It was like the lasso had acted on its own.

This lasted for only a split second before a deep voice roared from behind them.

"CJ!"

They turned. Nick, dressed in one of his collared golf shirts, was rushing toward them, a look of anger and urgency on his face.

"Dad?" Peter said, and a whole different set of troubles emerged before Peter.

"Uh, oh," CJ said under her breath.

The Return of Dad

Chipper remained on the ground while a woman held a bloody golf towel to his face. Many adults huddled around, offering their care. The greatest bully Peter had even known was now the victim.

Peter stood on the outskirts of the crowd next to CJ, who wouldn't look up from the ground. Adults pointed and stared at her. Their dad was talking on his phone in the street, punctuating his words with hand gestures. CJ's lasso was in his grip. Peter knew his mother was on the other end of that call.

The bloody towel and the circle of people prevented Chipper from looking over at Peter, which made Peter thankful. He knew he was officially dead now; there was no turning back. It was going to be a short school year.

Nick hung up and charged past Peter and CJ without saying a word. He kneeled in front of Chipper and put his hand on Chipper's knee, talking softly to the boy. Peter looked away; he couldn't bear to watch. It was hard enough to watch strangers treat Chipper like an innocent sparrow with an injured wing, but his own father? The looks from people in the crowd, as though CJ and Peter were the worst kids in the world, were enough to make Peter want to crawl into the nearest golf bag.

Nick stood and started walking toward them. The soft features on his face he used when talking with Chipper dissolved, and his face hardened. He grabbed CJ by the wrist without slowing.

"Let's go," he said.

Nick pulled CJ down Ranch Street, and she had to walk with a gallop to avoid from being dragged. Peter stayed one step behind, and even that took a lot of effort. He didn't dare say a word, though he was curious when his father had returned home.

Nick let go of CJ's wrist only upon kicking open the screen

door to their home. He pulled CJ through, and she stumbled to regain her balance. Unconsciously, she straightened the tiara on her head. Peter entered behind his father.

Abby was sitting on the edge of the couch with Uncle Herb facing her. Both looked concerned.

Herb asked CJ if she was okay.

"Of course she's okay, Herb. She was the whipper, not the whipped. She could've blinded that kid! Then we'd all be out in the street," Nick said, tossing CJ's lasso in the middle of the living room.

Herb didn't respond. Nick's presence instantly charged the air. He knew a family meeting was necessary, and Herb knew Nick wouldn't want him present. He excused himself to his bedroom. No one said anything, but both Peter and CJ watched him go.

Abby asked, "Is the boy okay?"

"It looked worse than it was. She got him in the forehead, which bleeds a whole hell of a lot. He might need some stitches," Nick said. He sat on the opposite side of the couch from Abby and rubbed his face with his hands. "We'll definitely be hearing from Kenneth. Out of all the boys to hit—"

"That boy is not exactly a saint, Nick."

"Who is?" Nick answered. "Knowing Kenneth, he'll still probably sue us. That boy is his pride and joy, his chip off the old block. That's why they call him Chipper, right? They'll blackball us around here at the very least."

These potential problems didn't bother Abby as much as her daughter's actions. She shook her head and looked over at her little girl. "What were you thinking, Cynthia Joy?"

CJ's head dropped only slightly at the sound of her full name.

"Go to your room for a minute. You too, Peter. We'll deal with this, but I want to talk to your father alone for a bit."

Peter started to make his way down the hall, but CJ veered off to pick her lasso off the living room carpet.

"I don't think so. Drop that right there. That thing is headed for the garbage, pronto," Nick said.

CJ froze, but she didn't let go of the lasso.

"You heard me," Nick said, his voice deepening.

Peter's knees weakened.

CJ didn't budge. She stared at the lasso. It was like the lasso had power over her, spoke to her, and now was saying, *don't you drop me—you'll regret it.*

Nick said, "I'm counting to three, CJ. If you don't hand me the lasso, there will be consequences. Serious consequences. Trust me on that."

He said "one" through gritted teeth, his face flushed with anger. He didn't like his authority challenged anywhere: at home, at work, on the golf course. But most of all, his ire was drawn highest when tested by his petulant daughter. His friends had the type of girls that Nick thought he would always have: fragile, nurturing things who liked dolls and Disney crap, and thought their daddies were the greatest guys in the entire world. He had CJ. She could have been the daughter of a pair of rams.

"Listen to your father, CJ," Abby said.

"Two!"

CJ glanced at Peter, and their eyes locked for a second, right before she darted out of the living room with the lasso still in hand and down the hall toward her room, but she turned sharply into Uncle Herb's room.

Uncle Herb was sitting in the middle of the room, listening to the situation escalate. He'd wanted CJ to drop the lasso but had a feeling she wouldn't. CJ slammed the door shut behind her and locked it from the inside. She looked at Uncle Herb and hesitated, as though waiting for him to take the side of the other adults and demand her to unlock the door. When Uncle Herb remained quiet, she walked tentatively to the wall farthest from the door, not taking her gaze off him until she passed. He followed her with his eyes.

Uncle Herb stared at the locked door. All of a sudden, he was an accomplice. The sound of determined footsteps came and stopped in front of the door. The doorknob rattled.

"CJ, open this door *right* now," Nick's voice penetrated clearly through the door.

More footsteps. More knob rattling, then a heavy banging on the door. "CJ, right now, open this."

Then Abby asked, "Herb, please tell CJ to unlock the door."

Herb couldn't see CJ, but he sensed her presence.

"This behavior is coming to an end right now," Nick said, the anger still in his voice but not as loud this time. He must have said that facing Abby, not the door.

"Herb, if you can, unlock the door for us, please," Abby pleaded.

Herb paused before steering to the door. He maneuvered his chair several times, spurts forward and reverse, until the side of the wheelchair butted up against the door.

"Ah can't," Herb said to the door, though he didn't even try the knob. He was not surprised to hear Nick's exasperated groan.

"Find the key," Nick ordered. Footsteps fell away. More banging on the door. "CJ, OPEN THE DOOR!"

Herb strained his neck to see his niece, but she must have been huddled in the far corner. Between the bangs, grunts, and rattles, he was deliberating if what he was about to do was right.

"Where is that damn key, Abby?!" Nick shouted.

The damage was already done, Herb decided. He would be just another obstacle after the door. Nick could use some time to simmer down.

"Dad, can't you calm down? CJ was just sticking up for me," Peter said. His voice was small and timid, but Uncle Herb felt pride for his nephew anyway. That must have been very hard for Peter to say to his father.

Nick made an ugly sound, both dismissive and disgusted.

Footsteps approached accompanied by the clanging of keys. Then Abby: "Peter's right, Nick. Calm down a little."

Herb heard the click of the unlocking door and then a weighted push against his wheelchair.

"Herb, can you get out of the way, please?" said Nick, his voice fraying with each syllable.

"Can-t."

Abby asked, "Are you stuck, Herb? Is the battery dead?"

There was a long pause before Herb answered.

"No."

"Then get out of the way!" Nick roared, jarring the door so hard it crashed into Herb's elbow and rocked the wheelchair.

Herb took a deep breath and braced himself the best he could.

"No."

The wheelchair falling sounded like a tray of plates crashing to the ground. Herb landed on the side of his head, and the wheelchair rolled onto him, sandwiching him to the floor.

Next thing Herb knew, Abby was kneeling at his side and Peter was lifting the wheelchair off his body. Nick stepped over him and went to the window. The screen was lifted open.

CJ was gone.

Peter stared at the opening. There were benefits to living in a ranch after all.

Gray Sheep

Josh found CJ crouched behind the recycle container in the far corner of his garage. He didn't ask questions. It was his idea to have her finish the painting. She jumped at his offer. It detached quickly from the ark with the help of the screw gun. Josh propped it against the back wall of the basement, and CJ got lost in the work, hidden from those looking for her. She had to stand on her tippy-toes to paint black streaks near the top of the door, where the sky was in her painting. Josh was in and out of the house—"spring cleaning," he told her.

CJ was rinsing her paintbrush in a cup of muddied water when she heard her father's voice from outside the garage. She stopped what she was doing.

"Have you seen CJ?"

Though it was impossible to see her unless you were standing at the foot of the garage, CJ slowly backpedaled and crouched at the side of her painting.

It seemed to take a long time for Josh to respond. "Who are you?" he eventually said, in a tone that lacked warmth.

"Don't get smart," Nick said.

Josh then said, "I found you can learn a lot about your neighbors in the summer. You see everyone outside, or when they're inside you hear everything through the open windows—"

Nick cut him off. "Did you see which way she went or not?"

"Haven't seen a thing, sir," Josh said.

CJ heard her father mutter something then listened as his footsteps walked further away. After determining enough time had passed quietly, she returned to rinsing her paintbrush.

Josh's whistle sounded like a bird call. It started at a low pitch, then went high. CJ had heard it before; Josh used it to get the attention of the cats or Mr. Terry's dogs, but she paid it no mind this time. She was almost done with her painting. She only turned when she saw shadows approaching on the driveway.

Peter appeared in front of the garage. He stepped in quickly. He didn't want his parents to see him after they returned from their search up the block. In hindsight, Peter believed CJ jumping out the window was a brilliant maneuver. She was in big trouble anyway; maybe this would give everyone time to calm down. Peter wanted to sneak CJ back in the house before her parents returned and realized she'd been in Josh's garage the entire time. Josh was in enough trouble already, but he never seemed overly concerned with what other people were thinking.

"CJ, we better go home. Dad's not too mad anymore. Everyone is really worried," Peter said, hoping she wouldn't put up a fight.

"I'm almost done."

"CJ, please. Uncle Herb is really worried," Peter said.

"Not yet."

Peter looked over to Josh for some help, but Josh was busy digging through his pockets to find a lighter for the cigarette dangling from his lips. He lit the cigarette, leaned against the garage's frame, and inhaled as he studied the sky. He acted surprised when he noticed Peter staring at him, and he pointed the cigarette at him. Peter knew where this was leading.

"I promise I'll never start to smoke."

Josh exhaled and smoke streamed out and up into the air like steam from a freight train.

"Good boy."

"There!" CJ said. "I'm done."

CJ stepped away from the painting, and Peter drew near. It was unlike anything she had created before, and she had made a point to show Peter everything she'd drawn since she was two. Usually her work consisted of a rainbow of bright colors splashed across the page in a fireworks display. This painting had only dark colors; it had a caveman, story-like quality. Peter wasn't quite sure what he was looking at.

"It's really good, CJ," Peter said. He'd learned a long time ago never to ask *what is it?*

CJ beamed beneath streaks of black paint on her face. "What do you think, Josh?"

Josh flicked his cigarette into the driveway and walked over. He studied the painting, nodding his head and smiling. "Awesome," he said, and if he didn't mean the compliment, it was impossible to tell.

CJ nodded in agreement. "You know what it is, right?"

"Of course," Josh said.

"Peter?"

"It's—it's sheep, right? Gray sheep," Peter said.

CJ smiled, eager to explain. "When I first started painting, I was going to make the rain storm, like the one Josh thought was coming."

Peter cringed.

"You see, here are all the dark clouds," she said, pointing to what Peter thought were sheep. "But then it didn't rain, so I said to myself, *what should I paint? What's fluffy like clouds?* Sheep! Then we went for that hike in the woods, and Mr. Terry said it was like a parade, and I thought, *I'm going to draw the sheep on a parade,* and I made them like us. There's me, Peter, you Josh, Uncle Herb, Mr. Terry, and Mr. James."

Peter watched CJ's finger as she pointed to each cloud, or sheep, which represented one person on the hike. As he looked closer, he saw the attention to detail. There were wheels on Uncle Herb's sheep, Mr. James' sheep was skinny, and Mr. Terry's was certainly not. Josh's sheep had longer hair than the others, and CJ's sheep wore a tiara on its head and lasso around the neck. Peter's sheep was big and strong and seemed to tower over the rest. Though he disagreed wholeheartedly with the depiction, he appreciated the artist's vision.

They slipped into the house unnoticed, and when their parents returned, CJ got into trouble, but nothing she couldn't handle. Somehow, the lasso didn't even come up, so CJ didn't even have to go through the trouble of hiding it under her bed. The dinner table was very quiet; Uncle Herb barely looked up as Peter fed him. Nick mostly watched everyone as though he'd forgotten what his own home life was like. Curfew was strictly enforced, and Peter found himself lying in bed earlier than he had in weeks. The summer light faded around his room. Far from sleep, he tilted his head when he heard voices from outside. He went to the windowsill and saw people slowly gathering in the street, including Josh, Mr. Terry, and Mr. James. It was a strange sight to see them with a group of golfins, but they were on the outskirts keeping mostly to themselves. Even the old smoking lady hobbled down the street to the group. They were all looking down Ranch Street in the direction of the pavilion—maybe there was a community event that Peter wasn't aware of. He heard his front screen door open and saw his parents join the group, walking past their neighbors silently to some golfin friends of Nick. Peter put his ear to the screen and tried to separate the voices, but all the conversations came to him in one jumbled ball. An elderly, hunchbacked neighbor shuffled to the group leaving his slower-paced wife behind to talk to another elderly woman. The old man talked to some members of the group, then shouted back to his wife, "See, Liza. I told you. It's smoke. That's all smoke. It's coming from the forest."

That's when Peter realized the Pine Barrens were on fire.

Day 70

Uncle Herb sat in front of the television, watching video of the Pine Barrens burning on the local news network. All you could see were smoke and flames reaching for the sky.

"Some crazy old coots on the links this morning were talking about the evacuation plans of the Creek. Gimme a break—it's miles away," Nick said, laughing. He was lying on the couch behind Herb, staring at the laptop on his knees.

Uncle Herb often struggled in conversation with Nick—always had. When Nick said something, Herb was unsure if he was looking for a reply or just speaking aloud. In the early years of his sister's marriage, Herb would always answer Nick out of politeness but found that Nick rarely tried to engage Herb in an extended conversation. So now he didn't answer unless spoken to directly. Herb was no expert on forest fires, but he knew the fury of Mother Nature was not a laughing matter. She was unpredictable and unsympathetic. The weeks of draught provided great fuel, and all it would take is a change in wind direction right now and those old coots might be right. The newscaster reported that firefighters from the bordering county and as far as New York City were on call to relieve the local firefighters who had been trying to suppress the blaze through the night and the entire morning. That was a little disconcerting.

Uncle Herb wondered if there would be any trouble returning to his group home tomorrow. He was ready now, mainly because of the man sitting behind him. Nick changed the dynamics of the house and the overall mood. Abby, Peter, and even CJ (to an extent) walked on eggshells around the house, while Herb rolled over the shells trying to stay out of the way. Maybe things would settle down in a couple of days, once Nick got comfortable again and felt like he'd re-established his role as ruler. Herb found the whole thing sadly telling. No one was particularly eager to spend time in the house. Peter took CJ to a hill on the golf course where many of the residents were gathering to watch the smoke bloom on the horizon. Abby was all too willing to let them go, as she had a very interested buyer, in her words, come out of the blue for Josh's house. She said he was a recently divorced and, surprisingly, still wealthy guy, who wanted to ease the grief of his failed marriage by becoming a scratch golfer. His enthusiasm for the gated golf community had led to a hastily and unusually scheduled Sunday morning appointment. Abby obliged immediately, completely forgetting about her idea of everyone going to church together before Herb returned home.

Herb chose to let it pass.

The sound of a hammer broke the quiet, and Nick looked out the window. "That nut job just doesn't give up."

Herb smiled. *Josh.*

"It sure as hell would never float," Nick added.

Herb had no desire to engage in this conversation, but Nick never needed someone to engage with.

"Abby will have a fit if he's out there when she shows the house. He's drinking a friggin' beer, for chrissakes! It's ten in the morning!"

Herb was glad his back faced Nick. He smiled at the television as though the burning of a natural preserve was the funniest sight he'd ever seen.

"That kid is ridiculous," Nick added.

I think you're wrong, Herb thought.

"He's hanging a painting now. What, is he planning on moving in there once he's thrown out? Jesus."

Wrong again, dear brother-in-law, Herb thought. *That's the door to the ark that your own daughter painted.*

Herb was enjoying the secret volley he was holding with Nick. His words came out faster in the arena of his mind.

"Ah owen house eyed," Herb said, and pointed his chair in the direction of the front door.

"Have a good time," Nick said automatically.

Herb nudged the screen door open and rolled out onto the

walkway. Josh was indeed installing the door onto his ark. Herb couldn't make out the details of CJ's painting, but he was surprised by the lack of color—lots of gray and black. It was different than her past work.

Herb stayed close to the house, as still as the potted plant at his side. He could hear sirens in the distance. He thought he could smell smoke in the air but didn't know if that was his imagination.

He missed Peter and CJ and hoped to see their faces appear soon from down the street, with CJ's little tiara bobbing in the air. He was slightly disappointed that the kids weren't with him on his last day, but he understood. A forest fire was a lot more exciting than him.

Abby pulled up to the curb in Nick's sporty Mazda. She stopped between her house and Josh's. A black Cadillac Escalade that was following her parked inches behind her car.

Uncle Herb watched as Abby, sharply dressed in a silky blouse and skirt, walked over and met the man stepping out of his fancy SUV. He was probably around Herb's age, fit, and wore the style of sunglasses you'd see on a race car driver. From the tip of his visor to his khaki shorts, this guy was ready for a round of golf. All he needed was a golf tee behind the ear. *He'll fit right in*, Herb thought.

They took a wide turn around Josh's driveway, as if they were walking the perimeter of an invisible fence which contained Josh and his ark. Abby had her head tilted down and toward the man, whispering something. The man seemed curious and slightly perturbed, listening while casting quick glances Josh's way. In this moment, Josh looked to Herb like a zoo lion. Josh stopped working and watched the visitors walk near him with a look of indifference and superiority despite the circumstances. A beer bottle dangled from his fingertips. Once Abby and the man entered the door and fell out of sight, Josh finally moved. He finished his beer and went to his cooler to retrieve another.

Herb watched Josh intently, looking for a sign that revealed what Josh was feeling, but there was none. Only a small smile when Josh stepped back to see how the painting looked on the ark.

He's finished, Herb thought. *The ark is complete.*

Abby and the man were only in the house for a short time. Herb thought that was a bad sign but Abby had a smile on her face even after the Escalade drove off. Herb could tell by the way she walked that she was happy inside. It was a sibling thing.

"I think I have a sale," she told Herb in a singsongy voice and with a shimmy of her shoulders.

Herb forced a smile, trying to be supportive. Hopefully she'd have a different approach when she told the kids, one with a little more consideration for their feelings.

"I didn't think I had a chance when we pulled up, but Josh actually did a decent job of cleaning up the inside. And when the guy saw the golf course out back—forget about it! He called it an oasis for a thirsty and tired man."

Herb nodded. What else could he do?

"He wants to get in as soon as possible, but he kept bringing up the ark. I assured him it would be gone by Monday. I don't think he believed me. I don't think it's a deal breaker, but I'm not taking any chances."

Abby pulled her phone from her purse and hit a button. She put her hand lightly on Herb's shoulder as she passed.

"Hello, Kenneth," she said, as she entered the house.

Herb remained outside. He knew it wasn't a big deal, but it annoyed him that Abby had the father of her son's nemesis on speed dial. He told himself he was being a baby.

Herb wished he had a good feeling about leaving, but he didn't. Hopefully things would improve once summer ended and school started. But with Herb leaving and Josh on the way out, his niece and nephew were losing two of the small handful of people who had spent any time with them in the last two weeks.

Life is hard, Herb thought. *Sometimes the only thing you can do is give it up to God*, which Herb planned to do.

He stayed outside, waiting for Peter and CJ to come home. He was so deep in thought, he didn't notice the wind had changed directions and was blowing his way.

A Golfin Rally

When Abby saw Kenneth Kassel Sr. pull up in a golf cart to Josh's driveway later that afternoon accompanied by one of the Creek's security team, it had yet to dawn on her that the phone call she placed to Kenneth had authorized him to act like the adult version of his son, a role he quickly jumped at. Abby had handed Josh over to him gift wrapped.

Of course, like Chipper, Kenneth didn't want to bully on his own. The Keeme boy was unpredictable and did not possess that inherent fear of an authority figure. Bringing one of the mild-mannered security guys, who had one foot in retirement and the other in the grave, wouldn't work either. So Kenneth enlisted Brutus, the quiet caveman. He knew the man with the shaved head, goatee, and tattooed bicep was a source of many conversations around the Creek. Of course, the actual subject was never a part of these or any other conversations.

"Oh, no," Abby said from her view out the kitchen window. Deep down, she knew Kenneth very well might resort to this behavior, but her drive for that personal victory and that partial commission check had won.

There was a big difference, though, between hearing after the fact about unfortunate things happening and seeing them take place in real time; these sins were harder to absolve, especially if you played a part. When they're in the past, you can convince your brain that you might have acted in an honorable way.

Abby went into the living room and sat next to Nick on the couch, fidgeting in her place. He looked up for only a second and then turned his body slightly, shielding the laptop screen from Abby.

"Do you do work all this time you're on that thing?" Abby asked, trying not to sound *too* accusatory or exasperated. He'd been home for a little more than twenty-four hours.

"I'm researching," Nick said, not a complete lie. He was searching for his high school crushes on Facebook.

"Can you go out there? Kenneth brought Brutus with him to confront Josh. It's overkill and unnecessary."

"You called him," Nick reminded her.

"I know, Nick."

"Scare tactics work. Nothing wrong with a threat as long as you can back it up. You should know that better than anyone."

Here we go again, Abby thought. *The subtle, underhanded jabs are starting.*

"I'll go," Abby said, not wanting to pursue the conversation any further.

Nick watched her to the front door. He clicked out of Facebook and moaned, "I'm coming, I'm coming."

Abby stepped around Herb, who was in the same place on the walkway that she'd last seen him. His wheelchair was aimed at Josh's house. She didn't say anything as she passed, preoccupied with the tactic she planned on using when she reached Josh, Kenneth, and the henchman. She didn't want to look like the bad guy to Josh. She knew he had been good to the kids over the last couple of weeks. But she also didn't want to send mixed signals to Kenneth. As Nick had reminded her, she had started the ball rolling with her phone call. She noticed the Willow Creek truck had an empty boat trailer attached.

Kenneth smiled confidently as Abby and Nick approached. Brutus stood statuesque a step behind Kenneth, his eyes covered behind his dark rectangular sunglasses. Kenneth patted the air in front of him as he turned to Abby. "Everything is under control, we were just reminding him that tomorrow—"

"Everything was always under control," Josh interrupted, calmly. "Just not by who you might think."

Abby had to give Josh credit. He didn't get intimidated easily.

Kenneth Kassel Sr. continued, "We were just reminding him that sheriff deputies will be here tomorrow morning, and anything or any person still on the premises will be physically removed."

"I'm well aware," Josh said.

Kenneth was determined to finish his speech. "And we're very willing to help here. We had offered the community's truck and trailer when the eviction notice was posted, and since we didn't receive a response, we thought it would be in everyone's best interest to ask again. It won't be easy to get back once the sheriff steps in."

A passing golf cart holding two seniors slowed to a stop. The passenger leaned out and shouted in a creaky voice, "It's about time you did something about that, Kassel. We're tired of looking at it."

Nick smirked. A quick snort escaped through his nose.

"Is there anything we can do to help, Josh?" Abby asked.

Josh gave her a look that could only be called disdain.

The street suddenly became knotted with residents, many returning from the golf course hills where they'd watched the fire's smoke paint the sky gray. Abby hoped Peter and CJ weren't part of this cluster. She would definitely be grouped in with the dark side in this situation.

The two seniors in the golf cart, sensing the situation, decided to park at the curb: this was a lot more entertaining than having drinks before dinner with their wives.

"They're finally getting that eyesore outta here," the driver said to a middle-aged couple who were rubbernecking as they strolled by and came to a halt when they noticed Brutus, the chairman of the board, and the crazy, long-haired kid who thought he was the twenty-first century Noah in a stare down. Plus, standing on the outskirts was the bald guy who lived in the clubhouse for two weeks while his wife and kids lived down the block. On one driveway stood four of the most talked about figures in Willow Creek Landing.

"The hippie kid was the one who was skinny dipping at hole eleven, scaring all the geese," said the golf cart driver, Karl, who as the first eyewitness on the scene felt like an authority on the situation.

More people stopped. They watched and spoke together in the street and were comfortable enough with their standing in the community to throw out questions and suggestions to the parties involved.

"How they gonna lift that hunk of junk on the trailer, Karl? A pulley system?"

"I knew from the framework it would turn out like that. He never worked from a blueprint. No experience."

"Unprofessional."

"Amateur hour."

"What a waste of time and materials."

"Why don't they let Brutus give it a nudge with his shoulder? It'll collapse into a heap. We can use the scrap wood to build a walking bridge over the stream at hole fourteen."

Some members thought this was a great idea.

It was around this time that Peter and CJ were walking home, talking about the different animal shapes the smoke made in the sky. As they passed the pavilion, people were pouring out the doors heading toward Ranch Street, and they overheard a lady talking on her phone, advising her friend to rush down to "that house with wood art in the driveway."

Peter and CJ broke into a sprint.

The cluster was now two or three deep in front of Josh's house, so Peter grabbed CJ by the wrist as they weaved through the people.

"What's going on?" CJ said.

Peter felt her hot breath on his arm but didn't answer.

When they reached the front, Peter's heart sank as he saw Mr. Kassel and the scary-looking Brutus standing an arm's length away from the stoic face of Josh, ignoring the large collection of residents now gathering at the bottom of his driveway. Peter's heart sank further when he noticed his parents to the side of Mr. Kassel. Their nearness to Chipper's dad made their allegiance known.

CJ whispered into Peter's ear, "What are Mom and Dad doing there?"

Peter couldn't take his eyes off Josh. Josh stood straight and still, his stare slightly above the heads of the crowd.

"Do something, Kenneth!" a faceless voice shouted from the crowd.

"We have enough men here, we can lift that piece of crap on the trailer ourselves!" another shouted.

"He can get it from the dumps when the flood comes!" someone shouted, earning some snickers from the crowd.

Peter had a bad feeling churning in the pit of his stomach. He could practically feel the pulse of the crowd, and the negative tide aimed at Josh and his ark. He turned to see the faces of the golfins: men and women, parents and grandparents, looking on with varying degrees of aggravation. Some of the less interested residents huddled in the back, chatting away yet still a part of the pack. It had turned into a Creek social event.

Peter's eyes fell on Chipper right as Chipper yelled, "Let's burn it!" then hid in the crowd as his goons elbowed and grabbed at him, laughing.

Above the crowd, the sun sank into the sky. Gray clouds collected around its descent.

Kenneth Kassel Sr. wasn't facing the crowd, but he felt his back tighten with each shout of his name and demand for action. For the first time ever, he told himself he was too old for this garbage—the job of chairman wasn't worth the small pittance, power, and prestige. The nonsense wasn't worth the choice dinner reservations and tee times. But who could have predicted he'd have to deal with a mob mentality in this place, filled with the elites and one percenters? The only reason he undertook this stupid battle with this stupid kid in the first place was because he had thought the kid would be a pushover. He had assumed that the intimidation tactics learned from thirty years as a power broker would make this an easy play. Obviously, with this kid staring down the crowd like he was Wyatt Earp or someone, Kenneth realized that the best he could hope for here was a draw, and hopefully not of the Western cowboy kind.

"Why don't you just let us take it?" he said softly to Josh with his head lowered, out of earshot of everyone except Brutus.

Josh's eyes left the crowd and met Kenneth Kassel Sr.'s. His inexpressive face then revealed only the slightest crooked smile.

Kenneth felt rage flare within himself; his moment of compromise disintegrated. *Who is this punk to smirk at me? I've earned this life, this exclusive community.* He turned to the crowd and was surprised by how many residents had gathered since he'd last looked. They were people of new money and old money, people who expected and demanded the best this world has to offer, from the dinner plate placed in front of them to the cars they chose to drive. And as he raised his hands to address them, he couldn't help but be impressed with himself. They were waiting for his word.

The Stand

Peter didn't like the weird look in Kenneth Kassel Sr.'s eyes when he lifted his hands to speak. He looked like some crazy cult leader you'd see in a scary movie.

"Let's put it on the trailer!" he said, in his deepest, most presidential, chairman of the board voice.

Some people cheered, others complained about the unnecessary time taken to make a decision that seemed so obvious. Bureaucracy.

Peter looked down at CJ, unsure of their next step, or if there even was a next step. Every grown-up in attendance was in agreement.

No one noticed Josh walk calmly over to his work table and lift a hammer. "I'm tired of you golfins," he said, matter-of-factly, but his eyes showed defiance.

The crowd had started to move forward in a semicircle mass but stopped at seeing a sign of resistance. Some of the residents were surprised, having believed they were doing Josh a favor, a Good Samaritan deed.

The ones who were expecting Josh's opposition ordered him to drop the hammer and step aside. They called him a loser and worse. They said he should seek help (once he left Willow Creek Landing was implied). Once they saw this was getting nowhere, they insisted Kenneth Kassel Sr. do something. Kenneth, not liking the look of the hammer dangling at Josh's side, nodded to Brutus.

Brutus didn't respond immediately to the request. It was hard to tell what or who he was even looking at behind the dark sunglasses. His facial expression was as unreadable as Josh's.

"Drop the hammer," Brutus said.

Peter was actually thankful for that initial push from the crowd. His entire body, starting with his feet, had started to deep-freeze again. The problem with freezing during such a tense development was that you couldn't fight *or* flee. Freezing isn't listed as the third survival instinct, and it's not hard to figure out why: most species that chose the action were probably extinct by now. But now his feet were moving, though he had no idea if he was fighting or fleeing.

"Where are you going, Peter?" CJ said from behind him.

Peter kept walking. He had no idea what he was doing. Maybe that was the trick all along, to turn off the brain and not worry about the consequences, the possibility of doom, and just let another body part navigate for you, somewhere between your heart and the gut of your stomach.

Peter realized he was the only one walking now, and he didn't stop until he stood next to Josh. He turned to face the crowd.

Brutus, who never seemed like the kind of person to kid, shook his head slowly. Peter bet that behind those dark sunglasses were pieces of charcoal.

"Drop the hammer," Brutus repeated.

The crowd inched forward, not to rush Josh but to get the best view of whatever would happen next.

Peter scanned the crowd. His desire to belong, to be accepted, was never so out of reach. Peter saw the look of sheer hatred in Chipper's eye, as if Peter had the gall to do anything more than be punched. He knew if this turned into a free-for-all, he'd have to keep an eye out for him.

"Peter! CJ! Get over here," Abby said, waving them over to the semineutral place on the side she had drifted to with Nick.

Peter tried to find CJ in the crowd, but she wasn't in the place he had left her.

"I'm here," said a little voice from beside him.

Peter turned enough to see the shiny tiara, and a small hand gripping a lasso in front of her body.

"Peter!" Nick's voice cut through the static noise of the crowd and smacked Peter upside the ear. Nick pointed to the ground in front of him. "Right now, Peter. Right here."

Historically, this approach usually worked very well on Peter. He'd listen obediently and return with his head down like a puppy that piddled on the floor. He looked down at Josh's driveway and noticed all the cracks and crevices. Then he looked at the ark, the ark that he'd helped build. Maybe it wouldn't float, maybe it couldn't float, but that didn't matter anymore. Actually, he came to the realization it had never really mattered.

"Brutus," Kenneth Kassel Sr. said impatiently.

Brutus breathed audibly out his nose and stepped forward.

An electric whir came from behind the people, and the crowd parted reluctantly. Uncle Herb steered his wheelchair to the ark and did a six-point turn to face the crowd.

"This is unbelievable," Nick muttered.

Not sure where she stood on anything anymore, Abby stepped further away from the crowd but kept her children and brother in full view.

Brutus stepped forward and slowly turned his head toward Kenneth Kassel Sr. "Forget it, guy. I don't do kids and wheelchairs."

"What?" shouted Kenneth Kassel Sr.

"You heard me. I'm done," Brutus said. He started to leave. "No hard feelings, Josh. I got two kids to support."

Josh nodded. "See you around, Harold."

The name *Harold* echoed throughout the crowd.

Before leaving, Brutus looked at his phone and then put it back in his pocket. He stuck his finger in Kenneth Kassel Sr.'s chest. "It's 8:28. I'm being paid until nine, got it? No more nickel-and-diming me. Even if it's my last day."

Kenneth Kassel Sr. massaged his chest as Brutus walked away.

The crowd was already deflating as Mr. James walked over and stood next to Josh. Mr. Terry followed, holding his phone over his head.

"I've pressed nine, and I've pressed one. Don't tempt me to hit that other one. It will really screw up your tee times when you're locked up in county on charges of inciting a riot, or a lynch mob, or something else that will surely embarrass and shame you old divas," Mr. Terry shouted.

Mr. James looked at Peter and rolled his eyes. "He can't help himself. He loves an audience."

Abby sprinted to the house, her hands covering her face. Nick watched her go, then sighed. He held up two fingers to Peter and CJ, but his message was anything but peace.

"I want you inside in two minutes, you hear. Two minutes," he said. Then he jogged into the house after Abby.

There were murmurings and stare downs as Kenneth Kassel Sr. led the slow retreat back down Ranch Street. He offered to buy drinks for everyone in the pavilion, and this satisfied many.

Chipper and the goons hung back, hoping to get a piece of Peter, but he was surrounded the entire time by the people who had stood by the ark. For the first time, Peter did not freeze at the mere presence of Chipper or look for an opportunity to flee.

Rather, he walked toward Chipper.

Peter couldn't put a name on exactly what he was feeling, but he felt a tingling in his legs causing him to move. Maybe whatever Josh possessed that gave him the ability to stand up to the most powerful golfins in the Creek was contagious and had spread to Peter. He was uncertain about what was about to happen, but for the first time he didn't fear the outcome.

Peter stopped directly in front of Chipper. As he stood straight, he noticed that Chipper was definitely a little taller and wider than Peter, *but not by too much*. Having shoulders that were not hunched, a head not leaning to the ground and knees that stood firm and unjellied had leveled the open space between them. He wondered if Chipper sensed the same thing, because as he looked at Chipper's eyes and the flesh-colored Band-Aid on his forehead brought about by CJ's lasso, a flicker of uncertainty seemed to pass over his face.

"Howdy, Kenneth Jr.," Peter said, because in all his fantasies of standing up to Chipper, and on all the lists he created of things he would do when he finally faced this fear, it all started with repeating Chipper's infamous greeting.

The goons stared at each other in disbelief and laughed. But there was not the usual confidence in their laughter.

"Oh, man! Looks like Nemo is tired of swimming away, Chip," one of the goons said.

Chipper shook his head in disgust. "Or he thinks he can act tough now because he knows all the people behind him will come to his rescue like they always do," he answered.

Peter wasn't even thinking about the people behind him. His

entire body was tingly now, almost shaking. There was something freeing yet terrifying about living out something that you've pretended to do hundreds of times in the safety of your bedroom. He could only hope that the outcome would not be drastically different. Not once did he imagine that he would swallow all his teeth or get his nose rearranged. Anyway, he couldn't think about that now. The shaking wouldn't let him.

Chipper took a step toward him. "Do you know what I am going to do to you and that crazy little sister of—"

Without thinking, Peter did everything that Josh had taught him that dawn on the boat to perfection. He didn't telegraph the punch; Chipper had no idea it was coming. He led with his knuckles, powered by the rotation of his hips and aimed for Chipper's body. He felt Chipper recoil at impact but still followed through as Josh had instructed. All the air-punches he had thrown as he imagined this moment led to a blow that instantaneously knocked all the air out of his target's lungs.

However, Chipper did not go down. He staggered back and placed his hand at on his chest. The look on his face was a mixture of shock and pain.

"What?" was all Chipper could muster.

And before he could ask another word, Peter hit him again.

This time, Chipper went down to his knees.

Even if Peter decided to run for his life now or experience the humiliating beating that he had successfully avoided all summer, he would declare this moment a victory. He had hit back. And now he said: "Don't you ever bother me or my sister again." He wished it came out stronger and meaner than he'd intended, but threats and warnings just weren't Peter's thing, and he was okay with that.

The goons didn't know what to do with themselves. They looked at Chipper. They looked at Peter. They looked back at Chipper. Then they saw a group of adults approaching. They knew now that they wouldn't have to decide—a decision would be made for them. Chipper saw this too and remained on the ground.

Josh walked over and bent down to him.

"He hit me first," Chipper said.

If Chipper was expecting sympathy or first aid, he was about to be disappointed. Josh whispered to him, "You're lucky he didn't give you the grasshopper kick that I taught him. Then you would really have a problem."

Chipper didn't reply, but he looked at Peter and then his legs. Peter kept a straight face, but inside he was smiling. *What the heck was a grasshopper kick?*

Josh stood and eyeballed the goons. "Don't you think it's time to get a new hobby?"

They too looked quickly at Peter then back at Josh. They nodded.

"Good. Get out of here. You live by the sword, you die by the sword."

Peter wondered if Josh got that expression from *The Three Musketeers*.

They helped Chipper to his feet and quietly walked away.

Smoky Night

An hour after Chipper and the goons shuffled away, Peter, Mr. James, and Mr. Terry sat in lawn chairs leaning against the side of the ark. The sky was starless. Uncle Herb sat nearby, with CJ sitting on the ground in front of him, leaning on his knees. Herb couldn't have been happier. It was a good way to end his vacation.

"I feel like I'm camping," Mr. Terry said.

"God, do I despise camping," Mr. James said.

Josh let out a small laugh from his position on top of the ark's hull. He was sitting in his usual cross-legged position and staring at the dark shadows drifting across the sky.

"Are those clouds or smoke?" he asked.

Everyone looked up, but no one said anything. No one had the answer or wanted to exert the strength to think about it. The evening's events had left them all spent. They hadn't rehashed what happened. For now, the crickets would have to do all the chirping.

Earlier, Nick had called the kids in from the front door, but Peter ran up and asked very respectfully if they could spend another hour outside as long as they stayed in eye's view. Nick said thirty minutes. Peter smiled upon his return, happy with his negotiation tactics; he told everyone he would have settled for fifteen.

He'll be just fine, Herb thought. *He's a smart boy*.

Josh hopped off the ark and kneeled in front of Peter. "Listen, Peter. I want to tell you something that's been on my mind. What those people were saying about me tonight was true. Well most of it, anyway. I *am* a loser—"

"C'mon, Josh," Mr. James interrupted.

"No, no, let me finish. This is important. I am a loser in many ways, Peter. I flunked out of college after five years. I don't have a job. No money, no girlfriend, nothing. I don't even have a place to live after tomorrow."

Mr. Terry polled the circle. "I'm depressed now. You?"

"I mean, c'mon. I've been arrested three different times, hit a damn horse once," Josh said, shaking his head. "I've been out of my mind for so long. Seriously, I believed God spoke to me and told me to build an ark. Who does that?"

"Noah," CJ answered proudly.

Uncle Herb smiled down at CJ.

"But the thing is, and I don't even know how to explain it really, but for the first time in a long time, I feel okay with myself. Okay with where I am. And I don't even know where that is!" Josh laughed. "I started feeling it when I was standing in front of all those people. I don't know why, and then when you stood next to me next like that, young Peter . . ." He paused. "It all fell into place. I figured if I earned your trust, how bad can I be? Does that make any sense?"

"S," Uncle Herb said. "Odds-plan-s-not-e-aim-or-ef-e-un."

Peter started to interpret his uncle's longer sentence, but Josh held up his hand to stop him. Josh stood for a moment and appraised Herb silently. He climbed back up the ark and lit a cigarette. The end glowed against the backdrop of the sky.

"I like that, Herb. I like that a lot," Josh said, sounding like he was talking more to himself than anyone else. He took a long drag from his cigarette and exhaled slowly before repeating what Herb had said to him.

God's plan is not the same for everyone.

"That was some punch, kid," Mr. Terry said. "Wham-o! We were all watching, but it was Josh's idea not to break it up at first, to let it run its course."

Josh nodded but kept his eyes on the sky. "Great form, young Peter. Great form. I knew you had it in you."

Peter felt his ears getting warm.

Mr. James asked, "Now you answer me something, Josh. Were you going to swing that hammer?"

Josh paused before answering. His eyes followed something bright moving across the sky. An airplane? A shooting star?

"Probably," he answered.

Day 71

Beyond Willow Creek Landing, the thick cloud of dark smoke grew in the far distance. Overnight, it was joined by several smaller, yet just as ominous, clouds in the sky. That was the current headline: smaller fires breaking out throughout the Pine Barrens. Embers from the original fire were being carried by the wind some several miles, and with everything dried out from the drought, a spark was all it needed.

But Peter was still on a high from the night before. There were no repercussions from his father last night when he'd finally returned home, no phone call from Chipper's dad about the punch, only his father saying from above his laptop, "Crazy night. Go to bed," which Peter dutifully obeyed. But he didn't fall asleep right away. Actually, he didn't fall asleep for hours. Lying in bed, he replayed the night's events over and over in his head.

For the first time in a long time, Peter felt optimistic.

His father didn't seem too concerned with the fires either, but he was so occupied with his laptop and phone that he probably wouldn't have noticed if the couch he was sitting on was in flames. So Peter was surprised, to put it mildly, when his dad looked up from his laptop and suggested a bike ride and lunch at a restaurant. It sounded like a great idea until Peter remembered it was Uncle Herb's last day.

However, Uncle Herb insisted they go. He would see them when they got back. When Peter found out that his mother would also meet them for lunch after she checked in at the office, he had to jump at the opportunity. It was a long time since just the four of them had been out together. Maybe things really were starting to get better?

Peter felt strong as he pedaled through the streets of the T section. He, his dad, and CJ had been gone all morning, biking most of the time except for a stop at a local park so CJ could play on the swings. Peter's stomach grumbled as he cut the curb short and U-turned back to CJ and his dad.

"I'm hungry," Peter said.

Nick was pedaling slowly and steering his bike with one hand, texting with the other. He didn't answer. This was how he was for most of the day. There, but not. Still, Peter took whatever attention his father gave him.

CJ used this moment to blow by Peter and finally take the lead. The training wheels on her pink bike were uneven and the bike tilted to whichever side her weight was leaning.

"You need to learn to ride a bike without training wheels," Peter said, hoping his father would hear him. She was too big for that bike. Peter decided that if his father didn't get the hint, he would ask Josh to take the wheels off and raise the seat. Peter remembered the time he played catch with Mr. Terry and thought maybe the neighbors could help CJ learn to ride.

On Main Street, a fire truck crept silently past as firefighters stared blankly out the open windows, their faces covered in ash. The normally shiny truck was a muted red. Everyone on the street stopped as the truck passed, heading back to the firehouse. Some people waved, others nodded respectfully. The firefighters didn't wave back.

"Why aren't they at the fire?" CJ asked.

"They're taking shifts now," Nick said.

They pedaled in silence, until they reached the parking lot of the Sleepy Beagle Café. Nick put his phone in his pocket, then said, "Your mom will be a little late. She's stuck at the office. She said to start lunch without her."

They walked into the dark restaurant and stopped at the hostess stand. A pretty girl walked over carrying menus and greeted them with a friendly wave.

"Hey, I guess you won't be eating at the bar today," she said. Peter thought she had confused them with someone else. They never ate at the bar. The hostess stooped over and smiled at CJ. Peter saw a red bra underneath her low-cut shirt. His face turned a similar shade, and he looked away.

"What's your name, beautiful?"

CJ looked at Peter and frowned.

"We'll take a booth today, Holly," Nick said.

She walked them past the bar, but they all slowed at the image of the Pine Barrens burning on the big screen television.

"Don't you live in that golf community off of Slocin?" Holly asked.

"Yeah," Nick said, distracted now by the large visual of the fire's rage.

"Didn't they issue an evacuation alert?"

"For who?" Nick asked.

"Willow Creek."

This shook Peter away from the television. He glanced at CJ, who was looking at him, then at his father for some sort of direction like an order to backtrack immediately. But all Nick did was smile coolly at Holly and ask, "Why? The fires are still miles to the south."

A short, solid man in a sweat-stained T-shirt and black-and-white checkered pants dropped a heavy rack of glasses on the bar. He said, "Where you been? A fire sparked out east this morning. The wind is pushing it west. If it connects to the other fires, forget about it. Way worse than the Sunrise Highway fires. Time to get on a ferry to Connecticut," the man laughed.

"We have to go, Dad," Peter said.

Nick held his hand up. "Relax a minute, Peter."

"Uncle Herb is still at the house," CJ said.

Now Nick pressed the air with his hand impatiently. "Hold on a second. Let me make a phone call."

Peter couldn't believe he had to stay confined to this stupid, small booth as the world seemed to burn around him. Only a few tables were occupied in the restaurant; Peter had never seen the place so empty. Most of the people were gathered around the bar in front of the big television, his Dad included.

CJ leaned in from across the table. "Peter, we have to go back," she whispered.

Peter leaned down on the bench to get a better view of the television in the bar. "They declared a state emergency. The Catskills and Adirondacks are on fire too."

"We have to go back," CJ repeated.

"I heard you the first time."

Peter was stalling as he made a plan. His father had told them that there was indeed an evacuation alert at Willow Creek Landing, along with several communities that border the Pine Barrens, but it was a precaution. The fire was still miles away.

"They always play these things safe," Nick said. "We do need to pack up some things just in case, but by the time we bike all the way home Mom will be here with the car."

He told the kids to sit tight. Nick took his own advice and stood between Holly the hostess and a female server at the bar as they watched the fire unfold on the large screen. They would wait until Abby met them at the restaurant; she was just finishing up at the office (Peter had heard that before), and the family would drive over together.

Peter stirred the lemonade in front of him. If last night didn't get him in trouble, what he was about to do surely would. He started feeling that tingling sensation again.

"I'll be right back, CJ. I have to pee."

Peter slid out of the booth and slowly headed to the back of the restaurant, watching to see if his father would turn around to check on them. He never did.

Peter walked down the corridor, past the kitchen and bathrooms, and pushed open the back door. Squinting from the daylight, he ran around the back alley to the front, keeping low to the ground to stay beneath all the restaurant windows. He jumped on his bike and pedaled out of the parking lot.

He took a deep breath when he hit Main Street. Two fire trucks, this time filled with clean, rested firefighters with a look of urgency on their faces, raged past. If his father followed him, Peter knew he'd take the same back roads they took coming, so Peter decided to follow the course of the fire trucks and take Slocin Road the entire way even though he didn't want to.

As Peter biked past the stores on Main Street, picking up speed, he heard a voice call his name from behind him. CJ had just turned onto Main Street, her body and bike leaning dangerously unbalanced.

Peter had not involved her in his plan for several reasons. He didn't want her to get into trouble or danger, but he also didn't want CJ to slow him down. He couldn't just leave her on Main Street, so he waited, waving her to hurry, all the time expecting his father to turn the corner.

CJ stopped in front of him and avoided making eye contact.

"I had to pee too," she said.

"Get on," Peter said, and nodded down to his bike seat.

"I'll bike."

"Get on if you want to come with me. We have to get off Main Street before Dad sees us."

"My bike?"

"We'll leave it in front of the store and get it later. No one will touch it. Either you come on my bike with me, or you don't come at all."

CJ contemplated her choices. Realizing there was only one that suited her, she stepped off her bike and climbed up to Peter's seat.

Black Feathers

Peter's bike wobbled the first few yards as he got used to CJ's weight on the back. Secret Project No-Camp had provided good practice. He fell into a stride, glancing back only once for his father. Main Street dog-eared, and once the bike completed the bend, Peter knew they were in the clear. Their dad would turn off a lot earlier for the back roads without any sight of them.

"Stop wiggling, you're making the bike turn," Peter yelled back to CJ. If she did that on Slocin Road with cars traveling seventy miles per hour, they'd be pancakes.

"I can't help it. My butt hurts."

Something strange was happening on Slocin Road. Cars weren't speeding at all—in fact they were barely moving in both directions. They sat bumper to bumper as far down the curvy road as Peter could see.

"What's going on?" CJ asked.

The drivers looked either impatient or at a loss. Horns honked, some short and stuttering, other prolonged and angry.

"Look up there!" CJ said.

Huge feathers of black smoke colored the sky, much closer than ever before. Peter noticed the air suddenly had a burnt, crispy smell to it. This was not the smoke from the original fires.

"Is that the Creek, Peter?" CJ questioned softly.

Peter couldn't tell but found himself pedaling faster.

As they got closer, cars were sitting in the shoulder trying to make their own lane. Peter navigated around mirrors and elbows hanging from windows.

Before they reached the corner gates of Willow Creek Landing, Peter could see flames and smoke coming from the woods outside the gates. Peter pedaled furiously. Two police cars were parked in front of the entrance, and the officers were managing traffic from the middle of Slocin Road. As Peter feared, the Creek was the reason for the traffic snarl. One officer held his hand up to oncoming traffic, as he waved on the vehicles from the Creek. Cars poured out, despite the red traffic light above. A group of people was standing out front—some just watching, others using their phones to take video—and another small group paced and shouted at the officers.

Nick and Abby were part of that last group. Abby had left work to get Herb after Nick's phone call. She had run the last quarter mile to the Willow Creek entrance, abandoning her car on the side of the road once Slocin turned into a parking lot. Her eyes never left the smoke in the sky. She still had her heels in her hand.

"Officer, you have to let me in! My brother and maybe my kids are still inside. My brother is in a wheelchair," Abby yelled at the policeman for the third time.

The officer, who was a good deal younger than Abby but trained in this type of scenario, kept his composure and tried to diffuse the combative woman in front of him with his polite form of verbal judo. "Ma'am, like I told you, my orders were to let no one inside. We have sent an officer down to your home to make sure no one is inside." But what he really wanted to say was: *what the hell were they doing alone in there in the first place?*

Abby turned away from the officer and punched the air. Her scathing eyes locked in on Nick.

"I can't believe you lost the kids. Unforgivable," she hissed.

Nick had no response. There was no way to twist this. He looked down Slocin Road, hoping to see a glimpse of them, but all he saw was an ambulance with its lights on and siren blasting moving slowly up the shoulder. The sea of cars parted reluctantly. With the speed he had pedaled, he would have caught up to them if they took the back roads. He could only guess that they decided to take Slocin, outsmarting their own father, but they were still nowhere in sight.

"How could you sound so calm on the phone?" she asked, looking like she was ready to hit him.

Nick tried to defend himself. "No one could have predicted this. It was only an evacuation alert."

Nick knew that was a horrible answer, but it was all he had. The evacuation alert was set in response to the fires in the south and east. Now that a fire from the north had sparked, it made the evacuation immediate. Nick knew this was the worst possible scenario. The first homes a northern fire would reach were those on Ranch Street. He also realized, though he was not dumb enough to share with Abby, that the developers built all the homes so close together to maximize their profit, that once one home went on fire it wouldn't be long until their neighbor faced the same fate with the eaves of their roofs practically touching. They would burn like a matchbook. "I'm sure Herb is fine, and if the kids had just listened to me—"

Abby watched Nick's lips move, but she didn't hear his words. Did it even matter anymore? For a second, she wondered when was the last time something came out of those lips that warranted being heard. When was the last time he said something helpful? Complimentary? Something nice? She turned her back to him and started walking away before he finished speaking. It didn't matter. She was done.

In all their years of marriage, Nick never saw that look in her eyes. It was a look of something breaking, something irreplaceable now in pieces on the floor. The quick stab he felt hardened into something vengeful as he watched her walk away.

"No one forced you into the office today, Abby!" he shouted. He didn't think she would turn around, and she didn't. He would stay until they found the kids, then worry about what happens after that.

The ambulance approached, and the officer ordered everyone to step aside. Only the combative woman stood frozen in her spot, and he had to guide her away by the elbow. She moved zombie-like with an empty look in her eyes.

I'm never getting married, he thought.

If anyone was looking under the ambulance's carriage, they would have noticed the two bike tires keeping pace along the other side of the ambulance all the way through the entranceway.

Inside Willow Creek Landing, Peter and CJ stemmed off from the ambulance and hopped the sidewalk curve. Idling cars lined the street filled with anxious faces and valuable possessions piled in the backseats and strapped to the roofs. All the color of the community was washed out, blanketed by a gray haze. Peter swerved around people who were running through the street, some holding cardboard boxes filled with an assortment of personal objects.

Peter cut past the pavilion and turned left onto Ranch Street, pedaling down the center of the road because the sidewalks were blocked with people and cars being packed with last minute items.

Then Peter saw the flames. Down at the end of Ranch Street, the two houses bordering the woods were on fire. It was hard to see the trees beyond the two homes due to the smoke. There was not a fire truck in sight. The air had a burnt smell, and the temperature rose instantly. A police officer holding an oxygen mask to an older woman's face as he escorted her to his squad car saw Peter and CJ and ordered them to stop.

CJ choked back a cough. "Go, Peter."

Peter had no intention of stopping. They heard the sound of broken glass, then a loud cracking noise as the roof of one of the homes collapsed. Peter hopped the sidewalk of Josh's house, passed the ark, and rode on the grass of his front lawn.

CJ coughed again, sliding off the bike. "It's too smoky."

Ash and insulation dropped like snow. Peter knew he had to act fast. Only one home now separated their house from the fire. Peter dropped his bike and ran to the front door, yelling for his uncle.

The house was quickly filling with smoke through the screen windows. The smoke hovered at Peter's eye level, so he dropped to his knees and started to crawl in the direction of Uncle Herb's room. His eyes burned.

A hand swiped his ankle as he crawled. He turned and caught a glimpse of the gold tiara at his heels. CJ was crawling behind him, the lasso in one hand.

"Go back, CJ."

"No. I'm coming with you. Stop, drop and roll."

He didn't have time to tell her that the lasso wouldn't do much against smoke or that rolling only helps if you are on fire, so he just reminded her to "stay low and stay close." The visibility was getting worse.

Uncle Herb was not in his room, or his parent's room, or CJ's. If he was in the kitchen or living room, he would have noticed or heard CJ and Peter when they barged in the front door. That left only Peter's room, the room furthest from the front door and closest to the fire. Peter called out again, but no answer.

The door to his room was closed. He couldn't think of any reason Uncle Herb would be in his room behind a closed door, but if he didn't check, he couldn't be one-hundred-percent sure that his uncle wasn't in the house. The crawl down the hall seemed like it took an hour. His doorknob was hot. He opened the door, and smoked poured out of the room. He was blinded, and he coughed immediately, but before he covered his eyes he thought he saw a figure in the corner of his room.

"I'll be right back," he yelled to CJ.

"I'm coming with you," he heard her answer, but he couldn't feel her behind her.

He held his breath and beelined to the place he thought he saw the figure. He felt around; it didn't feel like a person or wheelchair. It was his broken air conditioner.

"CJ, he's not here. Let's get out."

Peter heard a small cough.

"I can't see," CJ said.

Peter couldn't see where she was. He told her to head toward the door. He hoped she knew his room as well as he did.

"I can't see, Peter," she said again, choking.

He rubbed his eyes, trying to ease the burning sensation. He tried to breath, but his lungs filled with dirty air. He thought he saw a shadow lying still in the corner of the room, and he rushed toward it only to see another shadow rush into the room and pull and lift it off the ground and into the smoke.

"My lasso!" he heard CJ yell.

He crawled after the voice but was knocked down by something hard. He felt something around his belly lifting him forcefully into the smoke.

"And here I thought *I* was crazy," a voice said.

It was Josh.

Snowing Fire

Josh carried Peter over his shoulder to his garage. CJ, her face and clothes blackened by smoke, was sitting on Uncle Herb's lap, her head against his shoulder.

"I don't know, Herb," Josh said, gently placing Peter on the grass. "I don't know how many people would run into a smoking house for me."

Peter looked over at his uncle, who looked tired and worried.

"My lasso is gone," CJ said softly, then coughed.

"How did you get here?" Peter asked his uncle.

Josh answered. "Police came by half hour ago telling us we needed to leave immediately, and that was before any of the homes were on fire. I don't think anyone expected it to move so fast. I told the cop I would take Herb with me in James and Terry's car." Josh looked down at the Bible between Herb's leg and the arm of the wheelchair and added, "Thankfully we both travel light. They should be here in a second."

A smoldering ember fell gently on the driveway. Josh peered at the sky. "With everything so dry, this place is going to go up in flames fast."

Mr. James appeared at the bottom of the driveway with a handkerchief over his mouth and nose. Black smears ran across his face, and his hair looked tousled. He pointed in the direction of the exit. "Look at the line. The pavilion is on fire. I think we need a change of plans, Josh. I don't think we are getting out of here by car anymore."

Trucks and cars were lined up from the exit all the way back to the circular drive around the pavilion and back into the three residential streets from which everyone was trying to escape. But it wasn't an organized evacuation: people refused to wait, driving around the shoulder onto the grass, only to get cut off by another car trying the same maneuver or an immovable object like the guardhouse. Some people abandoned their cars and left by foot, but did not leave the keys so the car could be moved, turning it into another obstacle. The cars made it mazelike for the walkers. And now the policemen directing traffic were yelling at cars to make room for fire trucks that were on their way. The people in the car were yelling back at the police officers to let them out first.

"Chaos," Mr. James said.

A familiar yelping came from down the block. Mr. Terry was being pulled by the dogs. He dropped a knapsack at his feet.

"What's that?" Mr. James asked.

Mr. Terry bent over, then looked at them. He spoke in bursts. "Old photo albums—that and dogs—all we need—everything else replaceable."

All of a sudden, the sound of exploding glass filled the air, and they all watched as part of the roof of the pavilion sank in.

"Catering hall kitchen?" Mr. Terry asked. "I would not want to be one of those cars sitting in line next to all those gas lines."

Not long after that, a series of explosions from the pavilion sent fireballs and clouds of smoke billowing into the sky. People jumped out of the cars surrounding the pavilion and ran for cover.

"I hope we have a plan B," Mr. Terry said.

"We need to run for it," Mr. James said.

Josh started running across the lawn in the direction of the pavilion. He stopped and held out his hand. "I have an idea. Five minutes. Don't go anywhere for five minutes!"

He ran off into the smoke.

"You are not supposed to run toward the explosions!" Mr. Terry yelled after him, but Josh was gone.

Josh's Ark

"It's getting really hot," CJ said. Uncle Herb told her to drink some water.

Peter went to the bottom of Josh's driveway where Mr. James and Mr. Terry were looking down the street for Josh. Smoke and heat were coming from both directions now.

"Has it been five minutes?" Mr. James asked.

"Close," Mr. Terry answered. "We will give him a little bit more, James, but I think we should make a break for it with the kids and Herb soon."

"Agreed," Mr. James said.

Peter's eyes burned. He wasn't thrilled about the idea of going anywhere without Josh. They had seen one man hit another, and many others yelling at each other trying to get out. They all thought that they should get out before the others. Peter was scared to see how ugly people can get.

"Really? That's his plan?" Mr. Terry said as they suddenly saw the Willow Creek Landing truck driving through smoke across the once-manicured lawns of Ranch Street. The truck maneuvered slowly around empty cars and trees too large to push aside. It was the only vehicle going deeper into Willow Creek Landing. The empty trailer bounced behind the truck.

Mr. James held his arms up in surrender.

Josh laughed when he saw the look on everyone's faces. Peter was amazed at how Josh seemed unfazed by the fire on two sides. He acted like he was having fun. "Have faith, friends. Listen to my directions."

Peter and CJ helped Mr. Terry and Josh lift the front of the ark and hold it in the air while Mr. James backed the trailer underneath. Then they all pushed from the back, and the ark slid onto the trailer.

"That wasn't too bad," Josh said.

"Speak for yourself," Mr. Terry said, walking away holding his lower back.

Josh started securing the ark to the trailer, and Mr. James lowered the drawbridge of a door.

The ark was loaded with boxes of dry goods and fishing poles, all the stuff Josh had prepared for the flood. He suggested that the dogs sit in the cabin, pointing at the two cats lying on a blanket at the back of the ark.

"Good idea," Mr. Terry said.

Mr. James assisted Uncle Herb up the ramp. CJ followed.

"I lost my lasso, Mr. James," she said.

"I'm sorry to hear that, dear. You sit next to your uncle, lock his wheels in place and hold onto his handles in case we hit any bumps."

Peter jumped into the bed of the truck and looked up and down the street. Homes and the Pine Barrens blazing one way, the burning pavilion and a line of abandoned and angry cars the other way.

"How're we getting out of here?" Peter asked.

"Are you doubting, young Peter?" Josh said, as he finished securing the last strap of the ark.

"No." He wasn't. He actually felt better now that Josh was back.

Mr. James took the wheel, and Mr. Terry accompanied him in the cab, pushing the barking dogs to the center of the seat. CJ sat in the ark, holding the handles of Herb's wheelchair. Peter stood in the truck bed with Josh.

"Take it slow," Josh said.

They had rolled only a couple of feet down Ranch Street before Josh yelled stop. Peter looked over the side to see the old smoking lady, the one who had recited the Bible verse, clanking her walker down the driveway of her friend's house.

"Get in," Josh ordered.

She was dressed in the same floral jacket but had a red kerchief covering her head now instead of the sun hat. Behind her thick glasses, she took in the sight of Josh standing in the ark, hooked up to a truck, and the collection of faces staring back at her.

She shook her head no.

All Peter could taste was smoke.

"Please come with us" Josh said calmly, while all the other faces around held a picture of urgency and impatience.

"What business of it is yours?"

Josh smiled. "Everyone's leaving, if you haven't noticed."

"Don't be a smart ass."

"Come," Josh said and waved her over.

"You can sit here." Mr. Terry said, opening the passenger door and pushing the yapping dogs off his lap and away from the window. He coughed. "Isn't this air bothering you?"

"Not in the slightest," she said.

The smoking lady turned and started up the walkway to her house. She turned and said, "Henry would have loved this excitement." She looked at the burning Pine Barrens and homes. "Wait until I tell him about this."

"We have to go," Josh told her.

She waved them off and slowly headed back to her home. She shouted back at them, "And if you are going to try to put that piece of crap in the water, put a life preserver on the cripple, will ya? Or else it's like drowning kittens."

The truck slowly rolled forward in the direction of the pavilion.

"Tell me again why we are heading toward an explosive fire with no way out by car, much less a truck with a trailer?" Mr. James asked through the small, back window of the cabin.

Josh laughed. "Have faith, brother."

Peter couldn't help but think again that while everyone had a sense of urgency and panic to them, Josh seemed to be having fun.

The truck moved at a walking pace. They had to move slowly for several reasons—Uncle Herb and CJ in the ark, poor visibility and maneuverability, and people were running randomly into the street not paying attention.

Then the truck came to a complete halt again and Mr. James pressed on the truck's horn.

"Dad!" Peter heard someone yell. "Dad!"

Through the smoke, Peter saw a boy standing on the side of the road. He had a backpack strapped to him and was holding a small suitcase.

"Josh! Stop!" Peter climbed over the side of the truck and for the second time in his life, approached Chipper head on rather than run away.

The Pond at Hole Number Eleven

Chipper sat in the back corner of the ark on four unwrapped cases of baked beans. It hadn't taken much persuasion from Peter for Chipper to join them. As Chipper told Peter how he was separated from his father in the rush, Peter thought for the first time his enemy looked more like a "Kenneth" than a "Chipper"—a scared and alone "Kenny," even. Peter promised he would help him look for his family once the fires were under control.

"I'm sorry, Ne—Peter," Chipper whispered before Peter yelled to Josh that he was staying on the ark with his uncle and sister.

Before they reached the next piling of cars, Josh yelled for Mr. James to turn off the road. "Hold on," he warned, and Peter held the grips of Uncle Herb's wheelchair securely, taking a second to glance down and make sure the tire brakes were in locked position. The truck, followed by the trailer and the ark secured to it, hopped the curb, and the wheels tore at the dry grass underneath.

Between two of the homes, Josh pointed and shouted to enter the golf course.

Mr. Terry leaned out the passenger window. "But there's a fence!"

"But we have a truck!" Josh yelled back.

Mr. James turned his head as he drove, and through the open, rectangular rear cab window Peter saw a slight smile appear on his face. He tightened his grip to the wheelchair and tried to balance his body as much as he could through the bouncing. He remembered how Josh taught him to let his legs be the power, from lifting heavy things to throwing a punch. CJ kneeled next to the wheelchair, gripping Herb's forearm. The truck picked up speed, and the fence bounced away, but the collision was jarring enough that Uncle Herb started falling out of the wheelchair. It was CJ who grabbed and held on; if Peter had let go of the wheelchair, there surely would have been more problems. Uncle Herb helped right himself and smiled. He told CJ that she didn't need her lasso. She was a hero without one.

The group drove slowly over the hills and fairways of the golf course. The air started to clear as they drove deeper into the golf course. There was something calming about finally being off of Ranch Street even though they were still surrounded by fire. Peter turned around and saw flames coming through the windows of his home.

"It's over there," Josh said, pointing to the pond at hole eleven, the place where Josh had skinny-dipped and scared the geese.

They drove across greens and around hole flags and patches of fire. When they reached the pond, Mr. James turned the truck around and revved the engine.

"Here we go," Josh said quietly.

The trailer tires splashed into the water as the truck moved slowly in reverse into the water.

"Go as far back as you can, James," Josh said.

The trailer sank into the water. When the water level was almost as high as the top of the truck's tires, they stopped. Josh started unstrapping the ark.

"Everybody in."

Mr. Terry handed the dogs over to Peter, then stepped on the tire that was just above the water level and climbed from the back of the truck to the ark. Chipper held out his hand to help on the last step.

Josh flipped the last of the straps into the back of the truck.

"All right, here's the true test. Go ahead, James, slowly." He reached over and tapped the top of the truck's cabin.

The truck and trailer moved forward. When the ark was completely freed, it slowly started to wobble and tilt as it drifted backward toward the center of the pond. Mr. James turned off the truck, quickly took off his shoes and rolled up his pant legs and climbed aboard.

"C'mon, baby, a little further," Josh said.

They were headed in the right direction, but Peter felt like he was on escalator going down.

"Uh, maybe we should get Herb to higher ground," Mr. James said.

The boat sank low enough for Mr. Terry to start paddling with his hands.

"A little further," Josh said, urging his ark. It was a race against time.

Then the boat scraped and hit bottom with a thud, not in the center of the pond but close enough. Not a drop of water seeped over the sides.

Everyone cheered.

The immediate danger was gone. The air was cleaner here. The group sat in silence and watched the fire engulf the homes of the Creek. In the evening, the flames lit up the sky. Peter heard the distant shouting of people and sirens. CJ placed one pillow behind Uncle Herb's back, then sat on another one next to him. Chipper quietly pet the two cats at his feet.

Mr. Terry was on spark watch, ready to sweep off any burning embers that floated onto the ark. None did. The air was still smoky at times but manageable in the open space of the golf course.

Josh stood and handed Peter a fishing pole.

"You like sushi?"

"I don't know," Peter said. "Are there fish in here?"

"I doubt it."

They fished until it was completely dark, catching nothing and saying little. Peter didn't care.

"You were right, Josh," Peter finally said. "The ark saved us. You did it."

Josh shook his head. "No, young Peter," he said, an unlit cigarette hanging from his lips as he looked into the dark waters surrounding his creation. "We did it."

"Osh," Uncle Herb said.

When Josh turned around, Herb struggled to say something to him. Everyone patiently waited until he finished. Chipper hung outside of the group but showed interest in the conversation. It was the most Peter ever heard his uncle speak in public. He was pretty sure Josh understood, but just in case, CJ repeated her uncle's words.

"He said, *Blessed are those who have not seen and yet have believed.*"

"Is that from the Bible?" Josh asked.

Herb nodded.

Josh thought about it for a second, then turned back around and lit his cigarette. "Maybe I should read more."

Everyone laughed at this, even Chipper.

As they grew tired, some tried to find comfortable sleeping arrangements. Peter couldn't stop taking it all in, like the time they saw the sunrise together: the homes burning, the silhouettes of the ark's passengers, the sirens and the sound of a helicopter in the distance. *All of this will make a great list*, he thought.

The End of Summer

"Things I Like/Don't Like About Our New Apartment"
A List by Peter Grady"

Like:
I'm not surrounded by gates to make me feel like a zoo animal anymore.
There is a 7-Eleven across the street—had every Slurpee flavor already.
CJ made a friend who lives in the complex—Juliana.
Dad and I played catch four times so far, and he told me I can get a phone for my birthday.

Don't Like:
Dad never stays the night anymore.
There is only one bathroom, and the place is too small for Uncle Herb to sleep over, Mom said.
No one is my age in the apartment complex.
I miss seeing Josh, Mr. Terry, and Mr. James every day—a lot.

"CJ! Hurry up! I want to walk Peter to the bus stop on the first day."

Abby was running around the kitchen trying to make lunches for the kids, making sure they had everything in their backpacks from the back-to-school checklist. She was trying not to be too hard on herself, but she was already falling back into her old ways again—the prefire Abby. The headless chicken running around. She told herself that it was only because it was the first day of school, and they had barely unpacked in their new apartment—that her mind was clear and her focus was where it should be now. There was just a lot of unpacking, rather unwrapping, to do. Everything they had was new—the fire had burned their old house to the ground. Abby didn't mind that part too much. It really felt like a true fresh start. She looked out the front window. She had a surprise for the kids on the first day of school, but it wasn't there yet.

Peter looked in the bathroom mirror one last time before heading to breakfast. He couldn't shake the feeling that he was forgetting something. Then he realized what it was. For the first time in a long time, he didn't have the jitters about going to school, the fear of being the fish out of water—laughed at, ignored or worse. He knew people would at least know who he was now, as it was his second year in the district. Plus, it didn't hurt that the news ran a story with a picture of the ark and everyone who was on it. Peter was front and center.

Abby kissed Peter on the top of his head as he sat down at the kitchen table.

"You are getting more handsome by the day," she said. "And you grew so much this summer. Dr. Gold thinks that was the reason you were having the seizures; you outgrew the medicine."

Peter hoped that was the case, but he wasn't going to worry about it. The new medication was working fine. What was the worst that could happen? He would have a seizure in front of all the kids at school? Been there, done that.

CJ came into the kitchen fidgeting in a new dress. "Do I really have to wear this thing? Juliana isn't wearing a dress to school."

"Juliana this, Juliana that," Peter joked. He was still getting used to not having CJ shadow him all day.

Abby put plates of pancakes in front of the kids when a van pulled into the parking spot in front of their apartment. "I have a surprise for you guys," she said.

"Uncle Herb!" CJ shot out of her seat and ran to greet him at the front door.

Peter watched as a smiling Uncle Herb navigated his motorized wheelchair along the walkway with a scowling Maria trailing behind. He waited for his turn to hug his Uncle. Herb had left for his group home the day after a fire truck discovered the ark and its passengers on the golf course. The confused stares on the faces of the firemen as everyone on the ark waved to them made Peter smile every time he thought about it. *Too much excitement here*, Uncle Herb had told Peter with a smile when he left. Peter had missed his presence instantly. He held his hug a beat longer than usual.

Maria stood in the doorway. The small apartment was a serious downgrade from their gated community, but she noticed it didn't seem to bother the family too much. Actually, they seemed surprisingly relaxed. Even the little girl (in a dress!) didn't have that edge to her—and the lasso was nowhere in sight! The love they had for her Hoobie was obvious—which made what was about to come a little easier.

Abby stood behind Herb and faced the children. "So, your father and I have been talking."

Peter's heart suddenly sank. Here it comes—what he had been waiting for—why dad never slept over. How could his Mother do this to him on the morning of the first day of school?

"As we look at new houses, we are looking at homes with at least four bedrooms, because . . . Uncle Herb is moving in with us!" Abby said, and after the kids cheered, she couldn't resist joining with a spirited yet awkward, "Yoo-hoo."

Uncle Herb smiled. Apparently he had been in on the plans, because he showed no sign of surprise. What Abby did leave out to the kids though was if Nick would be joining them in their new home. That was still something they were working through, but it was hard not to notice the change in Nick since the fires. He was trying. But Abby needed time with this. It couldn't hurt for Nick to work hard at something else other than his job.

"There is a second part to the surprise. This came in the mail yesterday," Abby said. She grabbed a box from behind the couch and handed it to Peter. He didn't recognize the name or address on the return label. Inside was a card, a bag of marshmallows for CJ, and a blue-and-orange baseball hat for Peter. The card read:

Dear Peter and CJ,
Thank you for lighting up our lives! Can't wait to see you at our housewarming party—as soon as your mother finds us a house!

Mr. James & Mr. Terry
P.S. I bought Mr. Terry the same hat, Peter, but he said his baseball days are over after playing catch with you that day. His shoulder still hurts. :) J

Peter smiled remembering that catch. It seemed so long ago now. That memory was replaced in his head by a more recent one of Mr. Terry washing the ash from his face with bottled water the second day on the ark, as Mr. James joked with him to use the water from the pond because goose poop was good for the pores. That was just hours before they were rescued.

"They want us to move to the East End with them. Mr. Terry has a lot of friends who live and work out there, and Mr. James is looking for a place to set up a private practice. They seem very happy and asked me to be their real estate agent," Abby said. "But I know that has a lot more to do with you guys than me."

"I miss them," Peter said.

"I promised to bring you guys out as soon as everyone is settled. And of course, they asked for you, Herb. You will go, right?"

Uncle Herb shook his head yes.

"We should go, Hoobie," Maria said softy from the back of the room, and Abby seemed startled, as if she had forgotten someone else was there.

"Oh, yes, I'm sorry, Maria. You got to get to work, and Peter, we should go find your bus stop—"

But something was itching Peter. "Has anyone seen Josh?"

A sad look came over Abby's face. "I tried, Peter. Mr. James and Mr. Terry said they didn't have a number for him, and Mrs. Keeme never returns my calls. I would have loved to invite him over, but he sort of disappeared as fast as he appeared."

"That's Josh," CJ said, cleaning up the syrup on her plate with her last piece of pancake.

The first day of school was pretty much what Peter had expected. He had difficulty finding his classes and opening his locker, but so did half the other students. He fit right in. A couple of the kids mentioned the story in the paper to him, but their minds were so lost in the confusion of school that the conversation just floated away. The one person who was talking about the fires and the ark was Chipper. Several times in the hall and in the lunchroom, Peter saw Chipper holding court, telling other students, even older ones, how he survived the burning of Willow Creek Landing. In the parts that Peter overhead, Chipper never mentioned who he was with—in fact it sounded like the battle was just Chipper versus nature, but Peter was okay with that. Especially after the first time they made eye contact in the hall. Chipper nodded to him, which Peter was cautious to return at first but slowly did. He knew then that there was an understanding there. Peter no longer had to fear Kenneth Kassel Jr.

When Peter returned home from school, there was a Post-it from his mother asking him to pick CJ up from the bus stop. She would be home within the hour. Peter decided to go out to get a Slurpee. The road to cross to get to 7-Eleven was busy, so Peter had to be mindful, but it was nothing like Slocin Road, and now he didn't have CJ to worry about unlike all the trips they had made over the summer.

There is nothing that signals the end of summer more than school starting, and as Peter entered the store, he wasn't even sure he wanted a Slurpee. There was a hint of autumn crispness in the air. It was not like the week when they had moved in, and Peter took 7-Eleven breaks, sweaty and thirsty, after helping his mom move stuff into the apartment. He felt like he should reward himself anyway for surviving the first day of school, so he poured himself a half cherry, half piña colada from the square Slurpee machines, but he went with a small instead of his usual medium.

"Aren't you a little young to be drinking piña coladas, kid?" a deep voice said directly behind him, so close that Peter felt the hot breath on his neck.

Peter turned around slowly. "Uh, it's only a Slurpee."

But there was no one there. A tall, skinny man in the soda aisle with his back to Peter was the closest person to him and there was an older man, an employee filling the hotdog condiments station, but the look on his face told Peter he wouldn't talk to someone unless it was in his job requirement. Peter quickly covered his Slurpee and got on line. When he reached the front of the line, the cashier stared at Peter and said, "No charge."

Peter was confused. He stared back at the cashier.

"No charge, young man. No charge. The man out there paid for it," he said dismissively, and pointed outside while waving Peter off at the same time.

Peter walked outside on full alert, waiting for some creepy-looking guy in a van offering him a ride home. His plan was to go back into 7-Eleven and ask the nearest customer for a phone to call his mom. There was no van in the parking lot—only a tall, skinny guy leaning on the fender of an old pickup truck. He was smiling at Peter and tapping a pack of cigarettes on his open palm.

"Hello, young Peter," Josh said.

Peter kept his lips on his straw as he walked to him, until his growing smile made it impossible to do so.

"You look weird, Josh."

Josh tilted his head to the sky and laughed silently to himself. Peter was only telling the truth. Gone was the beard, gone was the long hair. He could have passed as one of Peter's teachers if not for the cigarette hanging from his lips.

"So do you," Josh said, pointing at him, squinting as he lit his cigarette. "I almost didn't recognize you with how tall you got. Where is the amazing super shadow?"

"CJ has a friend now—Juliana."

"That's a good thing."

There was an awkward silence. Josh ran his hand through his hair.

"Yeah, feels weird, the short hair. Had too. Felt like I couldn't get the smell of smoke out of it."

"I like it."

Josh playfully smacked him in the head. "Haven't seen you since Golfin city burned to the ground. Too bad it took half the Pine Barrens with it."

Peter remembered what Josh had said about forest fires. "Sometimes things need to be burned down to the ground for rebirth to happen, right?"

Josh pointed his unlit cigarette at him. "You have a talent for listening, young Peter. That was crazy."

It turned out the firemen were provided with much needed assistance to extinguish the fire—four consecutive days of rain.

"Why are you here?" Peter asked. He hoped Josh was about to say he was looking to rent an apartment at the complex across the street.

Josh looked at him a little puzzled, then smiled. "Because 7-Eleven sells cigarettes and I, uh, needed a pack."

"Oh."

There was another uncomfortable silence then Josh said, "Hey, remember that first day with the nail gun and the ark. Man, I could have killed us."

Peter remembered. He would never forget. He loved that day.

"Guess what I'm doing now for a job? Construction!"

They both laughed.

"I love it, perfect job for me—a guy from the Creek actually got me the gig. Saw him at a gas station and said I was looking for work. Remember Harold from security?"

Brutus.

Josh stopped talking and looked off somewhere in the distance. The silence bothered Peter. He wanted Josh to keep talking.

"My mother is helping Mr. James and Mr. Terry buy a new house. They are going to throw a party. Will you be there?"

Josh grinned but didn't answer. He dropped his cigarette and put it out with the heel of his work boot.

Peter sensed Josh was ready to leave, so he said the one thing that came to mind even though he didn't really mean it. "Bye, Josh."

The goodbye was awkward too. Peter didn't know if they should shake hands, hug, or what. Josh gave Peter's head a half-playful push—then stepped into the truck and started it.

Peter waited for the red light then crossed the street. He never looked back. When he reached the grass of his apartment complex, he couldn't help but look back at 7-Eleven. Josh's truck was gone. He started up the walkway when he heard a shout. Josh's truck was in the middle of the road. The passenger window was down, and Josh was leaning as close to the opening without taking his hand from the steering wheel.

"Young Peter, J.R.R. Tolkien said, *Faithless is he that says farewell when the road darkens.* Do you agree?"

"I don't know, Josh." Peter yelled because Josh seemed so far away in that beat-up truck in the middle of the road. "I'm only twelve and—"

"A half! I know!" Josh yelled back. "Do you think it was chance we met in 7-Eleven? We are not farewell people, my friend! Tell Uncle Herb I'm reading more!"

With that, Josh flashed a peace sign and drove away. Peter followed the truck until it was out of sight, then he followed it some more.

As he climbed the last steps to his apartment, a sole raindrop fell on his bare arm.

Acknowledgments

This book would not be possible without all the love and support from many people.

First and foremost, I would like to thank my wife, Jacqueline, who took on my dream as her own. You always believed, and this couldn't have happened without you. I'm a lucky dude.

Special thanks to Kaylie Jones for not giving up on me. For over a decade, you provided vision, wisdom, encouragement, and unyielding optimism.

Thanks to Bill Landauer for his acute insights with character development; Kaitlin Martin, for capturing the spirit of the book with her incredible cover; Mindy Benze, for her keen eye and sharp editing skills; Kevin McEvoy, the amazingly talented artist (and second-rate fiddler) for the sketch map of Willow Creek Landing; and Johnny Temple and Akashic Books for providing the platform for this story to be heard.

To my amazing children, Maddy and Mikey. You inspire me and make me proud. You are my constant source of joy—and remember, the seagull is always watching.

Also, to my sister Cindy, the original CJ, who made my favorite meal (a pickle wrapped in bacon and steak) at every pivotal and celebratory point.

Lastly, a big bone to my crazy, sometimes lazy Kentucky mutt, Hazy, who sat faithfully at my feet and provided countless hours of companionship during the lonely process of writing and revision.

CPSIA information can be obtained
at www.ICGtesting.com
Printed in the USA
LVHW092024290819
629406LV00005B/712/P